The Fortune Cookie Writer

a novel

NINA NAVISKY

28 LEAVES PRESS

For Diana

A man with a bowl of half-cooked rice rarely declines an offer of roast duck.

My mailbox reeks of oregano.

Three parts oregano to one part rosemary and basil, to be exact. I realize this as I unlock the narrow metal door, and suddenly Mom's ulterior motive in offering to get my mail on Friday is clear. For a split second, her protective herbal blend, bound in a makeshift cheesecloth sachet and secured with a garbage bag tie, teeters on the ledge. But then, it succumbs to the weight of the mail resting on top of it and bursts. The contents of my mailbox tumble down in an avalanche of herbs, letters, and catalogs. Oregano clings to my sweater, dusts the mailboxes below, and lands on the drab beige carpet in clumps and sprinkles.

The mail room is empty, thank God. Not surprising for a Sunday night—I'm only here because I didn't have a chance to come by yesterday, due to the hectic Thanksgiving weekend. Mom and Dad flew all the way from California to Massachusetts to spend the holiday with Owen and me "just because," which is Mom-speak for "My grandson will *not* be scarred by his first postdivorce holiday."

I peek through the half-open door into the lobby. No one milling around. I shut the door with my foot while wiping my shirt clean as best I can, then scoop the herbs into a Dustbuster-ready pile. I've got to clean up this mess before someone from management walks in. What possible excuse could I offer? That I've decided to bake artisanal pizza in the mail room?

Now that I think about it, there's no way to explain it, *unless you know my sister.*

It was absolutely essential, Lindsay told me in August, that I "clear all stagnant energy" and "reclaim the space with intention" prior to moving in with Owen, but I had a few other things on my mind. Trivial things, like avoiding eviction, ensuring child support and visitation were in place, and helping Owen adjust to the fallout of divorce as well as kindergarten in a new school and town. There was no time for burning dried sage—number one on the list Lindsay emailed me. Even if there had been, setting off smoke detectors didn't strike me as the best way to ingratiate myself with the new neighbors. Putting a large black tourmaline stone in my five-year-old's pocket to absorb negative energy seemed dangerous, and making my own room spray required that I buy witch hazel as well as patchouli, lemon, and cedarwood essential oils.

Owen caught me scrolling through Lindsay's email, smirking, and he climbed into my lap and tried to read along when I refused. He put his finger on item number six—"play 528 Hz chakra cleansing music"—his attention focused on the unpronounceable *hz* consonant cluster. I explained the letters stood for hertz, a measurement of frequency, which was a fancy word for *sound.* He pointed to the text, so I gave in and read, "This healing music will cleanse your home of stagnant energy, and rejuvenate your mind, body, and soul." Then I noticed this gem in the next paragraph: "Stagnant energy that is unable to raise its frequency may transform into a negative spirit, or ghost." I tried to scroll past, but it was too late. Owen spotted the word *ghost*. Terrified, he said we should go back home to Nick's condo in Boston, where we all used to live together, since we'd never had to worry about the energy there. At which point I cursed my sister under my breath, and told Owen that while Aunt Lindsay was trying to be helpful, sometimes her ideas were a bit silly, and our new apartment in Natick would soon be home, too.

Mom found out about Lindsay's email after Thanksgiving dinner, when Owen assured her that my room—which she and Dad were about to unpack in—wasn't haunted, even though we never had time to clean the "stag-uh-nut" energy. Mom looked at me, straight-faced in front of Owen, and raised an eyebrow while I shooed him into the living room with Dad.

"Take a look at this list," I said on my way to the kitchen, pulling up the email and handing her my phone. I busied myself putting leftover turkey into plastic containers while Mom read. "Did you see what she wrote next to 'black tourmaline stone'?" I asked, when she looked up. "'Don't buy new for this venture. Listen to your collection. A stone will speak to you.'" I used my best whispery yoga instructor voice. "She is *ridiculous*. Maybe her L.A. spa clients have collections of stones they converse with daily, but that's not a big thing around here."

"What's this one?" Mom pointed to number nine on Lindsay's list. "An herbal blend. Basil, rosemary, yarrow, juniper, and anise. That must smell lovely."

"I'm sure it does. You know what else smells great? Febreze. But that doesn't mean it's a 'spiritual protectant against harmful forces.'"

"Well, it can't hurt," Mom said, poking through my alphabetized spice rack. "And it looks like you have most of these items already."

"That's not remotely true. I've never even heard of yarrow. I don't have anise. And juniper is a tree. I don't know if the recipe calls for crushed-up leaves or essential oils, but whatever it is, I don't—"

"So you substitute," Mom said, waving away my concerns. "Just like cooking. Let's see . . . looks like we'll have enough rosemary and basil left over from the roast, and I'll put in extra oregano for the ingredients we don't have. Perfect!"

I shook my head. "You have lost your mind. You can't replace three of the five ingredients with oregano. It will mess up the proportions. That's not how . . ." I stopped short as the flaw in my argument became apparent. Mom knew I had no idea how this nonsense worked, so who was I to tell her the rules? I changed tactics. "What are you going to put all the herbs *into*, anyway? Ziplocs don't breathe, and isn't that the whole point of this absurd exercise? To cleanse negative energy with scent? Do you really think you're visiting the daughter who happens to have empty sachets hanging around her apartment?"

Mom scanned my spartan kitchen, which was devoid of clutter or knickknacks that might be of help. Finally, she rested her gaze on the cheesecloth we'd used to cook the turkey, which was on the far side of the countertop.

"Mom, *no!*"

"Come on, Marissa, indulge your poor mother. It's no different than knocking on wood. What's wrong with wanting my daughter to have better luck?"

"Fine. I give up." I pounded the lid down over the bursting turkey container. "You can make one for Owen's room."

But Mom made a second one while I was busy scrubbing pans and loading the dishwasher, I realize now. And she decided to use one in my mailbox to ward off whatever negativity might come to me in the form of bills.

I scoop up the Stop & Shop circular, Val-Pak coupons, and Gap catalog. Hiding underneath are three pieces of actual mail, addressed to me rather than RESIDENT or CURRENT OCCUPANT.

All bills. Verizon. Visa. Eversource.

"Ha!" I hear myself say out loud as I rummage through my bag for my phone. I place the bills in a semicircle around the pile of herbs, open the camera, and line up the shot.

But I don't take the picture. Because whose behavior is the most ludicrous in this sorry chain of events? Not Lindsay's. She has no idea that one of her recommended negative-energy-cleansing techniques has been hijacked. Not Mom's, either. Her actions may be sorely misguided, but they're born of love. That leaves me. I'm the pathetic one attempting to document that Italian spices do not, in fact, have the power to stave off monthly bills.

My throat constricts, and then I feel the tears, and I look up at the ceiling and blink quickly. I was supposed to make something of myself. Yet here I am, working three jobs and still in debt, because three years at Yale is no better than zero when it comes to checking off *college graduate* on work applications.

Heat is pulsing through me now, traveling from my cheeks to my earlobes, across the base of my neck, and under my arms. I'm familiar with this humiliation-to-anger evolution, because my thoughts have turned to Nick, and what started all of this but his delightful Fourth of July surprise? When he told me his new boss was a jerk and would only let him take off the first three days of our annual week-long vacation to Cape Cod, I believed him without a second thought. Turns out he needed time to meet with his divorce attorney, so having a gullible idiot of a wife came in handy. A day after Owen and I returned, I got served.

I look at the time. 5:32. Nick will be back with Owen in an hour and a half. Which means I can't put off telling him about the Great Lunchroom Escape any longer. I got the call Tuesday: Owen told the lunch monitor he had to go to the bathroom and took off instead. He was found, after a panicked hunt, in the music room. Which means that my sweet, rule-abiding child *lied*. To a grown-up. It's totally out of character. I think I've figured out what's going on, but Nick isn't going to like my solution to the problem. I've been using Thanksgiving excuses to put off an inevitable fight over money, and those end tonight.

But one crisis at a time. Right now I need a Dustbuster.

I crack the door and peek into the hallway again. Still clear. As I pull it open, I spot a slim blond woman down the hall to my left, her back to me. She's in an elegant black sheath dress with a bateau neck and matching black suede pumps. She takes a couple steps and peers around the corner of the hallway, the red soles of her shoes visible as she walks. It's a dead giveaway. Red soles are the hallmark of Christian Louboutins—designer shoes that cost nearly triple my weekly child support. She takes a few more tentative steps down the corridor until we both hear the opening of a door, the exchange of pleasantries, and the steady hum of conversation. Then she spins back and strides down the hallway, head bowed. She brushes past me, veers left into the lobby toward the main doors, and stops. She turns around and regards me curiously, eyeing the mail key in my hand.

"Are you lost?" I ask, as she approaches me. "I, uh, I'm not supposed to let nontenants in the mail room, but if you tell me the name of the person you're looking for, I can find the apartment number on the mailbox."

"No, no, no, I'm fine. I know where they're . . . thank you anyway," she says with an embarrassed laugh. Now that we're close up, I can see she's much older than her figure suggests. Her makeup is expertly applied, but her foundation has settled into the lines around her eyes and mouth, drawing attention to the very imperfections she's attempting to disguise. "Do you live here?"

"Yeah."

"So you know Rose Klein?"

"No, sorry. I just moved in last August with my son. I'm still meeting people, but I haven't—"

"You have a little boy?" She clasps her hands together. "You *must* have known Bernie, then. Rose's husband? He loved children. The only man I've ever known who kept lollipops on him at all times. He was probably responsible for the rotting of hundreds of children's teeth."

"There's a man my son and I have bumped into a couple of times. Bald, usually wears a bow tie? We call him the Candy Grandpa."

"That's him. What a character. He was a wonderful man. They're sitting shiva for him right now."

"Oh," I say, uncertain what she means.

She offers a kind smile. "A Jewish condolence call."

"I'm so sorry for your loss," I say automatically. But how deep of a loss can it be for this woman, who knows where the gathering is but is choosing not to join it?

I wait for the reflexive "thank you," but instead the woman says, "I'm worried about Rose. Bernie took care of everything for her, always has. No sisters or brothers, and Bernie's brother lives in Florida."

"She doesn't have any other family?"

"Bernie's nephew is coming in, but he can't get here until next Saturday. Some big psychiatry conference in London that he's presenting at this week. So in the meantime, she's going to need some dinners, and someone has to check in on her until a more permanent arrangement is set up. She doesn't drive."

"She's lucky to have you, then." I smile politely. That should do for a sympathetic closer, shouldn't it? I don't want to be rude, but—

"Yes, well, that's the problem. I came in for the funeral, but I live in New York. Even if I were closer by . . ." She stops, clears her throat. "I didn't speak to Rose today. After all these years, you'd think things would be different, but, well . . . seeing me would probably be too complicated. I doubt she knew I was there, at the graveside. I made sure to stay in the back." She sighs, then fishes her wallet out of her handbag, cobalt blue with the gold Prada logo on the magnetic snap, and pulls out three crisp one-hundred-dollar bills. "Would you help? Just drop off dinner once a day, see if she needs to run any errands, maybe get her out for a little fresh air? You can keep the rest of the money for yourself."

"*Me?* But I don't even know her. I mean, she might recognize me from around the building, but we've never spoken. Doesn't she have any friends?"

"I'm sure she does, but they all seem pretty frail. From what I saw at the funeral, at least. And I don't know where they live or if they even drive at this point."

"Listen, I'd like to help." I try not to stare at the bills in her outstretched hand. Three hundred dollars. Almost a week's worth of take-home pay from my part-time admin job at Allerton Veterinary Care.

"Not enough?" the woman asks, catching my gaze. "That's all I have for cash, but I could write you a check. How about that?" She drops her wallet into her handbag, holds on to the bills with her left hand, and digs through the inner pockets of her bag with her right. She fishes out her checkbook, cloaked in cobalt blue Prada as well, and a pen.

"No, no, it's not that. It's . . . well, won't she— Rose, you said, right?

Won't she be suspicious if I start showing up every day? If I can't tell her that you've asked me to help out, she's going to wonder why some stranger is bringing her meals."

"Good catch," she says, nodding at me with approval. "I should've thought of that." She tilts her head, stares at the ceiling for a moment. "I know! Why don't you tell her that management sent an email to all tenants, and a bunch of people wanted to help out. Say you're the coordinator."

"But . . ." I pause, try to figure out how to point out the risk she's taking without painting myself as a criminal, but there's no tactful way to say it. "I could just pocket the money and not do anything to help."

"You could. But people who steal don't often confess beforehand. And at least I'll know I tried." She opens her checkbook, folds the bills in half, and stuffs them inside the empty slip pocket for the transaction register. Then she stabilizes the checkbook against the wall with her palm. "My phone number is on the check," she says over her shoulder as she fills it out. "Feel free to call if you have any questions. I'm Lena, by the way. The check says Darlene, but no one calls me that."

"I'm Marissa."

"Marissa . . . ?" She turns her head and looks at me expectantly, points to the payee line on the check.

"Oh! Marissa Karalis."

She writes as I spell it out loud for her, then tears the check out of the book and holds it up for me to see. Another fifty dollars. "Nice to meet you, Marissa," she says, as she coaxes the three bills out from underneath the leather slip pocket and piles them on top of the check. "Do we have a deal?"

— 2 —

*If you want to dine on pheasant,
find your bow and arrow.*

Nick and Owen have been in a horrible car accident. I'm sure of it. Why else would they be forty-eight minutes late and not call? I picture Owen's slight body bloodied and mangled, surrounded by EMTs. I can see the scraps of metal strewn across the highway, hear the police sirens blaring. Acid churns in my stomach; heat courses upward and leaves me flush; a bitterness fills the back of my throat. I'll kill Nick if anything happens to Owen under his watch.

Three solid knocks come from high up on my door, followed by a frenzy of them lower down. I lunge toward the door and fling it open with such force that Owen falls into my arms midknock.

"What happened?" I scream at Nick. "Why didn't you call me? Your phone is going straight to voicemail, did you know that? I thought you were dead!" I sit down on the threshold so Owen can snuggle into my lap. I bury my nose in the nape of his neck and breathe him in.

Nick looks at me like I'm crazy. "What? Why would you think—my phone died, that's all. And you said not to call from the car. Last time I did you got mad at me."

"This is different! This isn't a little late, this is *forty-five minutes*." I round down, make the time less exact to hide that I've been checking nonstop.

"What's the rule? I'm not supposed to call because it's way too dangerous, but at some magical point that only *you* know, I do have to call? It's either safe or it isn't."

He's right. But I've spent forty-eight minutes getting riled up and now it's going to take me a couple more to calm down. "Keep your voice down," I whisper-scold, even though I was the one who yelled first. Owen puts his arms around my neck and I bear-hug him as we rock side to side.

A twisted smile flits across Nick's face, vanishes before he can replace it with an acceptable one. I know that expression. *I love seeing Owen happy*, it says, *as long as he isn't happier with you*. Against my will, I feel a tinge of compassion for him.

"Listen, we left on time," he says. "The Pike was bumper-to-bumper. It took us more than double the usual time to get here."

"Well, it's one of the busiest travel days of the year. What did you expect?" I temper my critical words with the practiced, breezy tone I'm supposed to use in front of Owen. "Play nice," I used to say to Owen at playgroups when he was a toddler, never dreaming in a few years I'd be on the receiving end of that very advice from a coparenting instructor, rearranged into formal syntax.

"I assumed most of the traffic would be going into the city."

"Because no one who traveled to Boston, the easternmost city in the U.S., would need to go west to get home?"

Nick glares at me. I still find it hard to not be mesmerized by Nick's eyes, even when filled with contempt. They're bright blue, framed by thick black lashes and set against olive skin. The same color as the famous blue domed churches of Santorini, which I've always thought was fitting, since we met in Greece during my junior year abroad almost seven years ago.

"I'm pretty sure Maine has some cities that are farther east."

It's a generous attempt to defuse the situation, but he can't charm his way out of this one. "Fine. The easternmost *major* city. My point still stands."

"Jesus, I get it, we're late. I'm sorry." He sighs, then hands me Owen's backpack.

I smooth Owen's unbrushed hair and shift his weight so I can rummage through his backpack. "Where's Geri, O?"

"She's on the bottom." He fishes his stuffed giraffe out of the bag, the only animal in his vast collection who had the honor of joining him every day for his first year of preschool. Her plush has been worn to nubs, and her right ear is misshapen, a testament to his love. "Found her! She was tired, so she asked me to put her on the bottom. Guess why?" He looks up at me, grinning, as he waits for me to figure it out.

"Hmm . . . maybe so she could use your clothes as a blanket?"

Owen bobs his head up and down in delight.

I kiss the top of his head, then Geri's. "You make me laugh, you silly giraffe," I say to Geri, stealing a line from our nightly bedtime script.

Owen turns and gives Nick a withering stare, and then burrows into me.

"What?" I look up at Nick.

Nick rubs his eyes, then waves away my concern. "He's just tired."

Geri has been an integral part of Owen's bedtime routine since the day he got her, but last year she landed a speaking role. One evening, after I arranged the sheets and quilt the way Owen likes them—completely flat, except around his ankles and wrists, where they must be turned over so he doesn't get too hot—I gave him a kiss, an "I love you," and, for the first time, a breezy "See you later, alligator." Owen dutifully responded with "After a while, crocodile," then looked at me with a sly smile, as if to say, *Checkmate.* There was no follow-up rhyme, and we both knew it. But I surprised him with an ad-libbed "See you around, basset hound," and his face lit up with surprise. He scrunched his eyes and chewed on his bottom lip, racking his brain as I tried to gauge the likelihood of frustration tears. Finally, he held Geri up in front of his face and said, "See you soon, you big baboon!" I don't know why he decided the words needed to come from Geri—maybe he thought I'd get mad if he called me a baboon—but I burst out laughing in relief, and answered, "You make me laugh, you silly giraffe," as soon as I could catch my breath.

Nick taps Owen on the back, but Owen's face remains buried in my sweater. "Hey, bud. If Geri's that sleepy, maybe you should take her to your room."

"Dad's right, sweetie. That way she can catch up with all her friends, too. I bet she missed them."

Owen pulls away from me and nods solemnly. "Especially Grover." He cradles Geri in his arms, strokes her matted fur as he climbs out of my lap and heads toward his room, dragging his backpack behind him.

"Owen, hold up," says Nick.

"Oh, sorry." Owen shuffles back for a hug. "Love you, Daddy."

"Love you, too, bud. See you after school on Wednesday, okay?" He waits until Owen disappears around the corner, then glowers at me. "What's that about?"

"What do you mean?"

"'I bet she missed her friends'? Are you trying to equate visiting me with sadness?"

"I didn't mean it like that. Really. I was just trying to get him to move. And I knew he'd do it for Geri."

"Right," he says, with a snort. "Look, I've got to get going."

"Daddy?" Owen peeks around the corner.

"Yeah, bud?"

"Don't forget the cupcakes, okay?"

Nick blushes. "Uh, sure. Got 'em right here, kiddo." He pauses, then picks up a plastic CVS bag that's been resting to the right of the doorway, just out of my vision.

I turn away from Nick to make sure Owen has retreated to his room again, then pivot back. "Cupcakes! How *lovely*. Is baking a new hobby of yours?"

Nick rolls his eyes. "Is this a problem? Owen saw an ad on TV for red velvet cake, and he said he'd never tried it, so——"

"So your girlfriend came over and you played house."

"She works at a bakery, for Christ's sake! Why is it so terrible for me to ask her to help us out?"

"What exactly have you told Owen about her?"

"That she's my friend."

"Six months minimum! That's what all the literature says. No introducing someone new for at least six months after separation. Didn't you learn anything in that course? You didn't even wait for the divorce to be final!" Tears rim the waterline of my eyes, and I look up and blink quickly, just as I did in the mail room. It's such an obvious tell, and he's caught me in the middle of it. "You can't introduce him to a new girlfriend every couple of months from now on, Nick. It's too confusing for him."

"I won't." Then, after a brief pause, "I wouldn't introduce him to just anyone."

My breath catches. Courtney is more than a fling? The first time I heard her name was a couple of weeks ago, when Owen said that Daddy's friend looked like his kindergarten teacher, Mrs. Evans. If that's the case, I thought at the time, then this mysterious Courtney must be blond and slim—pretty in a bland, forgettable way. The opposite of me, which was rather poetic. She couldn't be more than a couple of years younger than me if she was the same age as fresh-out-of-grad-school Mrs. Evans.

My face is stiff with the effort of keeping my chin from trembling, and my torso quakes as I strain to hold in a sob. Stupid traitor of a torso. I cross my arms in front of me, dig my forearms into my stomach.

Nick glances at my crossed arms, the floor, my eyes. "Riss, I know it seems fast, but . . . sometimes you just know. Right?"

I shake my head, because once he whispered those same trite words to me about our future together, and he doesn't even have the decency to remember. I want to tell him not to call me by my nickname anymore, that he doesn't have a right to use it, but I know that would be juvenile and pointless.

"Nothing happened with Courtney until after we separated. I swear."

That depends on how you define "nothing," I want to say. *What* didn't happen until after we separated? Sex? That's a narrow definition of betrayal. I always suspected there was someone lurking in the background, because why else would he have been in such a rush to end our marriage? Even now, it's degrading, knowing that while I blindly packed our suitcases, carefully coordinating his swim trunks, tees, and shorts, even as I commiserated that he was a hard worker and *deserved* the whole week off, he was orchestrating the trauma to be inflicted on my return.

"Nothing happened. I promise, Riss."

It's the *I promise* that finally makes the trembling stop. "Oh, you *promise*," I say, choking on the words. "I see. I guess that settles that, then, doesn't it?" It's a pathetic comeback, but I can't do any better at the moment.

He bites his lower lip like he always does when he's deciding what to say. I hate that I still find it so endearing. "I don't . . . I don't want you to think I did anything slimy."

"Serving me with papers out of the blue wasn't slimy?"

"I had to, you know that! You would've taken Owen to California in a second if there was no legal restriction from taking him out of state."

"So instead you shackled me here! Where it would be super easy for a stay-at-home mom with no college degree to suddenly get a job that would make anywhere near enough money to support a child?"

Nick pales. I've hurt him, and it feels good. "That's not fair. I've never given you any trouble with child support. And I gave you a *lot* of money without a fight."

It's true.

Back in July, I wanted to make him miserable, sue him for every cent he had. Who the fuck was he to tell me that we should avoid a long drawn-out court battle? *I* was the one who sacrificed in the marriage, not him. The original plan, after all, was for me to take a year off from college. That was it. He was going to gain some work experience in Boston during the remainder of my pregnancy and Owen's first eight months, and then get a new job in Connecticut the following fall so I could finish up my final year. But we never made it back to New Haven, so when he bound me to Massachusetts with no education and no job prospects, I didn't feel particularly charitable.

My first instinct was to kick Nick out of the condo for good, because why should I have to move? Wasn't there some unwritten rule about wronged wives keeping the house? But my lawyer pointed out two stumbling blocks to my revenge plot: I didn't have the money to buy out Nick's half of the equity, and Owen's lousy lottery-assigned kindergarten placement wasn't worth staying in Boston for. My lawyer recommended finding an apartment in a suburb with a good school system and full-day kindergarten, but that wasn't possible, I told her, because Nick didn't have the money to pay for *my* share. She countered that Nick would, if he refinanced.

Nick said it was the worst deal he'd ever heard of. Why should he have to buy me out when it was *his* dad who'd paid our down payment in the first place, and he was the one who'd paid the mortgage month after month? Which is when I completely lost it and screamed at him that I didn't pay the mortgage because I was busy *raising our child* and *cooking our meals* and *cleaning our house*, and that if he'd wanted me to go back to work so badly, maybe we should've stuck to the plan and let me finish my degree *like he promised*. Oh, and lest he forget: this awful, unfair deal was going to net him a condo, and leave me homeless.

But as mutually unsatisfying as it was, moving out was the best choice for Owen, and we both knew it. Haggling over money meant we'd have to live together for months, wasting it while battling each other in court and sending Owen to a school neither of us were satisfied with. So we let our lawyers figure out what division was fair, created a separation agreement, and filed jointly so we could spare Owen that pain.

I can feel Nick staring at me, even though I'm concentrating on a stray scuff mark I've never noticed before on the doorway frame. I wipe the tears I've been unable to stop and look away, because even though I don't want him back, it's crushing to face how undesirable I must have been for him to have chosen this mess.

Nick kicks at a brittle leaf that's been tracked into the hallway. "So."

"So."

He passes me Owen's suitcase, royal blue with lime green sharks. "His keyboard is in there, too."

The keyboard. Right. The last thing I want to do is continue this conversation, but the I-don't-want-to-ruin-Thanksgiving excuse expires now. "Before you go . . . I need to talk to you about the keyboard. I don't think it's enough for him anymore. It's time for him to start piano lessons."

"What does he need lessons for? He's pretty good at fiddling around on his own."

I look back toward Owen's room, make sure he's out of hearing range, then lower my voice, just to be safe. "I got a call from school. He got in trouble last Tuesday for leaving the lunchroom. They found him in the music room, playing the piano."

"*What?* Don't they have lunch monitors?"

"Mm-hmm. He lied so he could go play."

"Owen's not a liar."

"Not until now."

Nick shakes his head. He opens his mouth to speak, raises his finger as if to make a point, then stops.

"Look," I say, "I think he's so fascinated by music that it drives him to do things he wouldn't ordinarily do. He's talented. We should nurture his interests."

"Come on, Marissa. He memorized a couple of songs you taught him on the keyboard."

"No, that's the point. I didn't teach him anything. He taught himself the theme songs to *Sesame Street*, *PAW Patrol*, even *Phineas and Ferb*. He gets the rhythm right, too, not just the notes."

"Really? *Phineas and Ferb* is fast."

"I know. I can't even keep the lyrics straight."

Nick sighs. "Okay, how much are lessons?"

"Around thirty-five to forty per half-hour lesson," I say, in what I hope is a nonchalant tone. "And he'll need to practice every day, so eventually he'll need a piano. Not right away, of course. We'll have a trial period with lessons before we invest, but—"

"*What?* Why can't he practice on his keyboard?"

"It doesn't have eighty-eight keys. And the keys aren't weighted, so when he plays on a real piano at lessons he won't have built up enough finger strength. He needs an instrument with pedals and a bench, not a toy."

"Weighted keys? Finger strength? You seem pretty well versed on the subject. Have you signed him up somewhere already?"

"No! I was just researching online. Look, I'm not talking about a ten-thousand-dollar baby grand. I found a couple of secondhand pianos on Craigslist that'll work for around six hundred. And I thought . . . with his birthday coming up next month . . . we could split it. Maybe some lessons, too, for a Christmas gift? It would make it special for him, knowing the gifts were from both of us, don't you think?"

Nick gives me a look that says *I know what you're doing*. There is no "us" anymore; it's all a charade for Owen. It was a weak attempt to make him feel guilty, and it's embarrassing that I've stooped to this level, but I can't afford any of this on my own. "Sorry," he says. "I already got Owen his birthday and Christmas gifts."

I fold my arms in front of my chest. "*Please*. No way are you prepared this early."

"Okay, fine!" Nick says, his cover blown. "Look, if he gets a lesson a week, that's two thousand a year."

"It's closer to fifteen hundred. No lessons in the summer. And that's the private instruction rate. I bet I could find a group class to bring down the cost. Trust me, I'd rather sign him up for online piano lessons—they're way cheaper—but I won't know if his finger positioning is wrong or if he's developing bad habits. Will you?"

Nick is shaking his head, has been since I corrected his estimate. "If this is so important to you, then you should've brought it up when we were budgeting for after-school activities."

"Not sure how I could've done that, since he didn't go MIA from the lunchroom until Tuesday," I say, with a shrug. Not a benign I-don't-know shrug—a textbook insolent teenager shrug. It's a bad move, pointing out Nick's fragile logic. That shrug is going to cost me. Literally.

Nick gives me a look of pure disgust. "I'm not made of money, you know."

I do know how much you're made of, I want to say. *We line itemed every penny, remember? You can afford this, easy.*

But escalating isn't going to get Owen what he needs, so I backpedal and concentrate on keeping my face neutral, my voice soft. "He fits the profile, Nick. I've been reading up on it. His singing is pitch-perfect—he doesn't have that little kid, out-of-tune type of voice. Every time he hears music he taps his fingers, and he keeps the beat. I always hear him counting in groups of eight, and that's the key to understanding music. I always knew he liked music, but learning songs by ear is a whole new ball game."

It's the wrong metaphor, because as soon as I say *ball game,* Nick's face lights up. "Ball game. *Exactly.* Owen's in a new school. He needs to make friends, and boys make friends through sports. He'll do soccer again in the spring and he'll give Little League a try. That's what we planned for and that's what makes sense for him now."

"But Owen *hates* soccer."

"It was his first season. He's got to get over his fear of the ball, that's all."

"Come *on*. He's the slowest runner out there."

Nick puts up his hand, traffic cop style. "Look, I have to head out. It'll be stop-and-go the whole way back, and I have to get some work done before a meeting in the morning." He turns and walks toward the staircase.

"I'm not imagining it," I call after him. "I really think we should support—"

"See you, Riss," he says, and disappears down the stairwell.

I close the door, careful not to slam it so as not to scare Owen. It's unbelievably frustrating—juggling three jobs, but still having to plead with Nick for money. My current salary at the vet's office doesn't quite cover the differential between child support and expenses—I'm still operating at a weekly loss of eighty-one dollars. That leaves me in the hole for a little over forty-two hundred for the year, and that's assuming everything goes according to budget, which it *never* does. I'm not without a safety net—I have my settlement money—but I can't touch it right now. If I want to leave behind microbudgeting and entry-level jobs, I have to finish college, and that means Owen and I will need that money to live on.

I pat the front of my jeans pocket, feel the outline of the check and bills that unexpectedly made their way to me tonight. If I'm careful, I can stretch seventy-five dollars to cover five days of dinners for—what's her name, again? An R name. Ruth? Rachel? No, *Rose*. That's it, Rose. That leaves me with $275, which I can add to the funds Nick doesn't know about from the two freelance jobs I've been working to cover my budget gap.

The only way Nick's going to pony up some cash is if the pressure comes from Owen, not me. Nick will be furious if I sign Owen up for a couple of lessons after tonight's delightful conversation, but what do I have to lose at this point? I'm sure I can get an introductory lesson for free, and now that I'm flush with bills, I can afford an additional class or two. Once Nick sees how much Owen loves it, he'll cave.

That's the plan, at least.

— 3 —

No sense in waiting for fish to season and steam itself.

The brisk air soothes my burning eyes as I walk out the door of Allerton Veterinary Care for my lunch break. I've been a sneezing, itchy-eyed mess since nine fifteen, when my body let me know that forgetting Allegra wasn't something it was willing to let slide. Petting the waiting room cats and dogs is the only enjoyable part of my job, but my immune system would be happier if I stuck to booking appointments and submitting purchase orders. I dig through my bag for a tissue to dab the corners of my eyes, then zip up my puffer jacket and head down South Main Street toward the crosswalk that connects to the Natick Town Common.

Last month, the trees that anchor the Common were bursting with crimson, ginger, and golden leaves, and I spent my free half hours sitting on a park bench, soaking up the remaining sun of the season and watching toddlers run up and down the steps of the gazebo. But today the trees are stark and the gusts of wind harsh, so I head on the diagonal through the Common and stride past the monuments to fallen soldiers, cross East Central Street, and walk up the steps to the main library.

The brick building is an architectural blend of past and present; as I enter, I pass what was once the exterior of the Victorian Gothic nineteenth century structure, and is now the centerpiece of three levels of modernized skylit space. I jog up a flight, sit on the carpet in a far-right corner aisle and face the lower-shelved books labeled with the now-familiar call number of 808.8. I tilt my head sideways to read the titles on the spines: *Bartlett's Familiar Quotations*, *The Oxford Dictionary of Quotations*, *The Oxford Dictionary of Literary Quotations*, *The Oxford Dictionary of Modern Quotations*. I've flipped through these books before. They're useless because the quotes within them are organized by person. I need books that classify by category, so I can look up *happiness* or *patience*, not *Shakespeare* or *Tennyson*.

I scan the row of books until I reach a title I've never seen before—*Someone Famous Once Said: Insights from Philosophers, Politicians, and Comedians.* This could be a good one. I pull it from the shelf along with two of its neighbors, *A Compilation of Quotations*, and *Toasts, Roasts, and Quips for Public Speaking*. Books on my hip, I make my way down the aisle and turn right toward my stall: an isolated corner desk abutting the window, perfect for flipping through pages while nibbling a contraband bagel.

Someone is sitting in it! No one ever takes my stall—it's the chill from the window that makes people decide against it. But there she is, in my spot. She's still wearing her down jacket and knit pom-pom hat, and she's eating *tuna*, the dimwit. I can smell it all the way down the hall.

I want to chuck my bagel at her head. *How do you not know the food rules, Pom-Pom Lady?* They're not complex. The smelliest you can risk here is a turkey sandwich. You don't pull out the Limburger cheese and garlic hummus if you're eating on the sly.

I sneer at Pom-Pom Lady's back as I walk toward the open tables in the center of the room. Her moronic tuna selection means the librarians will soon get cat food odor complaints, and now I have to nibble my bagel in full view of the reference desk. I pull a chair leg out with my foot, let my own books drop on the tabletop with a *thud*, and push the scattered books that have been left behind by others to my left.

Ten quotes per day is my rule; it keeps me on track to write the three hundred per month that Peking Foods, Inc. is paying me for. Three hundred *fortunes*, that is, not quotes. I can't plagiarize, but I've needed the quotes for inspiration over the past three months. Coming up with fortunes is harder than I thought it would be. It's tough to craft a witty comment that will appeal to an eight-year-old boy just as well as it will to his eighty-year-old grandmother. It's harder to write for kids—their appreciation of witticisms about the subtleties of life doesn't run deep— but if I think a fortune will get a smile from their parents, I consider it a win. They're the ones footing the bill.

I found out about the job several months ago through Digital Writer, an online freelancing platform, while searching for ways to earn extra cash at home after Owen's bedtime. Peking Food's ad, filed under "creative writing," explained that the company was a mass producer of Asian foods such as noodles, wontons, and fortune cookies, and that it was looking to update its database of fortunes by nine hundred—specif- ically, three monthly batches of three hundred fortunes. To apply, the ad stated, "email us three fortunes that combine Old World authenticity with contemporary flair." I sent them these:

EVEN THE CLEVEREST OF COOKS HUNGERS FOR TAKEOUT SOMETIMES

FORTUNE IS EARNED IN LIFE, NOT FOUND IN COOKIES

YOU WILL SOON LOSE MONEY; THE CHECK ALWAYS ARRIVES WITH THE COOKIE

A day later, I got the job.

My ability to create original fortunes maxed out around forty, though, so by the end of September, I turned to online horoscopes for ideas, and then the library. *Chinese Proverbs: 500 Ageless Adages* was my first selection, and it was easy to tweak some of the sayings. THE CAPABLE WILL BE ASSIGNED MORE TASKS simply needed the addition of SO ALWAYS STRIVE FOR MEDIOCRITY WHEN VOLUNTEERING to make it Peking Food worthy. I went through the book saying by saying, ignoring those that fared poorly in translation. ONE RADISH, ONE HOLE may be pithy in Chinese, but it isn't salvageable in English. Neither is AS A MAN CANNOT BE KNOWN BY HIS LOOKS, NEITHER CAN THE SEA BE FATHOMED BY A GOURD, or A LARGE BULL CANNOT PICK HIS OWN LICE.

I flick away a tiny bagel crumb that's landed on *Someone Famous Once Said* and put the book aside, since it's mostly filled with the musings of nineteenth-century philosophers. I open the book of toasts and roasts and skim the chapter titled "Worldwide Words of Wisdom." Hopefully, it will get my creative juices flowing for this last batch.

I'm supposed to be at 260 by the end of the day, and 300 by Friday, but I'm behind because of the holiday. I open Notes in my iPhone, tap "Peking," and check my running tally. 243. Yikes. The last thing I need is a bad online review for missing a deadline.

I scroll down and double-check my earnings. At seventy-five cents per fortune, I grossed $275 a batch, $180 after deducting Digital Writer's cut. The money from the first two batches is gone already, used to offset my monthly shortfall, and the wise course of action would be to do the same with the third.

But I don't want to make the sensible decision. I want to put the money toward a piano for Owen. Because piano and soccer aren't equivalent, no matter how Nick tries to conflate the two. Piano isn't just a fun after-school activity—Owen is getting into trouble at school because he doesn't have access to one. And it's not Owen's fault that money is tight now that Nick has replaced me with Courtney.

I hear myself sigh, conspicuous in the silence of the library. What I want doesn't matter when I can't make the minimum payment due. Once I put Peking Foods behind me, though, I'll be able to devote more time to Smartypants, an online educational toy company, which so far has been easy money. All I have to do is spruce up their existing product copy with phrases like *sensory development* and *hand-eye coordination*, sprinkle in some SEO keywords, and voilà—I've met their 150-word minimum. The trick, I'm learning, is to keep the work stream steady, so that eventually, I'll have some extra money to put aside for Owen.

Eventually.

The poor kid's in for quite a wait. If I manage to get into college next year—with grants galore, no less—then my burgeoning editorial career will be replaced with work-study, and most of my settlement money will go toward living expenses. This whole house-of-cards setup I have is *not* a career. I am one massive allergy attack away from not being able to go back to Allerton—and that's my main source of income. I can't allow myself to be in such a delicate situation, because if I were to lose my job, how would I defend myself to a judge if Nick sued for custody? Fortune writing doesn't ooze financial security.

Let's say I'm able to stick it out at Allerton until next fall. I'm still dependent on Nick's child support for almost half of my monthly budget, and that is a very dangerous place to be in, especially with Courtney in the picture. What if they have a baby? Will Nick try to weasel his way out of paying child support for Owen? Even if he plays by the rules, the payments will drop with a new bundle of joy. I *have* to be working toward more stability. I can't let my future with Owen be dependent on the fickleness of my immune system and Nick's love life.

The newfound $275 from last night, though . . . it hasn't been earmarked for budget deficits, or college transfer application fees. It wouldn't be irresponsible of me to put it toward Owen's piano needs.

"Have you finished with these?"

An earnest-looking blonde is standing in front of the left-behind books I pushed aside. She's slim, her hair in a ponytail—pretty in a bland, forgettable way. I can't smile at her.

She waits for a moment, swallows uncomfortably, then speaks louder. "I can take them for you, if you're done with them."

I want to explain that they're not mine, that I'm not one of those thoughtless people who expects librarians to run around collecting books that I can easily return to the desk, but my mouth won't cooperate. I try to force a smile, because this woman's Courtneyness is not her fault, but the best I can offer is a tortured, stretched-lip tremble. I nudge the books toward her without a word, attempt to convey with a few agreeable nods that I don't mean to be rude. She collects them and glances at me with an expression that wavers between *are you okay?* and *you're scaring me*, then leaves.

I slump down in my seat, cheeks burning, my interest in fortunes, educational toys, and college gone. I open Facebook and type in "Lena Scolani," even though I already checked out the mystery woman last night. She either doesn't know of or doesn't care about privacy settings, because I'm able to go through her photos and posts without a problem. It's pretty typical: she's uploaded vacation photos, shared some inspirational memes, contributed to several GoFundMe campaigns, and posted the occasional political opinion. There are several photos of her with her arms wrapped around a woman who appears to be in her midtwenties, who I assume is her daughter. Her maiden name is Jacobs; she has a golden retriever named Chanel and two cats named Ralph and Lauren. She's not subtle, this Lena.

I can't find her on Twitter or Instagram. A Google search provides links to multiple articles about the actor Peter Scolari, and to White Pages listings of several people with the last name Scolani, but none of the listings are Lena's. Not that it would matter—I have that information on her check. I'm not sure what I'm looking for, exactly. Social media can't explain why Lena is so interested in helping Rose, who apparently dislikes her, or what her connection to Bernie's nephew is. I could call her, but what would I say? "I need to know the specifics of your personal relationships before I can make lasagna"? It's none of my business. My role in this situation is simple: make some meals, earn some cash.

I check the time and see that I've only got fifteen minutes left. I wolf down the rest of my bagel while I sneak a peek at the reference desk. A brown-haired librarian is working on a computer, no Faux Courtney in sight. Time to find a book about budget-friendly dinners before I head back to work.

— 4 —

Not every rabbit is delighted
by a carrot.

Owen loves to cook. I don't know where he gets it, since he spent his formative years eating takeout. Not fast food, like McDonald's—healthy takeout, mostly from Whole Foods. But wild-caught Alaskan salmon with garlicky kale is no longer a weekly staple on our menu.

He's never been an only-chicken-fingers-and-pasta kind of kid. So now I have a five-year-old with gourmet taste buds on what should be a Ramen noodle budget. If it were just me, I'd bare bones it, but I've got Owen's health to worry about, so our culinary expenditures are far higher than I'd like.

I hate to cook, and it's not because it's time-consuming, or because I don't like making a mess in the kitchen. It's because I'm bad at it, plain and simple. Baking I can do. All it requires is diligence: follow the recipe precisely, and the banana bread will rise. But cooking is more of an art; it requires the ability to improvise, to use the recipe as a guide rather than a blueprint. This is the part that escapes me. I can't count the number of times I've followed a recipe to a T only to end up with an inedible Pinterest fail. So why not make an omelet instead and save time, money, and frustration?

Owen is the *why not*, of course. For him, I've learned how to blanch, braise, brine, and broil. He can identify all the spices in our overcrowded rack by scent, and he has far better instincts as to what might improve a lackluster recipe than I do. "Maybe we should put in a little more cumin" isn't a suggestion I gave to my mom as a child.

Our creation tonight is lasagna, made with sweet Italian sausage, beef, and three cheeses. I made one for Rose and one for us. I hold the stairwell door open for Owen with my foot, Rose's tinfoil-covered lasagna in my hands, and hear his footsteps behind me as we descend.

"So, Owen," I say over my shoulder, "I wanted to tell you that Mrs. Klein . . . Owen?" I hear scurrying, and turn around. He's at the top of the stairs again. "Owen, come on."

He walks down, two reluctant feet per step instead of one, and finally reaches the landing between flights. "Can I wait right here?"

"Why are you so tired, kiddo?"

"I'm not, I just . . . I need to stay here for a minute."

"No, you've got to come with me. The lady we're bringing this to lives around the corner and all the way down the hall. I won't be able to see you if you stay here. That's not safe."

"But—"

"Honey, there's nothing to be nervous about. She's . . . well, remember how I told you that the Candy Grandpa's in heaven now? This lady is—*was*—his wife."

"I know."

"So what's the problem?"

Owen sits on the step and buries his head in his hands. "Idonwansay," he says, his voice muffled.

"I can't understand you when you're talking into your lap, O."

Owen looks up, exasperated. "I don't want to say! You told me, 'If you don't have anything nice to say, don't say—'"

"All right, all right, I know what I said. I give you permission."

He looks at me, not sure whether to trust my lifting of the rule. "But, she's a grown-up, and I'm not supposed to—"

"Owen! Out with it, already."

"Okay." He takes a deep breath and scrambles to his feet. "She's mean. I don't like her."

That's the big reveal? "How do you know that? You've never spoken to her before."

"She always yelled at the Candy Grandpa."

He's right. Rarely in English, which is why I suppose she felt comfortable scolding him in public. The times we observed, hand gestures led me to believe that their squabbles were over mundane issues, like forgetting to wear a hat or taking too long to pull the car up front.

"Well . . . they bickered sometimes. That's different."

Owen's brow furrows. "They *biggered*?"

"No, *bickered*. It means they argued about silly things. Things that don't really matter."

"Like you and Daddy?"

Ouch. What am I supposed to say to that? "No, sweetie, bickering is something people do when they've had the same argument for decades, and Daddy ditched me long before that stage could begin"? Or even better: "No, honey, people who bicker are irritated with each other; Daddy and I are doing our best not to despise each other right now"?

The guilt washes over me, and I want to stroke Owen's hair, hug him, and breathe in his sweet little boy scent—but I'm stuck with the lasagna, which is starting to feel heavy.

"Daddy and I do fight sometimes, it's true. And I'm sorry you've had to hear it. That was wrong of us. But we . . . we both love you so much, and living apart is new and hard for us, too. We're still trying to figure some things out. Come on, let's get this over with and then we'll find something fun to do together. Maybe make hot chocolate?"

Owen nods, but he looks unconvinced.

"You'll be fine, honey." I walk down the hall, inventorying ingredients in my head. Milk, sugar, marshmallows, vanilla, cocoa powder. Hmm. I seem to remember scooping from the bottom of the cocoa tin the last time we made it. "Hey, O," I say over my shoulder, "what would be your second choice, just in case we don't have all the ingredients?"

Silence. So he hasn't been walking behind me the length of the corridor?

"Owen, let's *go*. Trust me, you're making this out to be a much bigger deal than it is."

I hear a sudden scurrying of footsteps, and Owen's breath coming in spurts. This hiding and then running to catch up is getting old. Rose isn't a monster, no matter what his imagination has her worked up to be.

"Huh?" Owen asks, as he falls in step beside me.

"You didn't hear me? I wanted to know what your second choice for dessert would be if—"

"Oh! Anything is good."

My heart swells as I look down at the sandy brown cowlick toward the back of his head. He hates it, makes me wet it and comb it flat every morning. By the time he gets home from school it's sticking up again, but by then he's forgotten about it. It's from me, not Nick, which is the reason I like it. My hair's too long and thick to have a cowlick now, but my baby photos are proof of the origin of that noncompliant lock of hair.

Besides my hair and dimples, Owen's all Nick. He's got Nick's gorgeous eyes, and thankfully, metabolism. After Nick and I separated, it worried me, how much they look alike. Maybe Owen will pull away, I feared—maybe he'll choose Nick over me because he knows, on some unconscious level, that genetics tie them together more closely. Or—even scarier—what if seeing Nick in Owen's face will somehow taint my love for him?

Neither turned out to be true. My little man is still a mama's boy. When he's upset, he wants me, not Nick. Nick even had to FaceTime me a couple of Wednesdays ago because Owen skinned his knee and wouldn't calm down until I took a look at it, agreed with Nick's Neosporin and Band-Aid treatment plan, and blew him a kiss. And as for me loving him less—I can't believe that crazy thought ever crossed my mind. When I look at Owen, I see the tiny person who made me understand phrases I used to think were corny, like *the light of my life* and *you are my sunshine*. I see Owen, not Nick. Owen, who is more than an inherited collection of features.

I jut my hip to the side, knock him slightly off-balance to break the tension. I get a tentative smile, but not the giggle I was hoping for.

"What number is she?" he asks, his steps slowing.

"Eleven. A little bit further down on the right." I count the apartment numbers as I walk by them. "Seven . . . nine . . . eleven. We made it! Do you want to knock?" I glance over my shoulder, can see that he's retreating to the hallway corner. "Owen, come on." I motion for him to catch up. "There's nothing to be scared of."

Owen shakes his head and backtracks farther.

"Owen, *stop*!" I hiss, as he reaches the corner. I can't drag him to the door by the hand while holding the lasagna, and we both know it, so I cave. "Fine. You win. But you have to stay where I can see you."

I knock on the door. No answer. I glance back at Owen, shrug my shoulders as I wait. I knock two more times, and finally—footsteps.

"I'm coming," I hear from inside. "Hold your horses, I'm coming." An elderly woman opens the door, but it's not Rose. She's under five feet, with a plump grandmotherly figure, and, above her lip, a mole with several hairs growing out of it. Her hair is the same style as Rose's—short, combed back from her face on the top and the sides, and meticulously sprayed into position.

The woman looks at the aluminum pan in my hands. "You're looking for Rose?"

"Yes. I'm Mar—"

"Rose!" the woman barks, without looking behind her. "You have a visitor."

"Coming, coming already," I hear over the murmurings of several voices, and then Rose appears at the doorway. It takes a moment to reconcile the woman in front of me with the picture I have of her in my mind, because of how frail she looks without her heavy winter coat. I was right about the hairstyle—it's the same as the woman at the door's—but Rose's is jet-black instead of ash blond, a jarring mismatch with the deep lines etched in her face, the age spots that dot her cheeks and forehead, the sagging skin under her chin. She looks at me quizzically.

I try again. "Hi. I'm Marissa. I live upstairs." I wait for some sign of recognition, but her face remains blank. "I . . . I knew your husband. He was a very kind man."

Rose glances down at my aluminum pan and frowns. "So you've brought a lasagna?"

The lighter-haired woman wrinkles her nose and mutters something that sounds like "tray." Rose gives her a disapproving look, although I'm not sure if it's because she disagrees with the woman or because I've made a faux pas by delivering the lasagna in a disposable pan instead of a formal serving tray.

I feel my cheeks flush. "Umm, yes, lasagna. How did you know?"

"Everyone brings lasagna," Rose says. "It's cheap, it's easy to make, you can freeze it for later. You get to be an old lady like me, you've made a lot of lasagnas."

"Oh, I didn't realize . . . well, I can make something you'd like better for tomorrow. I mean, I can have someone else make it. The management sent out an email, and a group of us pooled together and were hoping to help out with meals for this week." Lena's excuse tumbles out before I realize I hadn't planned what to say if other people from the building were in Rose's apartment. Other people who wouldn't have received the imaginary email I just referenced.

"No! No need. No space left in my freezer." She waves the lasagna away. "Milk doesn't sit so good with me, anyway. Now you have a lovely dinner for yourself, already made. So it works out for both of us if you keep it." She gives a curt nod, as if we've come to this conclusion together, and lets the door slam closed without a thank-you or goodbye.

I turn toward Owen, still hovering by the corner in the hallway. I open my mouth to offer some rationale for Rose's behavior, but can't. How to explain this woman?

"See?" he whispers. "Mean."

— 5 —

Even from one branch, two pears may not taste the same.

Common Grounds is a café named for its coffee as well its location opposite the Town Common. It also happens to be down the street from where I work, and some days, when the wind blows strongly to the south, the aroma of espresso and pastries wafts into Allerton's parking lot, drowning out its faint medicinal smell, and I have to steel myself against the financial and caloric splurge. I've budgeted for lunch there on Tuesdays and Thursdays only.

Those are the days I have the eleven thirty lunch slot, which means it's morning commuting time on the West Coast. It's the only time all week that I can reliably reach Lindsay or Mom. So I treat myself to a hazelnut coffee and a lemon scone for lunch, find a cozy spot in the back, and try to catch up with one of them. I tend to call my mom first, since a conversation with Lindsay requires a certain amount of—well, *restraint*—and some weeks I'm just not up for it. But today I choose Lindsay.

She picks up on the first ring. "Hey, Riss. Hold on a sec, okay?" I hear a man's voice, soothing and steady above the sounds of the seashore, followed by silence, and then, Lindsay's return. "God*damn* it. It's supposed to stop the book audio when I get calls. I don't know if the problem is with the Bluetooth or the app, but—"

"What book are you listening to?"

"You wouldn't know it."

"I do *read*, you know."

"It's nonfiction."

"I read nonfiction sometimes."

"Look, it's just not something you'd understand." She takes a deep breath, and then her tone switches from Normal Lindsay to Spiritual Lindsay. "That you'd be open to *processing*, I should have said. Exploring personal truth is often difficult for those who are more . . . guarded."

I bet my feeble mind could handle it, I want to say, but I bite my tongue. She's probably right about me not being interested, assuming she's listening to yet another book about discovering her life's path. But deciding against spending twenty minutes a day meditating on how to best fulfill my dharma doesn't make me an idiot. It makes me busy.

I don't know why I still expect us to be as close as we were growing up. You'd think I'd accept it by now—the disdain that creeps into her voice sometimes, the way her words seem poised to wound. I can't pinpoint when it started. There's no pivotal event that altered our relationship. Until high school, our life paths were the same, to use Lindsay's lingo. Same schools, same sports, same after-school clubs. Me first, then Lindsay two years later. By the time she started high school, I was a junior, worried about AP courses, getting my license, SATs, and the constant pressure for sex from my then-boyfriend, Todd. I knew she was struggling with schoolwork, and I offered to help, but her answer was always no. Mom said she was embarrassed, that it was hard for her because everything came so easily to me. That I should give her some space. So I did. Senior year came and went, dominated by angst over college applications and my on-again, off-again relationship with Todd. It wasn't until Thanksgiving break of my freshman year at college that I noticed any change in Lindsay. I came home to find that Todd no longer had any interest in me, which was more of a relief than a concern. What *did* take me by surprise was that Lindsay no longer seemed to have any interest in me, either.

I take a gulp of my coffee and swallow hard. Lindsay doesn't like when I eat or drink while talking on the phone, tells me that doing so isn't *mindful*, but I think the truth is that she thinks it's disgusting to listen to. I wish she would just say that to me outright. Because the old Lindsay would say, "Stop it, that's gross," not "One must show gratitude for nourishment."

I called Lindsay today, not Mom, because I wanted her advice about the bizarre Lena-Rose situation I've somehow become entangled in, but now, less than a minute into our conversation, I don't feel like bringing it up. I don't want to beg her to tell me about some stupid book that I'm too shallow to understand, either, so I switch gears. "I was just checking to see how your Thanksgiving went. Mom said you went to Eric's. But it sounds like I caught you at a bad time, so why don't I call back—"

"Eric and I broke up."

"What? Mom said—"

"Why would I tell Mom right before her trip to see you? I didn't want her to have second thoughts about going, or to feel guilty the whole time. And I didn't want you to be alone."

I feel a stab of guilt. Sometimes I get so caught up in feeling defensive around Lindsay that I forget she's one of the most selfless people I've ever known. Far more generous than me, always has been. Like that time I was sick on Halloween when I was nine and she was seven. She collected eight mini-Butterfinger bars for me when she was trick-or-treating, even though she hated them, because she knew they were my favorite. She did it all on her own, too; she went trick-or-treating with neighbors because Dad was on a job and Mom was home taking care of me. I wouldn't have done that, had the situation been reversed. I'd have picked up one or two, a token gesture. But *eight*? Besides a prized animal like Owen's Geri, there's no possession of greater value to a seven-year-old than candy.

"Oh, Linds, I'm so sorry. You've been together for such a long time. . ."

She chokes back a sob. "Six years."

"What happened?"

"We want different things from life. He wants kids, and that's not in the cards for me right now. That's what I get for dating an older man, I guess."

That's not in the cards. So she's moved on to tarot cards now? "Wait, do you mean—"

"Oh my God, Marissa. It's an expression."

I can't help but smile. Lindsay can read my mind better than anyone. Better than Nick, better than my parents, better than any of my friends. This is why it's worth putting up with all of her bullshit. "I know it's an expression. I wasn't thinking . . . what you think I was thinking."

I brace myself for the logical response *So what were you going to ask me, then?*—but Lindsay doesn't press further. "Whatever," she says. "Eric's just not as flexible as I thought he was. He's not willing to consider any alternate journey. I don't know if I ever want to get married."

"Ever? To anyone?" My eyes fill with tears. I've tainted the entire institution for her. "Is it because of me?"

She lets out a frustrated sigh. "Honestly, not every decision I make is in reaction to one you've made."

I stifle the irritation that flares again, suppress the urge to tell her off for lashing out at me, because I know she's in pain. "I'm confused. Did he ask you to marry him and you said no?"

"No, but we've talked about it before. Everything just came to a head." She takes in a deep breath, lets it out in a controlled, steady stream. I count to eight in my head, since that's the Lindsay number for relaxation exhalations. "Sometimes you have to listen to what the universe is whispering to you."

What the universe is whispering to you? Please. It's so self-indulgent, to think that the universe gives a shit about any of our problems. I don't know how many planets exist in the universe, but I do know the estimate has more sets of zeros than I can comprehend. The earth is infinitesimal in relation to the vastness of the cosmos, so why Lindsay thinks her mundane struggles warrant a ranking on the universe's list of concerns is beyond me. But I shouldn't be surprised. Lindsay and I can't even agree on definitions. For her, the *universe* means *wherever you live* and the forces within it aren't gravitational or electromagnetic. They're mystical, and apparently they're willing to reward the attentive with individualized life coaching.

"Okay," I say, keeping my voice neutral, "so what exactly does the universe think you should do?"

"I'm not sure yet. But I do know that I need to seek my life's path rather than passively accept society's dictates. Life's decisions need to be active; they need to be deliberated and birthed."

Birthed. It's an interesting word to choose, a Freudian slip, because six years of being a couple with no resulting pregnancy means birth control, a decision that Eric seems to no longer be on board with. It's ironic, actually, that my spontaneous go-where-the-wind-takes-you sister has done a far better job of being responsible with contraception than I have.

"But do you love him, Linds?" I ask. "'Cause that's the only thing that matters."

"No," she says bluntly. "It's not." She stops short of saying what I know she's thinking: *You know better than anyone that that's not true.* "Listen, I've got to run. I'm pulling in to work right now. Talk soon, okay?"

Silence. Lindsay gets high marks for spirituality, but she could benefit from remedial work in etiquette. At the very least, she could have given me a namaste. I assume *namaste* means goodbye—or both hello and goodbye, like *aloha*—because the instructor at my prenatal yoga class used to say it at the beginning and ending of each session. But then again, what do I know? Maybe it translates as a Lindsay-approved phrase, like *a full heart*, or *be true to your intention.*

I'll give Lindsay this: she's great for writer's block. *Explore personal truth, consider an alternate journey, listen to the whisperings of the universe, seek your life's path* . . . I can tweak these, no problem. I open Notes on my phone and type in the new Lindsayisms for later editing.

I finish off my scone, my finger hovering over Mom's name in the contact list, then think better of calling. If I tell her that some mystery woman is paying me to cook for a nasty old lady, it'll come out that I'm doing it to fund Owen's piano needs. Then Mom will send me money, and she shouldn't. I saw Dad's phone on Sunday.

He was checking online to see if their return flight was delayed before we left for the airport. Mom was perched next to him on the couch, Owen in her lap.

"You're going to slice your finger open, Dad," I said, looking at the spiderweb of concentric circles etched around the point of impact on the screen. "Aren't you going to get your phone fixed?"

He cleared his throat and glanced at my mom, then focused on the screen again. "Looks like the flight's on time," he said.

"Family is more important than a phone," my mom said, wrapping her arms around Owen and pulling him in close for a snuggle.

I take a sip of my coffee, the hazelnut flavor cloying now that the coffee is tepid. Grimacing, I push the cup to the side of the tray, and try to sort out in my mind what happened in that moment. There's the surface reading: my detail-oriented dad was focused on check-in procedures, while my child-focused mom made an offhand comment about the importance of family. But it isn't like my dad to flat-out ignore me. Is it possible he wasn't distracted, but embarrassed? Could it be that my parents had time to fix the phone, but couldn't afford to after buying tickets? Maybe Mom's comment about prioritizing family over phone was precise, not offhand.

I sigh, because I have zero objectivity when it comes to my parents and money. Every consideration is shaded by guilt, because I know why my dad still drives a beat-up Buick and my mom offers private tutoring after she's done teaching for the day. And what have they gotten for their investment in my education? A daughter who's barely scraping by.

So cross Mom off the list for a Rose consultation. That means I have one person left to call: Lena. It's clear that Rose doesn't want me to come back, and after last night's debacle, I'm not looking forward to making a return visit. I *could* keep the money and call it quits; Lena admitted it was a risk she was willing to take. And no one besides the two of us knows about our deal. It's not like I'd be setting a bad example for Owen that I'd then have to justify. And the money is for *him*, not for me.

Wanting to help my child doesn't make me a terrible person.

But let's be honest: it doesn't make me noble, either. I'm no Jean Valjean, stealing a loaf of bread to feed my family. I'd be taking money from a well-meaning woman who's trying to help a grieving widow, and there's no way to dress that up. I scroll to Lena's name under my contact list, my heart pounding as the phone rings. What the hell am I going to say? *Rose is rude and she scares the shit out of my kid* is what comes to mind—accurate, but hardly appropriate. Then again, Rose seems to scare Lena, too. I doubt she'd be surprised to hear a sanitized version of that character assessment.

Lena's voicemail comes on and relief floods through me, even though I know phone tag isn't going to resolve the situation. "Hi, Lena," I say, after the beep. "This is Marissa. From Rose's building? I, uhh . . . I tried to leave a lasagna with Rose last night, but she wouldn't take it and she—well, she slammed the door in my face. I can give it another shot tonight, but I don't have high hopes. She really doesn't seem to want visitors. Or Italian food. Please call me back today, if you can. I'm available after three. I hope . . . I hope we can find a way to make this work."

— 6 —

When water floods the crane's nest, she builds again.

Teriyaki chicken with broccoli is on the menu tonight. Owen is lying on the countertop, making lazy circles with a fork in the cornstarch and water solution we'll use to thicken the sauce, while I check to see if the water for the rice has started to boil.

"Why so sleepy, O?" I stabilize the bowl before it tips. "Usually you're excited when we cook."

Owen sits up with a shrug and beats the solution harder, the way he's supposed to.

"I'm not mad, honey. I can do it if you need to rest."

"It's okay. Are we making any dessert for Mrs. Klein?"

"Yep. We can't put any butter or milk in it, though, so that cuts down on our options. I thought maybe we'd make fruit salad for her? Think that's a good idea?"

Owen makes a face. "I mean, that's not really *dessert* . . ."

"For grown-ups, it can be. But if you think it's a bad idea, I can send it to school with you for lunch instead." I add the rice to the pot, stir the chicken and broccoli sizzling in the pan to the left of it, then turn to face him.

"School's better," he says, perking up. "Pack a *lot*. With a granola bar, or some Triscuits. But put it in my snack bag, not my lunch bag."

"But you have snack so early in the morning, O. Are you sure you're going to be hungry for that much food?"

Owen nods, his back angled toward me now, but I can tell by his hand motions and the steady clinking of his fork that he's trying to break up a pesky clump of cornstarch.

He must be having a growth spurt. God, this is going to be expensive, and I have zero dollars accrued in my Unanticipated Height Fund. I've got to stop being so organized with my preseason shopping. I bought him his winter-weight pants in September, and I've already washed them and thrown away the tags. And for what? To avoid the horror of a chilly morning in—*gasp!*—fall-weight pants? Please. There are plenty of kids at the bus stop still in shorts, even on fifty-degree days.

At least he's craving healthy food. I just hope snack time doesn't follow writing—that's a surefire way to guarantee he gets down no food at all. Mrs. Evans is a stickler for penmanship. I don't mean to make excuses—it's not pre-K anymore—but I know Owen is capable of writing four sentences about what he did over the weekend, or the plot of *Where the Wild Things Are*, or what animal he'd be if he could turn into one. And lately he's only been writing a sentence or two, max. The worksheets he brings home are worn through with eraser marks in spots, and I can see the imprint of multiple attempts in areas that haven't torn yet. What frustrates me is that every single letter was legible *before* she forced him to perfect them. It seems extreme for kindergarten. I like the idea of setting high standards, but at some point, I may need to schedule that parent-teacher conference I thought wasn't necessary when the sign-up sheet went around at the Open House back in September. I think it's more important at this age to teach kids how to express themselves than to be fanatical about—

My phone rings, and "Lena Scolani" lights up on the display.

"Lena! I'm glad you called." I tap Owen on the back, and he turns and hands me the cornstarch solution, then flips onto his belly and slides off the countertop.

"Hi, Marissa. Sounds like yesterday wasn't a huge success."

"That's an understatement." I stir the mixture into the chicken and broccoli pan, set the microwave timer for three minutes, and shoo Owen toward the living room. "I'm making Rose's dinner right now, but if she's as thrilled to see me today as she was yesterday, then I'm not sure how I can make the rest of the week work. Also, I thought the . . . I'm sorry, I can't remember the name . . . the, umm, condolence call . . . I thought it was only on Sunday night. But when I dropped by last night, Rose had friends over, and I interrupted her. So it wasn't the best timing."

"She did? That surprises me. I mean, traditionally, shiva lasts a week, but Rose isn't very religious, so I assumed she would just open her home the one night. But I should have prepared you for the fact that she might have some close friends over on the second day. I apologize. I can't imagine there'll be anyone there tonight."

"Well, even if that's the case, I have another problem. I don't have any good trays. They're all at my ex's house."

"What?"

"Rose didn't like my tray. Or her friend didn't. I made lasagna, and I brought it over in the aluminum pan I baked it in. I didn't realize it was customary to present the meal more formally."

"It's not. I'm not sure what you're talking about. What exactly did she say?"

"Rose didn't say anything. But her friend looked disgusted when she saw the lasagna. Then she gave Rose a look and muttered 'tray' under her breath."

"Just 'tray'?"

"Yep."

"Huh." Lena is silent for a moment. "Wait. What did you say you made for dinner?"

"Lasagna."

"Meat or veggie?"

"Meat—sausage and beef."

"This friend of Rose's—did she have a large mole above her lip, by any chance? Was she very short and plump?"

"Yes. How did you know that?"

"That was Dottie! She's Rose's best friend. I'm so glad to hear she was there. But that's beside the point. My guess is she said *treif*, which is Yiddish for 'nonkosher.'"

I flush with embarrassment. "Pork! I wasn't thinking! But . . . I didn't tell her there was sausage in it. Lots of lasagna recipes call for beef only. How did she know?"

"She didn't. But she must have assumed there was *some* kind of meat in it. And it isn't kosher to mix any kind of milk and meat in the same meal."

"So the cheese counts as milk? Why didn't you warn me? I feel like such an idiot! Do you think I offended Rose? Is that why she shut the door on me?"

"No, no, no. You did nothing wrong! I didn't tell you about any dietary restrictions because Rose doesn't keep kosher. At least, she didn't.

48

Maybe she's become more observant over the years. But again, I apologize. Here you did me this enormous favor, and you were met with . . . well, Dottie could use some lessons in tact, and Rose is . . . I guess you could say brusque."

Brusque. This Lena is the Queen of Decorum.

She sighs. "I know she's not easy. But if you would be willing to try one more time, I would be so appreciative."

"I'm willing to give it another shot," I say, since I'm already mid-double batch. "But honestly, I don't know if she'll even open the door for me. Any ideas?"

"Hmm . . . I bet her curiosity will be piqued if you tell her Joel Klein was the one who asked management to send out the email."

"Who's Joel Klein?"

"Her nephew. The psychiatrist I told you about, remember? Tell her that . . . tell her that he felt badly he couldn't get back until Saturday, so he set this up. It'll work, no question. He can do no wrong by her."

A new lie? So now Lena, the mystery woman, wants me to spin a tale about Joel, the mystery man? Who is connected to Rose—how, again? His last name is Klein, so he has to be from Bernie's side of the family. I'm about to ask Lena when I remember her words from when we met: *Bernie's brother lives in Florida.* So this Joel is Bernie's nephew.

This is getting ridiculous, though. Any normal person would be delighted, or, at the very least, appreciative, of someone cooking and delivering dinner to them. But not Rose. Yet here's Lena apologizing profusely on her behalf, attempting to butter me up with talk of the *enormous favor* I'm doing for her, when we both know this is a business arrangement, plain and simple.

What is the deal with your tortured relationship with Rose? I want to ask, but as I try to think of more acceptable phrasing, the microwave dings.

I turn toward the stove. The sauce is bubbling and splattering all over the stove top. I forgot to turn it down to simmer.

I curse softly under my breath, flip the stove dial to low. "Lena, I've got to go. I'm about to ruin dinner. Wish me luck tonight."

— 7 —

The owl may be small, but his eyes are large.

The stairs again.

I look up at Owen from the landing between the first and second floor staircases. He's retreated to the top and is hovering near the open doorway.

"Not again, O. She's not *that* scary."

Owen flashes me a look that says, *That's a lie.*

"Come on, honey. You're carrying the rice. You're going to have to come down at some point."

Owen shakes his head furiously and backs up farther.

"Okay, okay. You win. I'll wait."

"No! I . . . uh . . ." He motions me up the steps so he can whisper in my ear, even though there's no one around to overhear us. "I have to pee."

"Can you hold it? We're just dropping off—"

"*Mom.*" He puts the rice container on top of my chicken and vegetables, and fishes around in my bag for my keys.

"Owen! Stop it—I'll go back with you."

"No. I'll catch up." He spins me away from him, then sprints through the doorway.

What is going on with him? Is Rose intimidating enough to cause a bathroom run? Does she look like a scary character from a movie or TV show? Or from some clip he's come across on that hellscape known as the Web, despite my best parental control efforts?

My arms are starting to ache, so I make my way toward Rose's. I've almost reached her apartment when his hurried footsteps thump behind me. I look back and see him turn the corner that connects the main hallway to Rose's corridor. He's running, and his face looks flushed.

He stops as soon as he sees me. "I'll wait right here," he says, in a stage whisper.

"Fine. Just stay where I can see you."

I knock on the door lightly, then take a step back.

"I'm coming, I'm coming, enough with the *klopping* already," she says, as if I've been pounding on her door. She swings it open, glances down at my tinfoil-covered culinary gifts, and lets out a sigh that sounds like the one I made when Owen "helped" clean up after making veggie soup by flushing all the ends and skins down the toilet. "You again. Like I said, no room in my freezer. It would only go to waste here. You take it, you'll have a nice dinner for yourself for tomorrow." She nods, as if we're in agreement, just as she did yesterday.

"Joel asked if I could bring this to you!" I blurt out, before she can close the door on me.

"*My* Joel?"

"Uh, yes. Joel Klein."

Lena was right: a glimmer appears in Rose's hollowed eyes, a proud smile eclipsing her usual grimace. I let Lena's contrived story tumble out of me. "Remember the email I told you management sent? He set that up. So I didn't talk to him directly, but—"

"Such a smart boy! Always has been. He's a hotshot doctor now. And so good-hearted. Such a *mensch*, that Joel."

Boy. It's sweet Rose thinks of Joel this way. I have no idea how old he is, but if he's Bernie's nephew and an accomplished psychiatrist, my guess is he's a good four to five decades past boyhood by now. "He's at a conference until Saturday, I heard?"

Rose nods. "In London. I told him, so what's the rush? You think I won't be here when you get back?"

"Well, I think he wanted to make sure you had some help in the interim." I point to the dinner I'm cradling with my free hand. "Teriyaki chicken and vegetables—no milk to worry about." I point toward Owen. "My son, Owen, helped me cook. He's a great little chef."

Rose opens the door fully and looks in Owen's direction. "So this is the little *boychik* Bernie was talking about!" She clasps her hands together. "Not so many *kinder* in the building. Come, come! I have candies for you. In Bernie's office."

Owen eyes Rose warily, then scurries over and hides behind me. Rose retreats into her apartment, and since I'm not sure if she expects us to follow her, we hover in the hallway. I clear my throat loudly to get Rose's attention, then take a few tentative steps toward the kitchen, which is to my left. "So, I'll just leave all this on the table for you, okay?"

"Hah?" Rose's voice comes from a room down the hall to the right, the room that must be Bernie's office.

"On the kitchen table?" I yell. "Can I leave the food here?"

"No, no, no! If it's warm, it's not so good for the wood. On the counter is much better."

I pivot toward the countertops. Mounds of magazines, newspapers, and shopping bags blanket them; dishes, glasses, and food remnants fill the sink that divides them. There is one small, unclaimed area on the far-right corner, so I place the container of chicken and veggies on it and stack Owen's rice on top.

Rose reappears from within Bernie's office and takes several steps toward the kitchen. "You. Little boy." She beckons for him to come closer with her bony finger. "I will tell you where to find—" She stops short, as she notices where I've set dinner down. "No. Not there. That spot is for the phone."

"Oh! I'm sorry," I say reflexively, although there's no phone to be seen. I assume Rose isn't referring to a cell, but I don't see a cordless phone or a base, either. The contested countertop area is as far away from the electrical outlets as you can get in the kitchen, so its location doesn't make any sense.

"Go pick out a piece of candy," she says to Owen, pointing to Bernie's office as she walks toward me. "It's in a jar on the desk. I have to help your mama find us a new spot." She opens the cabinet above my containers and pulls out a desk phone that must be from the seventies. The only time I've ever seen a corded phone like the sturdy, fire-engine-red one in front of me is in the movies or old photos. It looks like a prop, like it should be sitting next to the Rolodex on the desk of an intrepid reporter. She hands back my containers and positions the phone in its rightful place. Holding on to the countertop with one hand, she lowers herself to a squat, leans forward while squinting at the floor—and loses her balance.

"*Oy gevalt!*" She clutches my leg to steady herself.

I hoist her back up to standing. "Are you okay?"

She takes in a ragged breath, and coughs. "Yah, yah. It looks like

I need to do more of my exercises. The jack is down below." She points to the wall-mounted plate just above the baseboard trim. "You will plug it back in for me?"

"Of course!"

"It was too much, with the phone calls. Too much talking about Bernie."

"I understand." I don't, really, but what else can I say? No one close to me has died, not even my grandparents. I can't offer her any comforting words about Bernie, a man I hardly knew. And didn't she just say she didn't want to talk about him?

I set the containers aside and plug the telephone cord into the jack. It's an odd place for a cord to be—out in the open, not hidden behind a couch or a desk. I'm a bit worried that Rose might trip over it. She notices me holding it and points to a small strip of rectangular plastic running from the base of the wall to the top of the countertop. "It goes there. Bernie set it up."

It's a cord cover. It's off-white, camouflaged against the cabinetry, so I didn't notice it. Ripping the cord out must have been easy enough, but laying it flat and feeding it back through the channel will require far more dexterity. From the expectant look on Rose's face, I can see the job is now mine, and that's fine by me. I'll take a tedious chore over a meaning-of-life discussion with a near-stranger any day. I can sense her monitoring my progress from behind as I push the cord forward in miniscule increments. "All set," I say, as I thread the final length of cord through the channel.

"Nuh-uh-uh." Rose shakes her head. "Not so fast." She picks up the receiver, puts it to her ear. She smiles, then holds it in front of me so I can hear the muted dial tone. "Now we are done! So. Time to find a place for your containers."

I don't know if Rose thinks that hiding the cord affects dial tone transmission, or if she's just a person who likes to check her work, but either way, I'm happy she's moved on to . . . stacking, it seems? She's taking magazines and newspapers strewn about the countertop and placing them atop her existing overburdened piles, in order to open up new space. She grabs my containers and shoves them into a spot that's far too small for them. She leaves them precariously perched over the edge, with the Leaning Tower of Newspapers looming from above. It's a solution that's doomed to fail, but Rose looks satisfied with her work.

I hear it then, from Bernie's office—the melody of a familiar song, although I can't put my finger on which one. Rose pales suddenly, and freezes, mouth ajar. The right side of her face pulls into a half smile; or—oh, God, please no—is the left side slumping and the right side neutral? There is a faraway look in her eyes. She is somewhere else.

Jesus Christ. Is this a stroke? Asymmetry is one of the classic signs, isn't it? "Rose! Rose! Are you okay? Rose!"

She looks at me, her eyes blank, and then, after an agonizing moment, she refocuses. "Wha—? Oh—yes, yes. It was the music, that's all."

Normal speech. I breathe a huge sigh. "Sit down for a minute." I lead her to one of her kitchen chairs to examine her face. Her expression is even now. "You can see me?"

"What? Of course I can see you."

What did I learn in that First Aid course I took for lifeguard certification back in high school? It's AAOx3, isn't it? Rose is awake, she's alert, she orients to her name. What are the other two Os? *Think.* Name . . . place and time!

"You know where we are?"

"What are you, *meshuggah*? In my apartment!"

"What day is it?"

Rose gives me a look. "Tuesday. Are we done now, with your questions?"

I turn toward the sink, pull the least dirty glass out of it, and refill it with water. I'm not sure why I'm getting it, to be honest; it just feels like I should be doing *something*. "Here." I plunk the glass down on the table in front of her. "Take some sips. I'll be right back."

I stride to the office to find Owen seated on the worn tufted cushion of a piano bench, his back to me, a trail of hard candy wrappers behind him. He senses me, turns, and smiles. "Mommy, look what I found! A *piano*!"

It's an upright, with mahogany wood and an intricately carved music rack. I don't know enough about pianos to assess how old it might be, but other than a few scuffs, it's in pretty good shape. "That's exciting, honey." I use the most even voice I can muster. "But I think you surprised Rose—Mrs. Klein, I mean—and she's going to need to rest. Now's not the best time to—"

"No, no, let him play." Rose has followed me into Bernie's office. "It's been such a long time."

"Rose! You need to sit." I swivel the desk chair around for her. "And I don't want to overstep my bounds, but maybe call your doctor? I think that would be—"

"Sha, sha!" She waves away my suggestion, listens intently as Owen begins to play again. She closes her eyes as music fills the room.

"Did you play?" I whisper.

Rose shakes her head.

"Bernie?"

"Nah, neither of us. Joey did. At our old house."

So Joel lived with you when he was younger? I want to ask, but for the second time in as many hours I have to remind myself that my job is to deliver meals, not pry into Rose's family history.

"What song are you playing, O?"

"The Kermit song," he says, over his shoulder.

"You mean *It's Not Easy Being Green*? How do you know about The Muppets? They're even before *my* time. I've only seen one of the movies. Grandma rented it from Blockbuster when I was home sick from school one day."

Owen stops playing, turns, and gives me a quizzical look. Video stores aren't in his memory. They are to him what corded phones are to me. The idea that a movie might not be accessible at all times, with just a few taps of a finger or clicks of a remote, is incomprehensible to him. "Daddy and I watch Muppet movies when I stay with him overnight. There are a lot of them." He hums the song that I still can't place, experiments with matching the sound of his voice to the notes of the piano. Whatever he's singing under his breath isn't *It's Not Easy Being Green*, I can tell now, but what other Kermit song is there? More importantly, Nick and Owen have a weekend tradition that I don't know about?

They have every right to. I know that. And I admit I'm selective with the information I share with Nick about Owen. But it still hurts to know I'm not in on the secret. And it sucks to be the do-your-homework mom when Nick gets to be the Muppets-and-cupcakes dad.

"We can watch the Muppets together, too, sometimes. I think it used to be a TV show also—maybe I could find episodes on YouTube Kids."

"No, it's okay. Daddy will get them."

Owen begins to play again, starts the song from the beginning. My eyes fill with tears, and I'm glad he's facing away from me. I don't want to make him feel guilty for having fun with Nick, and I shouldn't have tried to insert myself into whatever routine they've set up together. I know what I should and shouldn't do, what I should and shouldn't say—but knowing that doesn't make doing it any easier.

It bursts into my memory then, a hazy image of Kermit strumming a banjo in his bog. "Oh . . . *Rainbow Connection*. That's what it is!"

Owen swivels around on the bench. He nods, a serious look on his face. "Uh-huh. But I've only figured out part of it. Can you find it on the iPad so I can listen more? I can't remember the whole song."

"Sure. How many times have you heard it?"

"Once."

"And you figured out the whole chorus?" He gives me a blank look, so I clarify. "The chorus is the part of the music that repeats with the same words and music."

"He plays by the ear!" Rose grasps my arm. "Such talent, your boychik."

"Thank you! I'd like to get him lessons, but my ex . . ." I sigh. "It gets complicated."

Rose nods. "All of it, yes. Marriage, children, divorce . . ." She stops short of saying the word we're both thinking: *death*. Her chin is quivering, and I'm not sure what to do. Should I look away and let her compose herself? What if she starts to cry? Should I hug her? Fifteen minutes ago I was afraid to walk into her apartment, and since then I've helped out with home repair, evaluated her medical status, and twice skirted counseling after death.

She swallows twice, hard, and her chin stills. "So. It's a school night, yes?"

I don't know if she wants me to leave so she can cry, or whether she's graciously giving me an out, but either way, I'm happy to leave. "It is." I motion for Owen to come over. "But before we go, are you sure you're feeling okay? Because, before when Owen started playing, when you got, umm . . ."

"What, because I'm an old lady it has to be an emergency? I was surprised is all. I'm fine." She waves away my concerns.

"Uh, okay," I sputter, relieved. She really does sound fine, and she's walking normally, too. "I'm sorry Owen surprised you, but . . . thanks for letting him play. I hope you like the chicken."

"What are you talking? Of course I will." Rose follows us to the door. "Would you let me know who is being so kind by making the dinners? For the thank you notes."

Damn it. Now I need another lie. I force a smile, and hope it looks like a genuine one. "No thank you cards needed. I wouldn't even know who to thank. Everyone pitched in money, and I picked up the collection from the leasing office. Owen and I make all the dinners, since he loves to cook. We'll be by tomorrow with another one. Or—I will. Owen stays with his dad on Wednesdays."

"Mommy, come *on*." Owen pulls me by the sleeve.

"See you then!" I wave and follow Owen into the hallway before he knocks me off-balance. "Stop pulling me," I say, as we round the corner. "What's the problem?"

"You were talking a lot."

"Well, it's a sad time for Mrs. Klein. I think it made her really happy to hear you play, though. I don't know if you heard her, but she said nobody has played the piano for a very long time."

Owen's brow furrows. "I don't get it."

"Get what?"

"Her piano. It sounds just like the one at school."

"Of course it does. The notes sound the same on every piano."

He rolls his eyes. "Duh. Everyone knows that. But only if the piano goes to the doctor."

"What are you talking about?"

"We couldn't go to the music room yesterday because the piano doctor came for a visit. Mrs. Hollbrook, the music teacher? She came to our room instead. She said pianos have to have checkups at least once a year like people do, so they don't get sick. When a piano gets sick, it starts to sound funny." Owen stops, waits for me to put two and two together.

"So?"

"So why does she have the doctor come look at it if no one ever plays it?"

— 8 —

A spider must spin an intricate web for his dinner.

My body isn't conditioned to the Wednesday visitation schedule. Nick has Owen from after school through dinnertime, so it's the only weekday I *don't* have to rush from work to the bus stop. *Owen's not stranded*, I reassure myself every Wednesday when I enter the apartment without him. He's not crying and confused, alone because Nick's forgotten to pick him up. Owen is safe.

I wish Nick would text me when he picks Owen up. Just a simple *I've got him* would be enough to calm me down. I've asked Nick to do it a bunch of times, and he always says he will, but he never does. I don't know if he's being passive-aggressive or if my feelings just aren't important enough to capture his attention, but in either case I'm stuck with clammy hands and a heartbeat in the aerobic zone.

Today's anxiety is heightened by a Boston College brochure that arrived unrequested. Lindsay would say the universe is whispering to me, but if that's true, then why is it sending a brochure from a school that doesn't offer my major? Its glossy cover taunts me, with its photos of bespectacled professors and enrapt students, its smiling graduates with mortarboards. There's a tightness in my chest as I run my fingers over the cover, and sweat pools under my arms. I know how vulnerable Owen and I are until I get college squared away. But I've had no luck getting through to university financial aid offices the past couple of days—it's acceptance week for midyear transfer students. I'm in limbo, unable to plan for us. So I clean.

Today's challenge is the bathroom showerhead, which has sprouted a white flaky mold I can't scratch off with my fingernail. It's nauseating, the thought that every time I shower, fungus spores are being propelled via water jets onto my body. A quick search on my iPhone brings up the *Better Homes & Gardens* website, which instructs me to fill a plastic bag with vinegar, secure it to the showerhead with an elastic band, and let it soak for an hour.

This easy fix is disappointing news; I was hoping for a more labor-intensive task. I scan the bathroom for additional scrubbing opportunities. I could use an old toothbrush to clean the shower caddy while I'm waiting. And the caulking between the base of the shower and the tile floor—hallelujah, it's coated with brown film! That'll require bleach *and* scrubbing. I eye the shower fixtures for mildew as well, silently congratulating myself on my ability to make lemons out of lemonade.

Lemons! Nature's bleach. Exactly what I need for round two of cleaning, to neutralize the chemical smell. I grab two lemons from the fridge, juice the liquid into a bowl, then fill a quart-sized plastic bag halfway up with vinegar. *When life gives you lemons, make lemonade.* The saying won't leave my head as I set Owen's step stool in the center of the tub so I can reach the showerhead. There must be a way to extract a fortune out of that phrase. Hmm . . . What Chinese food is sour on its own but delicious when combined with a bit of sugar? Tofu, maybe? Not a great comparison—tofu's bland, not sour. Bean sprouts? I don't know what they taste like when they're not drenched in sauce. People would get the reference if I replaced *lemon* with a stereotypical Chinese fruit, but what fruit would that be? Lychee? The problem is that *lychee-ade* doesn't pass translation muster.

I'm teetering on the step stool now, the bag of vinegar over my head, when it dawns on me that *Better Homes & Gardens* has presented me with an impossible task. There's no way that the elastic I have on my wrist—a curly-haired girl's ever-present bracelet—is going to stretch wide enough to encompass the widest point of the plastic bag once, much less several times, in order to secure it to the showerhead. This pull-and-twist ponytail approach is going to leave me with a snapped hair tie and covered in vinegar. I suppose if I'd thought ahead, I could've cut the elastic in half so that I could tie it around the empty neck of the bag while holding it on, but . . . well, actually, no. That wouldn't have worked, either. You need two hands to tie a knot, so how could I have held the bag steady? Just how many hands do you think I have, *Better Homes & Gardens*?

Duct tape. It's my only hope. There's still a leftover roll from my move, which I snag from the kitchen odds-and-ends drawer. It takes several tries, but I finally manage to attach the bag onto the showerhead. I step down from the stool, back out of the shower to appraise my work. It looks sturdy—no puckering of the tape or tilting of the bag. I grin. It's a ridiculous accomplishment, if you can call it that, but I'm proud of my handiwork. You take your wins where you can get them.

This full three-to-seven stretch I have—it's because I don't lose any time to travel. Nick drops Owen back off at my place on Wednesday nights, which *sounds* generous, but I know he does it out of fear I'll injure Owen in a car accident rather than out of kindness. I tried to do the pick-ups when we first set up our transportation schedule. I was determined to prove to Nick that I could handle it, because who did he think I was, some old lady who needed to depend on a man to drive her around? Please. But the truth is I still can't find my way driving around Boston, even with Waze or Maps guiding me. Every street is either one-way or under construction—there's no grid of lettered and numbered streets like there is in New York or D.C., unless you're in Southie. Take the wrong turn in any other part of the city and it's impossible to get back to where you started, what with its winding streets and counterintuitive highways.

I got lost on the way back from Nick's the very first time I picked up Owen, which I tried to cover up by turning my incompetence into life lessons. "It's important to have adventures," I told Owen in what I hoped was a breezy tone after GPS directed me to turn onto a street that no longer existed. "Important to explore new avenues," I improvised. Owen asked how we could explore an avenue that wasn't there, which led to an explanation of figurative versus literal speech and the proper usage of the word *literally* before we were funneled onto Storrow Drive, a highway that strikes fear into the heart of any cautious driver. Traffic exits are on the left and the right, multiple merges must be made within short distances, and travel lanes become exit-only with little warning. It's notorious for its low overpasses, which trap the moving vans of college freshmen with enough regularity that this rookie mistake is now part of the vernacular: it's called *getting Storrowed*.

Our second mishap landed us near the Museum of Science, which I explained away as a chance to wave hi to the giant T. rex statue that greets visitors at the entrance. I thought I was in the clear, but Owen blew my cover by suggesting that Nick take him out on driving adventures like

Mommy does. Nick said nothing to me about it, but apparently he told Owen that walking adventures are way better, because you get to see things up close. The following Wednesday Nick offered to drop Owen off, and the week after that he said we should keep up the midweek habit and choose a meeting place on weekends.

I grab a spray bottle filled with diluted bleach, a scrub sponge, and some gloves from the cleaning closet. The shower caulking is next, and I intend to show it no mercy. But as I pass by the kitchen, I spy the brochure resting on the countertop.

"Stop looking at me like that!" I yell. "I can't get anything done today, okay? You don't even offer the classes I need, don't you get it? Honestly, you'd think the universe would know the details better than me, what with having access to *all of the information in existence—*"

That's it! How arrogant of me, to assume I knew better! *I* must have made the mistake.

I drop the spray bottle, sponge, and gloves on the counter, snatch the brochure, and flip through the pages. I'm sure there's a list of departments in here somewhere, and then, maybe, I'll have to give Lindsay a bit more credit. Here it is: B.A. in Accounting, African and African Diaspora Studies, American Heritage, Art History.

No Anthropology.

"I knew it!" I shout, hurling the brochure across the kitchen. "You had me doubting myself, Lindsay. On basic *research*."

I assumed, when I started researching, that my semester abroad would be a loss, but I hadn't considered that my education would be held *against* me. But top-ticr universities won't accept transfer students who've completed more than two years. That revelation knocked three universities off my list from the get-go, and eight more had to be discarded when I discovered they had no anthropology departments. The remaining four universities on my list all require two years of attendance. There's no showing up for senior year to nab a diploma . . . which brings me to my most pressing problem: money.

A sour taste fills my mouth as I think of the lengthy phone calls to financial aid offices that await me next month. You should *not* base aid decisions on Nick's salary, I'll have to explain to the reps, because I'm divorced now, and have access to none of it. Yes, I can provide my joint tax return, but I was a stay-at-home mom in April. I'm working now, but I'll have to quit my day job if I'm going to go back full-time and do work-study. Wait, please don't put me on hold! The good news is I won't need funding for room and board, since I'll need to live off-campus to maintain residency for schooling for my son. So . . . where should I note all of this for the admissions committee to take under advisement?

I let out a sigh as I pick up the brochure splayed under the sink. An anthropology degree isn't going to rake in the bucks the way a medical or law degree would. I need the quickest route from degree to career, and that means co-op. Think of it: six months of earning money, gaining business experience, and making contacts while I finish my studies. I'm in luck, because Northeastern has an anthropology department. Tech companies are hiring anthropologists to work on marketing research and consumer outreach, so who's to say I couldn't find, or create, a co-op on the business side of my major? Wouldn't that get me a worthwhile return on my investment—over, say, someone who spends her co-op conducting field research in a remote village?

Return on investment. I've got Dad to thank for teaching me that term. And for anthropology. Because you know what would be an even bigger uphill battle than anthropology? Archaeology, and that's what I was planning to study, before he put his foot down the summer after my sophomore year.

⌒

"What are you trying to do," he asked one evening as I snatched the car keys he'd tossed on the kitchen counter, "pick the major with the smallest possible ROI?"

I hesitated. I had no idea what ROI stood for.

"Return on investment, Marissa. In two years, you'll be done with college. Then what? You have to make that degree work for you."

"But Dad, everyone says college is for trying different things. It's not just about figuring out how to make money. I mean, hopefully that will come, too, but everyone says find your passion first, then—"

"I'm not everyone. Study a subject you find interesting, yes. But you have to find one that'll put you on a path to self-sufficiency."

"Yale's not a trade school."

Dad's eyes narrowed, and he swiped the keys back from me. "I'm going to assume you weren't talking down to me just then."

"I wasn't. I was just saying that—"

"There's no shame in being a plumber. We've done well enough to pay your tuition. You remember that, before you give me any more attitude." He let out his breath in one big huff. "Tell me something, Marissa. Why do you think I chose plumbing?"

I shrugged. "Because you like working with your hands? Or running your own business?"

"Uh-huh," he said, nodding. "So why not become a landscaper? Why would I pick a profession that requires me to get on my hands and knees and stick my arms in toilets?"

I shook my head. I'd never thought about why my dad chose to be a plumber before. He just *was* a plumber. "Umm . . ."

"Job stability. A plumber will never be out of work. People will go for a while without mulching their flower beds or mowing their lawns if cash is tight, but they're always going to come up with the money if their toilet isn't working or a pipe bursts. See what I mean?"

"Why are you telling me this *now*? I have to declare a major in the fall. And I just applied for my spring semester abroad in Athens."

"I know. Mom told me. I didn't know you had to apply so soon."

"I applied early. I really want to go. I *need* to go, because . . . because . . . " Because it would be so amazing, I wanted to tell him, to immerse myself in the city's rich history, to visit excavation sites and learn the basics of archaeological drawing. It would be my first step. One day, I'd travel the world, learning about the customs and traditions of ancient people. I'd join a team of people able to peer into the past and discover mysteries lost to time. I'd be a part of something spectacularly ambitious, something more significant than burst pipes and backed-up toilets.

I could feel the opportunity quickly slipping away from me, though, could see by the set of his jaw that his mind was already made up, that my words would carry no weight, no matter how polished. It was so unfair of him to destroy my plans because they didn't match his, but suddenly my throat was swollen and all I could choke out was, "Can I go, Daddy? Please?"

I brushed off the tears I hadn't been able to stop from rolling down my cheek, then turned away in embarrassment. I could feel his stare from behind. It was humiliating that I'd been reduced to this inarticulate, pathetic little girl.

"Oh, honey," he said, his voice softening. "I didn't know it was this important to you. Look, I'll make you a deal. You can go in the spring, but starting this semester, you've got to study something that'll offer you more flexibility in the future. Find a bigger umbrella."

Travel the world. They're laughable, my former plans, because now I can't even get out of Massachusetts without a court order.

But I can't pin all the blame on Nick. Waging a court battle to get the right to move out of state would be pointless. I've been withdrawn from college for more than two years, so even if I were to concoct some fantastic rationale for my extended academic negligence, I'd still have to take two classes *outside* of Yale just to prove that I'm up for the task of returning, and then hope I get readmitted.

So that's a dead end.

I'll admit I didn't handle things maturely when I left. I was told accommodations could be made, but I knew I couldn't go back to school. The prospect was unbearable. And what was I supposed to do once the baby arrived?

I couldn't fathom living at home with my parents, either, waiting for the baby to be born, weathering their disappointment day after day. So when Nick asked me to visit him in Boston, and then that visit became a halting *why don't we see if we can make this work*, I turned a blind eye to the pressure from his family to get married. I pretended it was true love, because it was close enough, wasn't it? I moved to Massachusetts to be with Nick, set up a nursery for the baby, and made plans to return to Connecticut the next year.

What I didn't anticipate was how madly in love I would fall with Owen. Once he was born, all I wanted was to spend every second with him. Every one of his firsts—his first smile, his first babble, his first crawl—was intoxicating. I half-heartedly pushed Nick to move back to Connecticut as my leave of absence neared its end, but I accepted his excuses to stay put when I knew I shouldn't have. Suddenly, my goal of traveling the world seemed like an absurd venture. What did I care about solving the riddles of the past when the future was bundled in a warm blanket in my arms?

Warmth.

I'm pulled out of my daydreams by the feeling of steam clinging to my chin and cheeks. I'm standing in front of the kitchen sink, hovering over a pail that is now filling with hot water. I check the trash can under the sink and find the refuse of my cleaning spree—a bleach-filled scrub sponge, a mold-filled toothbrush, a mass of soggy paper towels. Apparently I clean on autopilot now, because I don't remember throwing out any of those items. I add the lemon juice, stir, and head back to the bathroom for round two of cleaning.

— 9 —

Under the lake's placid surface lives a turbulent world.

I've made serious fortune-writing headway while the showerhead has been soaking. I'm up to fortune 261 on this third batch, and I'm gunning for my Wednesday-night quota of 280. "Worldwide Words of Wisdom"—the chapter I thought held such promise in the library—has come up short, though. Sure, there are stray Plato and Gandhi quotes, but the author seems to hold the opinion that Americans are responsible for a good 80 percent of insights into the human condition. Most of the quotes are from Twain, Thoreau, Lincoln, MLK, and a whole lot of Oprah.

Don't get me wrong: Oprah is the source for eight fortunes in batch two. I even made use of her famous "You get a car!" line, which I did by arranging it in a "Confucius say" format. (OPRAH SAY: YOU GET A COOKIE! YOU GET A COOKIE! EVERBODY GETS A COOKIE!) I was proud of that construction, because by making the subject American rather than

Chinese, I rid the offensive trope of its sting. But then I worried after I submitted it that Peking Foods wouldn't get it, that they'd think I was equating Oprah to China's greatest philosopher and fire me. But as of today, no comment from them either way about batch two's fortune 189.

I think I take this job far more seriously than they do.

It's probably best to shift gears and get some Smartypants product descriptions out of the way; the fortune creativity well is running dry and I can make up the remaining ones much quicker once I'm fresh. I'm midskim of the manufacturer's description of MagShapes, a knockoff of Magna-Tiles, when my phone rings. The main number of Owen's school pops up. I *knew* this day would come. Nick's forgotten Owen. Idiot.

"Hello?" I try not to sound panicked.

"Ms. Karalis?"

"Yes?"

"Oh, hello! This is Julia Evans calling. Have I caught you at a good time?"

"Is he okay? He's not still at school, is he?"

"No, no, no. Owen's father picked him up at dismissal. I'm calling because you haven't been able to make it in for a parent-teacher conference yet. I was hoping we could find a time that works for you."

Oh, God. I've already been marked as a slacker parent who doesn't care about her child's education. "Of course! I'm so sorry for the oversight. Uh . . . will this be about how he's doing academically in general, or do you have any specific concerns?"

Mrs. Evans clears her throat. "Well . . . first, let me say that Owen is sensitive, smart, and I'm delighted that he's in my class this year. I think we can save specific concerns for when we speak in person, but I did want to let you know that we have a handle on the lunchroom incidents. I can assure you they won't happen again."

"'Incidents'? I thought it was just that one time."

"He was found in the music room at lunchtime again today. But we now have all monitors alerted to the issue. Please know that the security of all our students is paramount."

"So, when he's found there—he's just playing the piano?"

"That seems to be the case. Mrs. Singleton—she's one of our psychologists, and she's such an amazing resource—she observed him in the lunchroom this week, and she's planning to visit the classroom Monday. By the end of next week I'll have more information to share with you. Would you—"

A psychologist? "Wait. Why does she need to observe him in the classroom? Is he trying to leave there, too?"

"Oh, no! I gave you the wrong impression. It's the focus wall that's become a bit . . . challenging."

"The focus wall?"

"Yes, the wall at the front of the classroom. It's decorated and separated into sections that showcase what we're working on each week—letters and sounds, sight words, math, writing. Anyway, Owen seems to be . . . intrigued by it. He gets up to touch it. Often. Actually, touch might not be the best descriptor. Tap is better. He taps it."

"Is there anything musical on the wall?"

"There's nothing that produces sound, if that's what you're asking."

"Maybe pictures of instruments or musical notes, then? Something that makes him *think* of music? Because clearly that's a big draw for him."

"I'm afraid not. The wall is academic, as I said. Why don't I email you possible times, and you get back to me when you have a moment? I'll reach out to Mr. Karalis tomorrow. Obviously I couldn't bring this up in front of Owen at dismissal. And in the interim, if you think of anything you'd like to discuss at the meeting, feel free to—"

"Writing."

"Hmm?"

"I'd like to discuss writing." Specifically, how your goddamn military precision writing assignments are stressing out my kid so badly that he gets out of his seat every two seconds and escapes whatever you're about to hand out. "I have concerns about the emphasis being placed on penmanship in the classroom. I respect your high standards, but to ask Owen to erase and rewrite his letters over and over is quite demanding for kindergartners, and, honestly, bordering on punitive. It gets in the way of him being able to express himself, and I think that's more important academically than actual letter formation."

Mrs. Evans is silent for a moment. Then, in a quiet, concerned voice: "Ms. Karalis, I've *never* asked Owen to do that. Did he tell you I did?"

No.

The answer, painfully clear, takes me by surprise.

I made up that explanation. I saw his eraser-worn paperwork, and I filled in the details.

Why would Owen put that kind of pressure on himself?

"I, uh—I must have misread the situation. I have to go. I'll get back to you with a time soon."

I glance at my phone: 4:17. I'm dying to call Nick, but there's no point. He can't talk about Owen right in front of him. I have to wait until drop-off.

I rewind the conversation with Mrs. Evans in my mind, analyze each new piece of information. Owen left the lunchroom again. That's not terrible news. All monitors are on the lookout now because of this second escape, and it might even be the proof I need to push Nick into coughing up some cash. I just have to bring up lessons again without an

I-told-you-so attitude. As for the tapping, I see Owen do that all the time with his iPad, in counts of eight. He's figuring out new songs. There must be something rhythmic Mrs. Evans hasn't noticed about the focus wall.

The writing, though. There's no good explanation for that.

Is it because of me? My need for neatness and order? Kids see everything. I assume his eyes are always glued to the iPad, but he's probably watching me dust the lampshades, recenter the chairs around the table, wash the light switch plates. Just last week I got mad at him when he was drawing at the kitchen table because he didn't put an extra piece of construction paper underneath the one he was using. My shitty, second-hand kitchen table. Does he think my love is dependent on meeting these exacting standards? What the hell is the matter with me?

I stare out the living room windows. He's watched me hand-wash them with vinegar and water how many times? I study the spindly, bare limbs of the one maple tree visible from my vantage point on the couch and notice the sun is setting, a depressing reality of daylight saving time in Massachusetts. Yes, the fall foliage is gorgeous and sipping warm cider on a blustery day is wonderful, but in my bleak mood all I can think of is the steep price tag that comes with an autumn replete with apple orchards and pumpkin patches: four months of a freezing steering wheel and furnace dependence. Soon I'll have no choice but to say goodbye to extended stretches of fresh air until April.

Fresh air!

Lena asked if I could try to get Rose out for a bit, and just this morning I made a mental note to give it a shot this afternoon, but between stress cleaning and fortune writing, I've blown it and missed the daylight. I doubt Rose has been out much since the funeral, considering she doesn't drive. That can't be healthy. I may have screwed up on the sunlight front, but maybe I can talk her into getting out to run an errand, just for a change of scenery. And it'll be a good way for me to take my mind off Owen.

I flip on the lights and head over to the kitchen to organize Rose's dinner. Tonight's menu is as low effort as it can get: salad with grilled chicken and a crusty baguette. I didn't even cook the chicken myself; I just grabbed the few remaining dried-out strips from the salad bar. I feel guilty, but I can't force myself to cook without Owen. Spending time with him is the only enjoyable part of the process.

I arrange the salad in a pastel flowered bowl to make it look less pathetic, cover it with tinfoil, and place the baguette on top. At least the bowl is a winner. It's a HomeGoods bargain, bought years ago, even though discount shopping wasn't a necessity at the time. Back when Nick encouraged me to buy whatever we needed to make our condo a home.

Might as well bring my culinary disappointment downstairs early. Even if Rose shoos me out of her apartment, I'll have done my part for the evening. Plus, I have to admit, now that I know about Owen's second lunchroom escape, I'm dying to get another look at that piano of hers.

Owen's "piano doctor" story prompted me to do some online research last night. Those $600 pianos I saw on Craigslist, the ones I told Nick about? They're not going to cut it. Turns out that bargain pianos are a rarity, even though the number of listings led me to believe otherwise. Most of the ads stated something to the effect of *great piano, but no one plays it anymore*. Bad sign, according to multiple YouTube videos. If no one's playing it, then no one's tuning it. Which means the piano might need a pitch raise, which is a primer tuning before the *actual* tuning. Together that'll cost at least two hundred, maybe three. And if the pin block is dried out, or the treble bridge is cracked—two areas of a piano I can now identify—beware. You may be taking a piece of junk off someone's hands *and* paying to have it moved. That'd be at least another hundred in my case, considering the flight of stairs it'd have to be lifted up. Consensus seems to be that anything under two or three thousand dollars should raise suspicion.

So how, then, might the piano experts of the Web explain Rose's old-yet-tuned piano? The best I can come up with is that Owen might be wrong. Just because I think he has a pitch-perfect ear doesn't mean he does. Who am I to judge his ability? I don't have the skill set, and even if I did, I'm the most biased person in the world. There's a Chinese proverb I've run across in my fortune research: THERE'S ONLY ONE PRETTY CHILD IN THE WORLD, AND EVERY MOTHER HAS HER. As the stage mom of a child who's yet to have a single professional lesson, I've got to own up to the truth in that adage.

But if Owen *is* right—if Rose and Bernie have had the "piano doctor" visit regularly even though neither of them play—then the piano must hold great sentimental value. Rose said Joel played it at her old house. So why would she and Bernie have paid to move it here? It's a safe assumption they've been living apart from Joel for decades at this point.

Now that I think about it—the piano is in Bernie's office, not the living room. And the office was sparsely furnished and organized, in contrast to Rose's nightmare of a kitchen. So maybe he was the one who tended to the tuning of the piano. Hearing Owen provoked a reaction from Rose—no question about that—but it was mixed, to say the least. With Bernie gone, she might reevaluate the piano's prized status. She may even need money now. I don't want to take advantage of her, but this could be mutually beneficial. Which means I've got to get a better idea of what that piano is worth.

YouTube has armed me with *CSI*-level knowledge of piano abuse, but the problem is that visible clues like scuffs and discoloration don't give much indication of how a piano is functioning. Where I'd like to take a look is the *back* of the piano. I'd be able to see if there are cracks in the posts, the ribs, or—most importantly—the soundboard. But I'd have to turn the piano away from the wall, and that's a sitcom-worthy premise if I've ever heard one. What am I supposed to do, pretend I've dropped my keys behind there? Funny on TV, next to impossible to pull off in real life. Even if I could, there'd still be two other places to check, and neither can be viewed without disassembling the entire instrument.

There's no way to remove the panel behind the foot pedals in the midst of polite conversation. That's what I'd have to do to see the treble and bass bridges—release the middle clip of the bottom board and slide it out. A cracked treble bridge is something any prospective buyer should look for. It's a deal breaker, plain and simple.

How about opening the top lid and unscrewing the music desk without being noticed? It's the only way to see the hammers, tuning pins, and strings. I have a feeling Rose might wonder why I'm checking to see if the hammers are in alignment or searching for white chalk on the tuning pins or a few shiny strings among a mass of dull ones. (Answers: White chalk is evidence that a piano has been serviced, but not the best news, as the marks are reminders of which pins are starting to loosen. Same goes for the strings: shiny ones have been professionally replaced, but that means the remaining dull ones are likely on their last legs.)

The most damning piece of evidence is a black stain on the plate around the tuning pins—the pin block. The discoloration is a remnant of what's called pin block dope, which is used in a last-ditch effort to save a piano. It's a liquid that seeps through the holes into the pin block, which temporarily swells the wood and keeps the pins tight. A post–pin block dope piano will never hold a tune. It's a disaster waiting to happen.

So now I'm a piano detective extraordinaire, with no way to examine the item of interest. But the piano's condition only matters if Rose is willing to sell it, so I need to take this step-by-step, and first find a way to casually broach the subject while I'm down there. If she's not interested, there's no need to waste any more time on piano investigation. The case will be closed. I pick up Rose's dinner and head down to her apartment.

— 10 —

If you are patient, the roaring tiger will eventually purr.

Rose doesn't answer her door. Not even after three rounds of knocking. It's possible she's out, I guess. I know she has some friends, like the lasagna-hating Dottie. There's no reason for me to assume she'll always be home.

I consider leaving the salad on the doorstep, then decide against it. The lettuce will wilt if it's left out too long. I don't have a cooler to leave it in, though. The only one I have—*had*—is Nick's. It wasn't high on my list of kitchen essentials when we split up everything we owned as a couple. I had to concentrate on keeping as many cooking utensils as possible, considering the needs of Chef Owen. So I am coolerless at the moment.

I turn to head back upstairs when I hear Rose. "Stop *klopping* on my door. You're giving me a headache." She talks between coughs.

The inside chain slides as the coughing continues. Ugh, please don't let her be sick. I didn't sign up for nursing care. I can't let myself be guilted into taking care of this woman. I barely know her, and I have problems of my—

Rose peers out the door, her face shiny with tears. Her hair is matted down on the sides, from sleep, I assume, but the top remains styled and sprayed. It looks a bit like John Travolta's pompadour in *Grease*. Has she not been out of bed today?

Rose cranes her head around the corner, looks into the hallway. "Where's your boychik?" she asks, her voice raspy.

"Oh, hi! He's with his—"

"Yah, yah, yah." She waves my words away. "Your ex. Now I remember." She looks down at my tinfoil-covered dinner. "So?"

It takes me a second to realize she's asking what's in the bowl. "Salad." I pass it to her. "With grilled chicken. And a baguette."

Rose eyes my salad and grimaces. "I'm not so much a salad person. *Ach*, such a waste."

I let out a reflexive, irritated sigh. No dairy, no dairy mixed with meat, and now no salads? "I didn't know. I can—"

"Nah, what are you talking? It's very healthy, Bernie was always trying to get me to eat healthy. But let me put it in a plastic and give you back your beautiful bowl."

"No, keep it. I can pick it up another time, really."

"Come, come, follow me." Rose talks over her shoulder, ignoring my protestations on her way to the kitchen. She's wearing a full-length fleece bathrobe, so she must have either changed into it late in the afternoon or she never bothered getting dressed this morning. She offers no explanation for her disheveled state, doesn't try to fluff out the sides of her hair or zip her robe up all the way. I can see the scooped neck of her cotton nightgown underneath it, the loose, wrinkled flesh of her chest, and her prominent collarbones, and I look away, as if I've caught her undressed. I doubt she'll want to go out for errands today, and it's a relief. As much as it'd be easier to take her out without Owen, I depend on my Wednesday free time. Best to wrap up this visit and get back to writing.

The kitchen is even worse than yesterday. Rose certainly didn't spend any portion of her day cleaning dishes or trying to clear space on her countertops. She rummages through the assortment of full containers piled atop the small table at the far end of the kitchen until she finds a satisfactory one. It's lidless, and I wonder if its position near the bottom is by design, to provide it with some measure of coverage after she discovered she ran out of lids.

"Two left, only," she says as she pulls out small, crescent-shaped pastries. One has swirls of chocolate filling between the rows of dough while the other has jam. She turns to me. "Rugelach?"

"No, thank you. But they look delicious." The truth is, they look like they *were* delicious. Unless she's been baking—and I assume I'd smell some lingering aroma if that were the case—they're left over from shiva, three days old at this point.

She nods sadly. "Not so good anymore, I bet." She tosses them into the sink. It's possible she's not hungry, or doesn't like rug—whatever that pastry is called, but the fact she tried to force the suspect bite onto me is annoying. If she thinks they might be stale, she should either try them first or throw them out. She shouldn't make me the guinea pig.

Rose empties the crumbs from the bottom of the container into the sink, dumps the contents of my salad into it, and opens the fridge. A putrid smell wafts out as she shuffles food around to make room. She balances the container on top of two rows of yogurt cups, holds her hands up to protect against collapse, and slams the door shut. "There!"

Two rows of yogurt. How did she put it, when she saw the lasagna?

Milk doesn't sit so great with me. Either she lied when I first came by on Monday, or the yogurt lover was Bernie. How heartbreakingly mundane, to expire before your yogurt.

My cheeks flush. Isn't it clear she needs help, this frail woman who's slowly being enveloped by the contents of her kitchen? Yet five minutes ago I was calculating my odds on how to get a good deal on her piano. I was planning how to make my escape from this brief visit. What if I'm the only person who's come to see her today? It's repulsive how self-involved I've become.

"You know, Rose, I imagine that cleaning is probably the last thing on your mind during a time like this. And I'm one of those crazy people who actually loves to do it. I have a little time now, before Owen gets back from his dad's. Would you like some help?"

The words come out before I consider that my offer might be insulting. Maybe she doesn't realize what a disaster her kitchen is. Who am I, a certifiable clean freak, to judge what's normal?

Rose's cheeks redden as she looks around the kitchen. "My Bernie's the cleaner. The organizer. I do the cooking, he does the cleaning. For seventy years."

Did. He *did* the cleaning and the organizing, but Rose doesn't notice she's talking about her husband in the present tense. When does one start using the past tense to refer to someone who's been a constant presence? Seventy years. I can't begin to imagine a marriage that long. I couldn't make it to six. "That's a long time," I say, because I can't think of anything better.

She nods. "How long for you?"

"Five. Years, not months." It slips out, my subconscious attempt to make the length of my marriage seem less paltry in comparison to hers, but even to my ears, it's pitiful. Successful marriages don't use months as markers.

My eyes fill with tears, because it's humiliating to know she's probably mentally calculating Owen's legitimacy as we speak. My chin trembles, and I clench my jaw to try to stop it. I suppose I shouldn't be embarrassed in front of Rose, who just answered her door with tears staining her cheeks. But her husband left her by death, not choice.

"It was his decision to end the marriage?"

I nod, brace myself for some well-meaning version of *good thing it ended before you wasted too many years with him,* as if all of my marriage was worthless. But we had good years, or at least I thought we did. That's what makes it so hard. I don't know what was real. And that matters, even though it's in the past now, because if our love for each other wasn't genuine, then I shouldn't miss it. It's nonsensical, to long for something that never truly existed. But if our love was real, then it's understandable to mourn. Not for him, but for *it.* It's exhausting, replaying every moment in my head, trying to pinpoint moments of inauthenticity, to spot clues I should have noticed. It's a pointless exercise, interpreting his actions and words in retrospect. But I can't help it.

What I do know is this: Even though I hate the Nick who betrayed me, I miss the Nick who loved me. Or at least the Nick who seemed to love me. The one who knew all my quirks and accepted me in spite of them. The one who knew I thought tomato soup was revolting, unless I had a cold, in which case, I wanted nothing else; the one who told me I should let go of my shame over my third grade failure to defend a classmate with special needs when my friend Heather mocked her; the one who thought it was amusing I was snobby enough to avoid having a second conversation with anyone who said "totes adorbs." I miss the Nick I met on Mount Lycabettus.

The boy with the impossibly blue eyes never came to lunch. That's the first thing I remember thinking about Nick, although I didn't know his name at the time. The semester abroad in Athens program provided one meal a day to its students, and you'd better bet every student made their way back to the main cafeteria for it. I'd see him from afar at the farmers' market in the early evenings, could guess by his exaggerated gesturing and Yankees baseball cap that he was American. He could've been from another study abroad group, I supposed, but he was always alone.

To be fair, I'd been alone far more than I'd anticipated that January, too. It was shocking how little I had in common with the other students on my trip, who seemed to prioritize alcohol above all else. They'd spend their Friday and Saturday nights in tavernas drinking retsina or ouzo until they couldn't walk straight, and then spend their days nursing hangovers. I had nothing against going out for a drink, but I didn't see the point in ruining my free time feeling nauseous and dehydrated when I could be hiking the Santorini Volcano or exploring the sacred island of Delos. If getting drunk was the biggest dream they could dream, I quickly realized my spring semester was going to be a lonely one.

I let myself get pulled along to tavernas the first couple of week-ends, but I never saw Nick. Which didn't mean he wasn't at a different one, or doing something equally immature, but I preferred to think I didn't bump into him because he also thought barhopping was a waste of a once-in-a-lifetime opportunity. That he was up to—well, not necessarily *loftier* endeavors, but at least not such a predictable, juvenile one.

He wasn't in any of my classes, and I never saw him in the Scholastic Center, which housed the entirety of the program's classes. I kept hoping I'd run into him in the common areas of my building, but no such luck. Not that this was a tremendous surprise; students weren't housed in one dorm. Instead, we were placed in residential apartments sprinkled throughout the neighborhood, in order to provide us with real-life immersion opportunities.

He must have been on vacation, I decided one mid-February weekend as I hiked up the winding walkway to the summit of Mount Lycabettus. He has to be back in the U.S. by now. And what did it matter? He was probably nothing at all like what I'd imagined. I awarded him with an aura of mystery because he was elusive, but that didn't mean he was different than any of the other—

"Is this yours?"

I turned, not sure if the question was meant for me. Surrounded by tourists, overlooking all of Athens, there he was, holding a slim, gold bracelet. *My* bracelet. I'd never seen him this close before. I hadn't realized he was so tall.

I looked down at my wrist. How had it slid off? "Yes! Thank you so much. I didn't even know it was missing. The clasp must have come undone."

"Good thing I saw it fall." He passed it to me. "I bet it would've had a new owner really soon."

I nodded. "It absolutely would've. Thanks again." I pushed my hair back behind my ear, not because it was in my eyes, but because it gave me a way to stealthily wipe the sweat off my forehead. It was a mild fifty degrees outside, but it had been a steep, nine-hundred-foot climb.

"No problem." He waved a casual goodbye, then turned and walked in the other direction.

"I'm Marissa!" I called out after him, before he disappeared into the crowd. The words tumbled out, desperate and breathless. All at once, being in a foreign country didn't seem like an adventure; it just felt lonely. How was I supposed to make friends with kids who didn't even bother to hide their yawning while class was being held at the Acropolis or the

Ancient Agora? I didn't want to spend the next three months with people who didn't understand what an incredible opportunity this was. With people who didn't understand *me*. And I might not bump into him again.

He didn't turn immediately. Had he heard me? And if he had, would he turn back with a smug, girls-always-throw-themselves-at-me smile? After all, I couldn't have been the first to notice the striking combination of his black hair and azure eyes, his broad shoulders and lean frame. I cursed myself, as my words hung in the air, for being just another one of *those girls*, when I was so willing to judge the sour, alcohol-tinged breath and groping hands of *those boys*.

But when he did eventually face me, he looked as if he'd been taken completely off guard, and . . . was he blushing? "I'm Nick," he said, with a lopsided smile and a nervous bob of his head. In front of us was a panorama of Athens: the red-tiled roofs of the Plaka district; behind them, atop a rocky flat-topped hill, the towering marble columns of the Propylaea, Parthenon, and Erectheion; beyond the historic site, a myriad of buildings until the Aegean Sea. "It's amazing, isn't it?" He gestured toward the view as he made his way back to me.

I nodded, relief washing over me. "It's unbelievable."

I want to erase the memory of Mount Lycabettus from Nick's mind. I want to take back every piece of myself I've ever shared with him, just as I took back my coffee maker and my laptop. He shouldn't have the right to know my past, my secrets, my motivations. But since memory-erasing guns are still science fiction, he's privy to a part of me he doesn't deserve.

Rose is studying me, and I can tell what she's thinking: that I have no idea what marriage is really about, that it's ridiculous to compare the measly time frame of my marriage to hers. But my marriage was also wonderful and messy and precious and poignant—it was still *meaningful*, and—

"You said the exact right word yesterday," Rose says.

"What?"

"'Complicated.' Marriage is complicated. No matter how long."

I can't think of what to say in response. Kindness is not what I've grown to expect from Rose. I nod and wipe away a wayward tear with my sleeve.

She studies me, opens her mouth as if to say something, and then closes it. "So," she says, with a clap of her hands. "I accept your generous offer. My kitchen could use a little help, yes?"

I smile, grateful to change the subject. "Should we start with the dishes?"

— 11 —

Even a well-fed donkey may kick.

I have to give myself a pat on the back—Rose's kitchen looks brand new. Don't get me wrong, there are still piles of bills, coupons, and magazines, but now they're in paper grocery bags in Bernie's office. The fridge has been emptied of rotten food and refilled with the containers that once cluttered the kitchen table. Microwave splatters have been wiped away, and the sink and countertops have been scrubbed. The dishwasher is running, and the stove top grates, now free of burned-on grime, are drying on paper towels, along with an inverted teakettle and the upper compartment of the coffee maker. With the exception of a stack of plastic serving platters left over from shiva, all items have been shelved.

I turn to Rose, who's stacking the dishes we had to wash and dry by hand once the dishwasher got too full. "Where should I put these?" I point to the plastic partyware. "I can't find any empty cabinets."

Rose frowns. "Top of the refrigerator, maybe? I can't see up there so good."

"They're too big. They'll fall and hit you on the head when you open the fridge. How about in the closet in Bernie's office?" I take a few steps toward his room. I'm not making it up; it would be dangerous to leave the platters above the fridge. The fact that I now have a legitimate reason to go to Bernie's office—or, as I like to think of it, Owen's piano studio—is just dumb luck.

"No! Stop!"

I freeze, taken aback by the unexpected outburst.

"I don't want them in Bernie's office," Rose says, her voice hushed.

"There's no space?"

She shakes her head. "It's not that. I don't want . . . *those things* in his office."

My face flushes. Of course. I didn't even consider that she might not want items associated with her husband's death in *his* room, *his* space. And now that I think about it, *office* is an odd name for the room. It's not like he was working from home. Maybe she calls it that because he was responsible for their bills and household paperwork? If so, I'm not sure why all that junk ended up on their kitchen countertops. But what else would you call the room? I bet *man cave* isn't a term Rose regularly uses.

"You don't have to keep them, you know," I say, in what I hope is a comforting tone. "They're just plastic. If it hurts you to have them, you should get rid of—"

"What?" Rose looks at me as if I've gone completely crazy. "Throw them out? Perfectly good serving pieces? With young people today, everything is disposable!"

"I mean *recycle* them, not throw them away." Now isn't the time to get sidetracked, but honestly, does Rose think she can go toe-to-toe with a millennial over the need to protect the environment? I doubt she knows what a carbon footprint is, or the difference between global warming and climate change.

Rose shakes her head. "Using again is better than recycling." To be fair, this is true. Reuse does come before recycle in the waste management hierarchy. Score one for Rose.

"Fine. Where would you like me to put them, then?"

Rose shrugs. "Bernie's shelf, I guess."

"But you just said you didn't want to put the platters in his office."

"Bernie's shelf in the *bathroom* closet. You have to go through his office to get there. It's the top shelf. You go, I can't reach it."

Rose's apartment has the same layout as mine, then—two bedrooms separated by a bathroom. I nod, grab the plastic platters and serving pieces, walk into Bernie's office, and find myself right in front of the piano. It's begging for me to put my detective skills to use. I turn to see if Rose is looking in my direction, but she's wandered over to her fridge, her back to me. She opens the freezer, the only spot in her kitchen I've yet to organize. She yanks out a plastic container from the back and holds it high, examines its contents from underneath. She pauses, then shoves it back in the corner. Why the woman refuses to dispose of food I don't know, but I do know why her refrigerator wouldn't close.

I place the platters on the ground quietly. I can't believe I'm getting a chance to look behind the piano! Cracks in the ribs, posts, or soundboard, I remind myself. That's what I'm looking for.

I drag the bench away from the piano, and as I do, the lid pops up. I see books, the glint of metal—and then it shuts. So it's a *storage* bench.

I close the door halfway—thank God, no creak!—and open up the bench again. There are gold locking mechanisms on both sides, which I press into place. On the left-hand side of the storage compartment is a worn copy of *100 Classical Piano Standards*, and on top of it, a metallic object I can't identify. It's comb-shaped, with four tines, and the initials J.A.K. are engraved along the side. Joel's initials. I flip through the book, which is filled with the scores of Bach, Schubert, and Handel, all heavily notated with different colored pencils. I assume they're a music teacher's markings—every *mp* lightly colored in yellow and circled with red, every *mf* colored with red and surrounded by yellow. Not that I know what either *mp* or *mf* stands for. The markings above the staff tend to be shaded in blue, and they highlight horizontal dots, Italian words I can't decipher, and what look like greater than or less than signs. I have to be careful not to tear the pages as I flip; the tops of those closer to the binder look as if they've been compressed and are beginning to tear. Mozart's *Turkish March* and Beethoven's *Moonlight Sonata* look especially fragile. I glance at the metal object in question and turn it ninety degrees so the initials read from left to right, as they should. The tines line up with the marks in the sheets! So *that's* what this metallic thingamajig is: a music book page holder.

Next to the music book is an assortment of ribbons and medals. My first assumption is that they must be piano-related, but upon closer inspection, I can see the medals are engraved with soccer balls instead of pianos. I push them aside in a slow, even motion, so they won't clang, to get a better look at the book underneath. The cover reads *Important Things About Me!* and has cartoon pictures of smiling children.

I peek around the corner at Rose, who's still engrossed in her freezer cleanout, then flip through the journal, which offers one topic per page, and space for the child to write in his thoughts. I turn to the beginning.

THINGS I LOVE:

1. Mom
2. Dad
3. Bandit!
4. roller costers
5. soccer
6. Laffy Taffy
7. building model planes with Dad
8. dolphins
9. M&Ms
10. my freinds

I'm careful not to chuckle out loud, because I adore this list. The placement of M&Ms above friends, the misspellings, the double selection of candy and random inclusion of a wild animal—it's a list Owen would make. I'm assuming Bandit was a pet, since he earned an exclamation point and clocked in just below Mom and Dad. Definitely an ego-saving ranking for Aunt Rose and Uncle Bernie, who must have taken in Joel quite young, since he thought of them as Mom and Dad. But building model planes is something an older elementary student would do, isn't it? I look for dates on the journal, or a listing of a grade or teacher, but there are none. So I turn the page.

I WONDER . . .

Why are there almost two hundred countrys in the world instead of one big country?

What is on the edge of the universe?

How are blue whales so big? Their tounges can wiegh as much as an elephant!!!

Why do people with brown eyes and people with blue eyes see the same colors?

Smart kid, this Joel. I make a mental note to Google the weights of both a blue whale's tongue and an elephant, then glance at the next page.

MY FAMILY . . .

Instructions:
Draw or paste a photo of your family doing your favorite activity!

Two photos, unbound to the page by hardened paste, fall to the ground. One is of Joel and a bushy-haired Bernie on the edge of a soccer field, Joel in a uniform. He's in profile, running full speed toward Bernie—his stride is elongated and the wind is blowing his hair back from his forehead. Bernie's mouth is open wide and his arms are outstretched in a victory stance.

The other is of Rose and Joel. They're both sitting on the piano bench, their bodies angled to the camera, Rose the closer subject. In the background are the remains of what appears to have been a fancy dinner; there is a damask tablecloth and candles. Joel is concentrating on playing—his expression is serious and his eyes fixed to the score—but Rose's is one of pure delight. Her eyebrows are raised and her mouth is slightly ajar, and her hands are raised in front of her. It looks as if she's waiting for him to finish, so she can break into applause. Joel is the focal point of her gaze just as she is the focal point of the camera's. I wonder if—

There is fumbling in the kitchen, followed by a high-pitched scream, and then a *thud*. I toss the journal into the piano bench and peer through the half-open door. "Rose! Are you okay?"

Rose is standing by the open freezer, a pint of chocolate ice cream at her feet, leaking onto the floor. "*Oy-yoy-yoy! Schmutz* all over my perfectly clean floor! Not five minutes was it clean, and already it's ruined. Ruined! All that work, work, work! For so long, and for what? What did it get me? Nothing." There's a sharp intake of breath from Rose, and then she squelches the exhalation and silences herself. She can't seem to stop staring at the ice cream.

Of course. It's Bernie's pint of ice cream. The last one she'll ever buy for him. That's what this is about. "Rose," I say quietly. "Let me clean it. It's no big deal."

She looks up from the ice cream trickling around her feet, then looks at my empty hands. "So. You're done with the platters?"

"Uh, well—I haven't found a spot just yet, but I can do that after—"

"No." She waves away my offer. "You already mopped once. *Genug.* Put the platters away—that I can't do. I'll clean up this mess."

I nod and close the door a smidge more as I rush back to the piano bench. I release the locking mechanisms, then grab the platters. I've got to hustle over to the bathroom and make it seem as if I've been rummaging around for a while in case Rose finishes up quickly.

I can see, when I arrive, why Rose didn't bat an eye when I said I couldn't find a spot for the platters. The closet abuts the shower stall, a variation from my bathroom layout. It's one of the most poorly designed closets I've ever seen. It only has three shelves, a sorry use of vertical space, and they're not even a uniform distance from each other. It's quite narrow— probably no more than a foot wide at best—but cavernous in depth. It's easily double my arm's length, which makes the items in the back inaccessible.

I don't know where Rose expects me to put the platters, because Bernie's toiletries are situated at the front of the shelf. There's a travel kit, several cans of shaving cream, two three-packs of Ivory soap, and a small box with shoeshine, brushes, and polishing cloths. They're all lined up as if displayed at a store—one of each item, label facing out, with duplicates stacked neatly behind. There are some medical items as well—a blood pressure monitor, two unopened bottles of men's senior formula multivitamins, and four half-full prescription vials. None of the drug names are familiar to me, although it wouldn't matter if they were. Bernie's medical history is none of my business, and, unfortunately, moot.

There's a large box behind these items, which I can see in the empty space above the prescription bottles. I can make out the words ULTRA-QUIET in bold, but that's all I can see of the manufacturer's labeling.

The only way to get the platters in is to use them as a battering ram to push the box farther back. I place Bernie's belongings onto the shelf below in preparation for the soon-to-be-waged platter battle. Now that my view is unobstructed, I can see all of the box's labeling. Assuming its contents match the packaging, the mystery object is a humidifier. Shouldn't be too tough to move, then.

Standing on my tiptoes, I try to push back the humidifier, but it doesn't budge. There must be other items behind it, but I can't reach them unless I pull out the humidifier and then stand on a chair and lean inside the closet to coax out whatever items are buried in the way back. I place the platters on the floor, turn toward Bernie's office to grab his desk chair, and bump into Rose.

"Oh, I'm so sorry! I didn't see you." I take a reflexive step backward and trip over the platters.

"*Oy vey*, watch it. I'm too old to pick you up," She grabs my wrist to steady me. Her hand is cold, but her grip is stronger than I expected.

I point toward Bernie's shelf. "There's a lot of stuff up there. The platters aren't going to fit unless we pull everything out and rearrange."

"Nah, just Bernie's broken humidifier is all. When he first brought it home, I asked him, 'Why do you think it's out on the curb, under a sign that says *free*? Because it's in perfect condition?' I told him to throw that *farshlugginer* humidifier out, but no, he said he knew how to fix it." She waves her hand in disgust. "You get what you pay for."

"No, there's more behind it. I tried to push it in, but something is stopping it."

"*Ach*, so he put more junk up there, where I can't see? Not everything can be fixed! Over and over, I tell him this, but he never listens!"

I shrug, because I have no desire to take sides in a fight she's having with her dead husband. "Do you want me to pull it all out or not?"

"Yah, yah. Let's see what else he's hiding back there."

I wheel in Bernie's chair, lock it from swiveling, climb onto it, and pull out the humidifier. Behind it is another box, this one corrugated and with no label. It's light, so I pass it to Rose. She places it on the desk and begins pulling items out of it as I lean inside the closet to try and budge what appears to be the remaining item.

It's a rectangular case made out of black aluminum and reinforced with steel strips along the edges. It must be positioned on its belly and backward, because I can't see any latches or a way to open it. I lean in farther and am able to graze the case with my fingertips. Pushing down on the shelf with my right hand for support, I swipe at the case with my left. It hits the inner side of the wall and shifts to the diagonal slightly, but I still can't grasp it. My arms aren't long enough, no matter how much I contort myself. I scan the shelf below for an object that might extend my reach, settle on an economy-sized bottle of shampoo, and nudge the case from behind. It finally frees, along with a cloud of dust that makes me cough so hard I almost fall off the chair.

"How many cords does one person need?" Rose says, digging through the cardboard box, as I make my way down from the chair with the case. "Look at this! Cords, more cords, and—connectors, I think Bernie calls them. I don't know what any of these go with. Now I have to—"

I turn toward her, the front of the case now in her view. Her washed-out complexion pales further, and she holds the cords in the air, frozen midtirade. I place the case on the counter and spin it toward me to see what she sees. I doubt it's a toolbox—there's no handle to cart it around. A storage container of some sort? There are two drawbolt latches on either end of the front face, the kind you see on a guitar case. Centered between them is a three-digit roll lock, secured by a latch.

She studies the case with a combination of curiosity and revulsion. "Is it—? Why would he—?" She shakes her head, pushes it away forcefully. "It doesn't matter. Get rid of it."

Throw it away? Didn't we just have a discussion about the horrors of recycling a few cheap, plastic platters? Isn't that why I'm covered in God knows how many years of dust from the back of a dead man's closet? "But it looks fine. You could put jewelry in it, or important papers. I was thinking about getting a locked case like this to store medication in, as a precaution for Owen. This one is way bigger than I need, but—"

"I want it out of my home! *Now*!" Rose's fists are clenched, her arms stiff and tight to her body, and she's shaking slightly. It looks like she's holding herself upright by the sheer force of her rigid arms, as if she's created a full-body cast for herself.

"Okay, okay." I put my hands up in an *I surrender* pose. "You win."

Rose flushes, and her arms relax. "You are going now, yes? You can put it in the trash room on your way out. Please."

— 12 —

A bee must land on many flowers before her work is done.

It isn't until I'm in the hallway, weighed down by the case, that I realize Rose didn't give me a trash bag. I pivot back toward her door, but it's already closed and I can hear her flipping the dead bolt and securing the chain. Getting rid of this mammoth case is going to be more difficult than Rose realizes. Then again, she must get the same ridiculous number of emails from management about trash disposal regulations that I do. Assuming, of course, she even uses email. It's possible she doesn't, unfathomable as that seems.

I've stopped reading management's incessant trash warnings. I read the official six-page disposal policy when I moved in—five pages too long, in my opinion—then skimmed September and October's barrage of emails outlining infractions and fines. For the past month, management's bolded, exclamation-marked messages have gone straight to virtual trash. I'm not throwing hangers, glass bottles, or pizza boxes down the chutes.

The basic trash disposal regulations are straightforward: second- and third-floor tenants must use medium-sized trash bags in the garbage chutes, and items that are too large must be brought to the first-floor trash room in a large trash bag. I obediently bought a box of medium bags when I moved in, but it turns out I was the only one. So now a day doesn't go by without several tenants clogging up the second-floor chutes with large bags, while I'm stuck dragging my trash downstairs in puny ones.

I hoist up the case and grasp its sides as best I can, my neck tilted up so it doesn't smack me on the chin. I shuffle down the hallway, then set it down outside the trash room. There's no way this oversized monstrosity will fit into one of my medium-sized bags.

But there's zero chance I'm buying bigger bags to get rid of Rose's stupid case. I just scrubbed her kitchen from top to bottom, and I know she has two boxes of them. And aren't I already doing enough for this woman, who seems intent on sucking the altruism out of me by kicking me out of her apartment on a regular basis? Bottom line: my too-small bags will have to do.

I jog up to my apartment, hoping someone will swipe the case during my two-minute round-trip excursion, but I return to find it right where I left it. I kneel next to it, lay the bag on the ground, and slide the case in sideways, which is the only way it will fit. The plastic stretches taut along the top of the case, but that's of far lesser concern than the six inches of it hanging out the end. There's no choice but to drop it off in the trash room as is. I peer in through the narrow rectangular window at the top of the door to see if the room is empty. *Damn it.* Freckly Maintenance Guy has shown up. That's what I get for trying to play by the rules.

It's Sean, I think. But maybe that name sticks out in my memory because I've stereotyped him as Irish due to his bright red hair and pale skin. He introduced himself when I first moved in, and when I ran into him a week later, I realized I'd already forgotten his name, or never registered it to begin with. I was able to salvage the awkward situation with the standard, "I'm so sorry, I'm terrible with names, would you remind me of yours?" But now I've forgotten it *again*, and you only get one pass with that excuse.

I glance down at the case, then back through the window. It looks like Freckly Maintenance Guy might be here awhile. His tools litter the floor, and he's standing on a stepladder examining a duct. I turn the handle, then think twice and let go. Why risk it? The better option is to take the case upstairs, wait for him to leave, then bring it back down again in its half-wrapped state.

I sigh and hoist the case. It's heavy, but not because of what's inside—at least, I assume not. It's too bulky for me to shake without dropping it, but there are no indications there's anything in it. I don't hear anything sliding around, and the weight doesn't shift as I walk.

Beads of sweat lace my forehead as I reach my unlocked door, which, thankfully, is still ajar. I back in and hurl the case sideways toward the kitchen, discus-style, but it doesn't make it far, landing on the hallway carpet with a thud. My arms have that pins-and-needles feeling because they've been contorted at odd angles for too long, so I shake them to get my blood circulating. I flick off loose flakes of dust on my shirt before righting the case and wiping it down with a sponge.

I *could* keep it. That'd solve my trash disposal problem. It's far too large for my purposes, but I wasn't lying to Rose when I said I'd like something similar. I know Owen's not a toddler anymore, but I'm used to having medications locked up in Nick's fire-resistant chest we hid under the bed. The one that also held our passports, marriage certificate, and Owen's birth certificate.

Nick's chest wasn't high on my list of items to push for when we divided our assets, although, in retrospect, it should have gone with whoever ended up with the household medications. And that person is me. I own every flavor of over-the-counter pediatric medication there is, and some of them are tempting. Like the grape-flavored ibuprofen tablets. They look like giant Smarties, and they taste even better. I know this because a couple of times when I've been out of regular strength I've resorted to Owen's stash. The probability of him getting a hankering for cherry-flavored juice and downing a bottle of acetaminophen is low, but there's a bigger problem than over-the-counter meds: hydrocodone.

It's hidden, with the less potent medications, in a shoebox on the highest shelf in my closet. Last year, I went to my doctor after a week of back spasms, and she prescribed it. I was embarrassed to take anything stronger than ibuprofen, because I hadn't been in a car accident or sustained a major sports injury. I'd pulled my back bending over to pick up baby carrots Owen had dropped on the kitchen floor. I told Nick an opioid for a veggie-induced injury seemed extreme, but he said Owen shouldn't have to miss preschool because I was being stubborn and refusing to take medication. Maternal guilt worked, but the hydrocodone didn't. It left me so dizzy I couldn't stand up, not even to get to the bathroom. Owen didn't make it to school that day, and I'm never going to take those evil pills again. But what am I supposed to do now, toss a month's worth of pills in the trash where they'll disintegrate in a landfill and seep into the water supply? Flush them and raise the contamination odds even more? I know my small bottle of pills isn't going to cause mass ecological destruction, but I still can't bring myself to do it.

But where could I store this decidedly *non*compact case? I have room in the cleaning closet, but, like Rose's bathroom closet, it's designed poorly: too deep and with limited shelving. Nothing would make me happier than to buy every bin and rack system available to organize the mess of sponges, buckets, cleaners, mops, and brooms. What could be more intoxicating for a clean freak than to clean the cleaning supply closet? But I don't have any excess funds for overpriced shelving, and there wouldn't be that much benefit. Everything would just end up smelling like chemicals—

Of course! Why didn't I think of it earlier? I grab the case, place it on the ground in front of the closet, and set cleaning supplies down on both sides, trying to estimate how many will fit inside. It looks like the case will easily fit the worst toxic offenders: bleach, ammonia, toilet scrubs, oven cleaners, and floor waxes. I can put the hydrocodone in, too, since I'm never going to use it. The over-the-counter meds will have to make do with my current shoebox setup for now.

I scoop a rag out of a bin in the closet and give the case a more thorough wipe. I run my fingers over its edges, looking for signs of age. There's some rust on the clasps and aluminum strips, but I don't know if that's due to time or being stored in a humid room. Other than rust, I'm not sure what to look for—hard black casing isn't giving me any clues. It's not a material that easily scratches or discolors.

Rose's reaction to seeing it still nags at me, though. I don't believe in curses, or bad juju, or whatever you want to call it—but the look on her face when she saw the case was downright weird. It's just a typical household item, like my filing cabinet or my waffle maker. Rectangular, metallic, functional. There's nothing horrifying about it. It's a regular combination-lock case.

There must be a simple explanation. She told Bernie to throw it out, he didn't, and so when she found out, she got mad at him. She still talks about him in the present tense sometimes, so it's understandable she'd have the same visceral response to his actions, even after his death. And then maybe she was embarrassed I was there to witness her making negative comments about her dead husband.

Or it could be that knowing Bernie wasn't there to quarrel with made her feel the weight of his loss for the second time in the span of a few minutes—first the absence of a husband to buy ice cream for, then the absence of a husband to squabble with—and suddenly, she needed time to herself. After all, she's under extreme stress. She's alone now, after a lifetime with Bernie. I only had a handful of years with Nick, and I can't manage to walk by the baking utensils in the grocery store without thinking of Courtney and wanting to scream.

There is a more pragmatic concern. I don't know the case's combination, and I certainly can't ask Rose for it, if she ever knew it to begin with. It's just a useless hunk of metal unless I can open it.

I turn the numbers on the combination to 123 and slide the square metal lock to the right, hoping the latch will fly open. No such luck. I try 000 next, followed by 999, and finally, 321. The latch doesn't budge.

I don't see any screws or a way of dismantling the hardware, which makes sense, since security is the whole point of having a lock. Bashing it until it opens is tempting, but it serves no point if I have any intention of using it again. Which leads me to the Internet—because there's no chance I'm the only person who's ever had to open a combination case without knowing the code.

There are twenty-two thousand results for the search *how to unlock a combination lock on a case*, and pages' worth of how-to videos. I scroll to the ones that focus on three-lock combinations. The first several advise me to look for markings on the side of each number—the logic being that fingertip oils would have caused darkening or discoloration, thus outing the secret combination. But even with the flashlight from my phone, I don't see any.

There are a thousand combinations in a three-lock combination case, I learn, and surprisingly, it's possible to try them all in under five minutes. The trick is to keep constant pressure on the square metal lock, so the latch will release when the correct combination is reached. That way you can get a rhythm going; you don't have to pause to try each combination. One video recommended wrapping a rubber band around the tab on one side and securing the other end around something stable, which is a good idea, but since I only have hair elastics, not wide, industrial-strength bands, my thumb will have to do.

YouTube's step-by-step instructions dictate that you start at 000, rotate first through the ones column (000 through 009), then add the tens column and try every combination (010 through 099). If you don't break the code with 0 as your first number, you've got to start the whole process over with 1 in the hundreds column instead of 0, and so on until 999. Or, in my case, 998, since I already know 999 doesn't work. It sounds like it'll take forever, but people in the videos seem to have latches flying open within a couple of minutes.

The thing is, there's no way of knowing whether you're doing it correctly. If the latch doesn't open—and I'm already past the ones column now and well into the tens column with no luck—is it because you haven't figured out the code yet, or because the lock is broken? Or maybe because this continuous system of checking isn't as foolproof as promised online?

Both thumbs are aching by the time I get to 082—one from scrolling through the numbers and the other from holding the tab in place—but I hold off until 100 to take a break and shake my hands out. Once the blood is flowing again, I get back to work, and I'm able to stretch the time between breaks over the next couple of rounds—shake-outs at 300 and 550. But the latch shows no sign of budging.

By 870, both hands are intermittently cramping and stiffening, and I begin to wonder if this worthless excuse for a case is worth the price of a carpal tunnel splint. But I'm too close to the finish line to quit, so I try the Ujjayi breathing Lindsay raves about to see if it will help suppress the pain. I breathe in deeply through my nose, constrict the back of my throat as if I'm about to whisper, and then exhale slowly to make a whooshing ocean sound. This is supposed to activate the first four chakras, whatever that means, and also "encourage the free flow of prana" and "create resonance within the body-mind." 996, 997, 998, and, why not, 999 again . . .

Nothing.

I slam my fist down on top of the case. "Piece of shit," I mutter, even though my deficiency in case hacking more likely deserves the blame. I don't know what I did wrong, but I'm in no mood for round two. I feel the blood, then—a trickle from my knuckle. It's just a scratch from the aluminum trim around the edges.

I walk into the bathroom to grab a Band-Aid and notice the showerhead is still soaking in my makeshift vinegar bag. I pull over Owen's step stool, peel the duct tape, and watch as the vinegar swirls down the drain. I appraise the shower caddy and the caulking as I let the water run to rinse away the pungent odor. I do good work, if I do say so myself. The brown film has been bested, and the lemons have done their job in disguising the bleach fumes. I pat the showerhead dry with toilet paper. It looks brand new! I can shower tomorrow without fear of giving myself a bathroom-borne fungal infection.

Final grades for the night:

Shower scrubbing—A.

Case cracking—F.

— 13 —

To reach the shore, both fishermen
must paddle in the same direction.

I t's been a super-productive evening thanks to Tranquility, the name
of the spa where Lindsay works. Not Tranquility Spa, mind you, or
Tranquility Spa and Skin Care or Tranquility Yoga and Spa Services.
Just Tranquility. I get it; they're trying to brand themselves with a Hindu
minimalist vibe, but there's an undercurrent of L.A. phoniness to the
name that just rubs me the wrong way. It's the nightclub attitude, the
cool-people-already-know-who-we-are mindset. The difference is that
Tranquility doesn't admit it's playing the client selectivity game.

I've purposely avoided the site during fortune-writing sessions so
as not to conflate Indian sayings with Chinese ones. I didn't want Peking
Foods to think I was yet another ignorant American who thinks all Asian
cultures are indistinguishable from each other. But tonight, desperate for
inspiration, I took a peek. And lo and behold, glorious web page after web
page of Tranquility lingo: a mishmash of Asian-sounding platitudes and

motivational phrases. In a description of a spiritual fortitude class—which is a therapy session with a spiritual wellness provider, apparently—the following is written: THE HINDU GURUS SAY: "IN LIFE, ONE SPRINGS FROM INSPIRATION, OR CLINGS TO DESPERATION." Catchy, right? But it makes me wonder: Which gurus? Because if it's not attributable to anyone, it rings false to me, like someone took the modern Western version of "as they say . . ." and replaced it with an ancient Eastern alternative. So I looked it up online. Not one matching hit with that sentence. The closest quote was Thoreau's, "The mass of men lead lives of quiet desperation, and go to the grave with the song still in them." I took out the *springs-clings* rhyme and left in just the key words—*life, inspiration, desperation*—and guess what popped up? A quote from Tony Robbins, the motivational speaker: "In life, you need either inspiration or desperation." So now I'm unsure what to think about the mystery author of these web pages. Is she a Tranquility employee—a Lindsay with a keyboard? Or is she outsourced, like me? If she's a freelancer, I don't know whether to be alarmed by her mixing of ancient wisdom with current self-help talk or impressed by her ability to write in her client's voice. At any rate, she's been a help to me tonight. I'm up to 274 fortunes, and I still have fifteen more minutes until Owen—

I hear the familiar three knocks high up on the door, and I wait for the flurry of Owen's fists lower down. Nothing. I rush to the door to find Owen slung over Nick's shoulder. Nick presses his index finger to his lips, the universal *shhh!* sign. "Transfer?"

Transfer. When Owen was a baby and we couldn't get him to fall asleep, Nick used to take him out for a ride in the car. It worked every time—he'd drift off within fifteen minutes, max. The problem was transferring him back from the car to the crib without waking him. A misstep meant he'd be up for hours, refreshed from his catnap. You'd think the beginning of the process would pose the highest waking risk, since it involved disentangling him from the five-point harness of his car seat and maneuvering him out of the car. Even the middle phase—walking up three flights and fumbling with keys to enter the condo—rarely caused him to stir. Reliably, it was being placed in the crib that posed the highest waking risk. I don't know whether it was the sudden separation from the warmth of another body, the creaking of the floorboards, or the unsettling sensation of being alone, but it wasn't uncommon to go through the whole process only to have him yowl as soon as his back touched the mattress.

It's weird that Nick and I still share this intimate shorthand. I know it would be even stranger for him to pretend our history didn't exist, to stand at the door and formally ask, "Would you mind if I come in? I'd rather not pass him to you now, he's likely in a light stage of sleep." But communicating in this code makes me uneasy, like I'm being disloyal to myself.

I move aside to let Nick in and don't even bother closing the door. I follow him into Owen's bedroom, then race in front of him to pull down Owen's window shade, turn off his baseball-bat-shaped lamp, and pull back his matching sports quilt and sheet. Satisfied with my preparations, I give Nick the go-ahead nod.

"Rub the sheets," he whispers.

I almost forgot. I run my palms back and forth in quick strokes over the fitted sheet, the underside of the flat sheet, and the pillowcase, warming them up as best I can so the cold doesn't wake Owen. Nick sits down in the bed and leans over, holds Owen as close to him as possible until the back of Owen's head touches the pillow. I pull the flat sheet and quilt up to his shoulders, then Nick and I look at each other. Five years later, and we're still waiting for the yowl. Owen mumbles something unintelligible, then flips over onto his stomach, pulls his hands up into a *W* position, palms down and even with his shoulders. I smooth his sheets and quilt perfectly flat, then roll them back so his wrists and ankles are exposed, just the way he likes. Nick holds his fingers up, one by one, counting to ten. He does this three more times, peers at Owen, then gives me a thumbs-up. We're in the clear.

"How come he's so tired?" I ask when we reach the hallway outside the kitchen. "He usually doesn't fall asleep in the car."

Nick shrugs.

"You can't think of *anything*? Because he was exhausted when you dropped him off on Sunday—"

"He's a little kid, Marissa! It's late! God, I am so sick of your insinuations. What exactly are you hinting at? Just spit it out already."

I give him a withering stare. "I was about to say that I've noticed it after school, too."

He reddens, which means he knows he's wrong, and also means he won't apologize. He's incapable of doing so when he's angry. We used to work around it when we were married, because there would be a time later that day, or the next morning, when he would give me a sheepish look and say, "Listen . . . about before . . . ," and that would be enough. But now we don't spend later that day or the next morning together.

I gesture to Owen's room, give Nick a pointed look. The last thing either of us needs is for Owen to wake up in the middle of this. "I'm worried about him, Nick. I got a call from Mrs. Evans today. She said Owen gets up from his seat all the time to tap the board behind her."

"Oh, that. So? Why didn't she tell me this when I saw her?"

"Because she didn't want to talk *about* him in front of him. But— that's not the point. What do you mean 'oh, that'?"

"He does it all the time. In counts of eight."

"Right. With his iPad. But only when he's trying to figure out new songs, or using music apps."

Nick gives me a strange look. "No. He does it anytime he thinks you're not looking at him. Under the table, thresholds of doors, sometimes the floor, if he's walking behind you. You haven't noticed?"

I haven't.

But does Nick honestly think he and Mrs. Evans, of all people, have picked up on something about Owen before I have? Please. I'm his mother. I know him better than anyone in the world.

But then again . . .

I *have* been distracted. Divorce, bills, jobs, college, custody . . . Is it possible I've been so invested in safeguarding our future that I haven't been able to see Owen as he is, right now? I fold my arms in front of my chest. "Well, if it's so obvious, I'm surprised it doesn't seem to concern you. It's really . . . odd behavior, don't you think?"

"It's a nervous habit. Some kids bite their nails. He taps. Not the biggest deal in the world."

"Mrs. Evans thinks it's a big deal. She wants the school psychologist to observe him, and she wants us to come in for a conference. And . . . have you noticed his writing? He erases his letters over and over again, tries to make them perfect. I accused her of being too hard on him, which is humiliating, because it turns out Owen's putting all that pressure on himself."

"He's like you."

"What's that supposed to mean?"

"You and your cleaning. Everything neat, ordered, in its place. He's the same way. What other kid cares if his socks are even, or if his sheets are completely flat and folded back at an exact angle at the wrists and ankles?"

"I don't know! I only have one kid. But I guess the fact that he lied at school today and ended up in the music room again is somehow my fault, too?"

Nick pales. "It happened again?"

"Mm-hmm."

He swallows, hard. Other than his Adam's apple bobbing up and down, he is frozen.

A shiver runs down my neck; my arms tingle. "You *know* something. I can tell. Spill it."

"I don't—"

"I have a right to know!" I yell, breaking my own rule about waking up Owen, but it's the only way I'm going to get through to Nick.

"Okay, okay," Nick says, waving his hands in a *calm down* motion. He takes a deep breath. "Owen's getting . . . teased at school. The first time he left lunch, it was because kids were mocking him—you know, tapping the lunchroom table and laughing, that kind of grade school shit. And then some kid stole his sandwich and stepped on it."

"Who told you that? Mrs. Evans?"

"No, Owen."

Tears spring to my eyes. Owen shared that secret with Nick? Not me? "So you didn't know he'd left the cafeteria a second time, but out of the blue today, Owen admitted what happened the first time?"

Nick sighs. "He told me last Saturday."

"Saturday? But I didn't even tell *you* about it until you dropped him off on Sunday night. So when I told you—" I gasp. "You already knew why he'd left, and you didn't *tell* me? You let me think it was only his love of music, and you let him continue to get bullied this week with no one to protect him?"

"See? This is why I didn't tell you. 'Bullied' is a strong word. Kids are mean sometimes. I thought you'd go crazy if you knew. Turns out I was right about that. I told him how to handle himself. I'm not happy that it happened again, but he can't run away from the lunchroom every time someone hurts his feelings, Marissa—it'll make him the easiest target in the school."

My poor kid. I know whoever is torturing him is someone else's little angel, but right now I want to *destroy* that child for hurting mine. I picture Owen, so excited about picking out his backpack and lunch and snack bags for big kid school, and I—

Snack bag. What did Owen say about Rose's fruit salad yesterday?

Pack a lot. With a granola bar, or some Triscuits. But put it in my snack bag, not my lunch bag.

"Nick, Owen's been asking me to pack extra food in his snack bag. Because he knows he'll actually be able to *eat* in the classroom, where there's more supervision. I wonder if this is happening more than we know. More than the teachers know."

"Come *on*, Marissa—a minute ago you didn't even realize there was a problem, and now it's an enormous one that's bigger than anyone suspects? The truth is he's getting picked on at school because he's anxious—a perfectionist—and honestly, if you didn't give in to him, then he wouldn't be so stubborn about it."

I take a deep breath, ready myself for the fight to come. "I thought the problem was that I cleaned too much. Now I give in to him? Care to give me an example of my faulty parenting?"

"The stupid nighttime routine! Why do the good-nights have to be in that exact order every time, with the basset hound, and the baboon, and all the other animals? Why can't you ever switch it up? Would the world come to an end if you tried it a new way?"

I pause for a moment, surprised by this unexpected line of attack. "The good-nights take less than a minute. It's comforting to Owen, a fun little thing we do together. Why would we switch it?"

"Look," Nick says, a pained expression on his face, "I don't know the bedtime routine as well as you. I know you start with 'see you later, alligator' and you end with Geri, but Saturday I messed up the order. I did big baboon before basset hound."

"So?"

"So he made me do it again. From the beginning."

I shrug. "He likes to hear the song in its entirety. He's musical. Partial phrasing bothers him."

"No. He made me start the whole process again. We had to leave the bedroom, come back in, adjust the sheets, the whole deal. And I didn't get the crocodile line right the second time. I said 'in a while, crocodile,' not 'after a while, crocodile,' so we had to start *again*, and after . . . I don't know, five or six times, I was really tired, so I said no, and I just turned out the light and left. And he lost it. Big-time. I heard him kicking, and by the time I went back in to tell him to cut it out, there were two huge holes in the wall and plaster all over his bed. He kept repeating 'we have to start over,' and I—I yelled at him, okay? And then he . . ." Nick swallows. "He bit his fingers. And he smacked himself in the head a couple of times."

Everything shifts. Like the turn of a kaleidoscope, a pattern that was once clear becomes murky for a moment, then transforms into a new reality.

I think of going down the steps to Rose's apartment, how I thought Owen was right behind me, and then, suddenly, he was at the top of the staircase again. Is it possible there's a set number of times he feels compelled to go up and down, an order that *must* be repeated—and he knew I wouldn't understand? I know the bedtime routine, but is there one for the staircase as well?

The bathroom. That's the excuse he used to leave the lunchroom, and it's the one he used with me, yesterday. Did he need to go, when we were heading down to Rose's apartment, or did he need privacy to retrace his steps on the stairs, away from my judgment? I assumed when he returned in the hallway, out of breath, it was because he'd run up to the apartment and back, but maybe he never went back at all. And on Monday, when he first used Rose as a convenient reason to avoid coming down the stairs . . . was that the truth, or just an explanation he thought I'd find less frightening than the truth?

"Did he draw blood?" I try to keep my voice calm.

"What, when he bit his fingers?"

I nod.

Nick gives me a dirty look. "*No*. He was just frustrated."

"Was there a mark the next day?"

No response.

"A *couple* of smacks?"

"Yes, two. You think I'd let him go for a third?"

"So you restrained him."

"'Restrained'? That's what you do to criminals, or crazy people!" Nick's neck is beet red. "I held his hands down. That's all."

I stare at the floor. "I've seen him smack his head before. When he's frustrated, or overtired. I've seen him do it in front of you. You've never held his hands down." I brace myself for Nick's response, but he's quiet, so I continue. "Those don't sound like smacks to me. They sound like punches."

I glance up. I should have stopped while I was ahead. Nick is pacing back and forth, waving his finger as if he's making a point, although he hasn't even started speaking yet. "See, I *knew* it! I knew you'd jump to—look, all kids tantrum sometimes."

"He needs to see his pediatrician! And get referred to—I don't know, a psychiatrist?"

"A psychiatrist? What are you saying?"

"Nick, he hurt himself! And doesn't what you described seem obsessive to you? Compulsive, maybe?"

He shakes his head. "You have lost your mind. I don't see him washing his hands all the time. And you can't get it this young. No. This is him trying to impress his Mommy the Neat Freak!"

"So this is just regular, run-of-the-mill anxiety? What could have caused that? Hmm, I don't know . . . maybe a dad who decides one day to kick him and his mom out of the house? And replace his mom a couple months later with a woman who looks like his teacher? Could that be at all confusing?"

Nick's face is bright red with fury. "It's been almost five months, not two! And if I'm such an awful parent, then why did Owen choose *me* to confide in, and not you?"

The front door is still ajar from when he entered, but he yanks it open farther, tripping over something as he lunges into the hallway. "Goddamn it!" he yells, hopping up and down while rubbing his hurt ankle. "Who the fuck leaves a bowl on the floor like that?" He doesn't recognize the HomeGoods bowl that was once ours, or if he does, he doesn't ask why it's outside the apartment. Instead, he turns to the right and punches the wall. The he hobbles off, his angry steps reverberating down the stairwell.

Rose.

Rose returned my bowl, left it outside my open door when she heard Nick and me arguing. How much did she hear?

I press my forehead against the door, let the silence envelop me. "Whatever happened to 'You're not supposed to give up on family,' Nick?" I whisper.

117

Nick had graduated from NYU the previous June, I learned that day on Mount Lycabettus.

"What are you doing here, then? Are you backpacking through Europe?"

He laughed. "No. That's not a concept my dad would understand. He's a classic Type A workaholic. I'm here because my great-uncle died."

"Oh. I'm so sorry."

Nick shook his head. "I only met him once, when I was four or five. But his wife, my aunt Nora, she's like a second grandmother. She's my *yiayiá*'s sister. She used to visit us in New York for a couple of weeks every summer, no matter what. She never missed. Until she got too old."

"So how long are you here for?"

"Up in the air right now. Nora's son, Alex, lives an hour away, but he's . . ." Nick abandoned this line of thought, then started fresh. "It's hard to explain. My dad thought it'd be a good idea to have me around while she decides what to do next. You know, to see if it's safe for her to live by herself, or to help her if she needs to move."

"What were you doing from graduation until now?"

"I had an internship at Fidelity last summer, but it didn't turn into a full-time position. Until I came here I worked a couple of boring part-time jobs. My dad has contacts in Boston, at an investment firm, but nothing's open right now. There's the possibility of something opening up in June, but who knows?" He shrugged. "It made more sense for me to be the one to come, once we heard about Uncle Theo. Plus, I get a chance to check out some sights while I'm here."

One such sight was right behind us—St. George's Chapel. The

small, nineteenth-century Greek Orthodox church is perched atop Mount Lycabettus, and Nick and I wandered through, staring at the muraled walls and ornate ceiling before ending up at the hilltop's outdoor café. We dined on moussaka with tzatziki and wine, and it wasn't until the lights came on in the Acropolis that I realized how long we'd been talking.

The following week, as we strolled through Anafiotika, a charming section of Athens known for its winding streets and whitewashed houses, I found out the critical information Nick had left out about his cousin Alex. Neither distance nor disability precluded Alex from caring for his mother. He was simply an irresponsible ne'er-do-well with more children than he could support and piss-poor business acumen.

That's what I suspected, at least, since Nick's vague and formal explanations sounded like he was parroting canned generic excuses. "Alex has important family obligations, many loved ones who depend on him," he told me, adding that over the years his dad had "attempted to assist Alex's entrepreneurial efforts."

"He's an entrepreneur? What kind of company does he run?" I stopped to pet one of the countless stray cats that roamed the narrow walkways.

"Uh . . . There's no company *yet*. He's still at the product development phase, so he's got a long way to go, but he's having problems getting patents." He glanced at the smile I could no longer hide and snorted. "Fine, you got me. My dad's funneled money to him for years. Indirectly, but he knew where it was going. He gave it to my *yiayiá*, who gave it to Nora, who gave it to Alex." He rolled his eyes. "Alex is family. And Dad always says you're not supposed to give up on family."

— 14 —

With an ox, the farmer ventures into fields he cannot manage alone.

I wake up to the sound of rain spattering against my window. The perfect pretext for lying to Owen.

"Hey, O," I say, as we're getting ready for the school bus, "I can't find my umbrella. We're going to need it for the bus stop."

Owen is concentrating on tying his shoes. "It's okay. I have my hood."

Shit. I didn't think about hoods. My jacket has one, too. "Yeah, but my hood isn't waterproof like yours, and the rain is supposed to get worse later. I'll need the umbrella at work, for dog walking. I think it might have slipped out of my bag. I'm going to go check the mail room, okay? Be back in two minutes."

"Uh-huh." Owen's attention is focused on the two enormous rabbit ears he's constructed out of his shoelaces.

I give him a kiss on the head and walk out the front door, then turn right and jog downstairs with exaggerated, noisy steps. There's no way I'd bring an umbrella on a dog walk and tie up both my hands, especially when the clinic is surrounded by a parking lot. It's a recipe for disaster. But these details are unknown to Owen.

I turn when I reach the base of the stairs and look up. The door to the apartment is still wide open. I climb the steps, this time as quietly as I can. When I reach the second-floor landing, I hide in the corner alcove. Back flat against the wall and head turned to the left, I peer inside the open door.

There's no sign of him, although I can hear him puttering around in the kitchen. It's a bad angle; all I can see is the hallway. I'd have a much better view of the kitchen if I were standing to the right of the front door, but there's no cover for me there, in case he were to walk out. It's possible I could—

Wait. Was that Owen's foot? It was lightning quick, its appearance and disappearance. He tapped the floor with his toe, then jerked it away, like you would if you were testing the water in a bath. I press my back harder against the wall, as if that will somehow make me invisible.

The toe again! This time less warily; he lets the ball of his foot rest for a second before it vanishes behind the doorframe.

A third time—the temperature of the floor is acceptable—and a fourth, fifth, sixth, seventh, and, of course, eighth.

The toe is gone.

What is this, now? A hand on the doorframe.

The first tap is cautious—the type you'd give to check if a stove top has cooled down. Then two-three-four taps in quicker succession, then five-six-seven-eight taps, rapid-fire.

The floor is on fire again—I can tell from the slowing of this second round of toe taps. But hasn't he already temperature tested the ground? I peer closer. Aha! He's switched feet. Symmetry. Why should I have expected anything different from my son, who needs socks and sheets to be folded at even angles? Will the floor be deemed tolerable this time? Will I soon see his other hand on the opposite doorframe?

I count toe taps to myself as I stealthily descend the steps, turn when I reach the midflight landing. My heart pounds; my stomach clenches.

His hand comes out, right on cue.

So this has been building for months. I've seen him by the half-open door as I've flitted from room to room, making beds, cleaning up breakfast, and assembling his backpack and my work bag. I even considered scolding him for not helping me. But he's little, I've justified, and it's sweet that he's so excited for school.

Did it start like this? This secret dance, this . . . ritual. Was it originally an occasional toe tap? What will it scale up to, if his compulsions go unchecked? Will he need an extra half hour to leave the house? An hour? Where else does he perform this ritual? I picture the busy streets around Nick's condo, filled with detours and disgruntled cabbies. What if Owen feels he must temperature test the road there? All that will separate him from an oncoming stream of traffic will be Nick's vigilance, and how much can I count on that when he thinks this is all in my head?

Stop it! I want to scream at him—but I know that's not fair, that it's not *really* Owen. It's some mysterious force deep inside of him, goading him, gripping him, overtaking him. I want to block the doorframe and hallway floor. Deny him access to them, make the problem go away. I could cordon the area off at night with my kitchen table, and sabotage his morning ritual. It's not that heavy, I don't see why—

No. Owen was furious when Nick tried to prevent him from finishing the bedroom routine. Actually, *furious* isn't the right word. People who are angry strike out at other people. Owen punched and bit himself, not Nick. And Owen is hiding this behavior from me. He knows it's strange, and he can't control it. He's ashamed.

Humiliating him won't make him confide in me. I've seen enough.

No hands or feet are visible now. Is he repeating the process in another room? Or are some rooms particularly compelling? How much of his day is devoted to completing these routines? And suppressing this impulse at school . . . it must be exhausting. Is that why he's been so tired lately?

I blink back the tears. "Owen," I call, my voice booming in the stairwell, "I'm coming up, kiddo. I couldn't find the umbrella. We're going to have to make do with our hoods."

I look in the rearview mirror before walking in to the clinic. My face is puffy, and my cheeks and forehead are covered with red splotches. Happens whenever I cry. It's bad this time—I look like I've developed a severe case of either rosacea or scarlet fever. I'm nowhere near present-able. But it's eight twenty; I have no choice.

"Allergies," I say to Megan, who works the front desk with me, when she looks up with alarm. It's a poor excuse—she knows it can't be my dog or cat allergies, since I'm just walking in.

"Oh my God!" The color drains from her face. "You didn't tell me you have food allergies, too. Your face looks . . . Is this an emergen—"

"No! Pollen, that's all." An even worse explanation, considering it's the end of November and all the leaves have dropped. I have to get better at lying.

Megan arches an eyebrow. "Look, you don't have to tell me if you don't want to, but . . . are you okay?"

Kindness—it gets me every time. I can be strong when people are rude or cruel, but the second someone is compassionate, cue the waterworks.

"I'll work the front." Megan pats me on the back as we both listen to me say over and over that everything's fine. She passes me a tissue. "Dab, don't wipe. You don't want to add black mascara streaks to your red spots."

"I'm good. Really. Thank you."

"No, you're not. Look, we're light on morning appointments and we're booked for boarding, so one of us needs to head out back and start the walks. Shouldn't it be the one who looks like she might scare off the customers?"

I smile. "Okay. Who should I take?"

"Belle. She'll cheer you up."

"That's right, Belle's here! I can't wait to meet her."

"She was dropped off last night. She's only here until tomorrow night or Saturday morning, depending on when the Andersons get back into town."

"How's she doing? Is she adjusting?"

"It's like I told you yesterday—a couple of days of boarding is a slice of heaven compared to what she's lived through. Besides, she's a superstar here, and she knows it."

Belle is a sandy-colored eight-year-old pit bull, well known to Allerton Veterinary Care because of the wounds she sustained prior to being adopted by the Andersons four years ago. She was abandoned at a gas station, and had been both malnourished and overbred. Her ribs and vertebrae could be seen through her skin, yet her body showed unmistakable signs of motherhood; her nipples hung low and loose from her body, and her back was bowed from pregnancies stacked too close together. Her ears were cropped, her teeth were filed down to nubs, and a huge chunk of flesh was missing from her left hind leg. She was shivering and in shock.

I asked Megan why Belle's piece-of-shit owners would do this to her. If they were breeding her to make money, why wouldn't they protect their investment? Which is when Megan told me a nauseating truth I wish I'd never learned: Once females are no longer able to produce quality pups, people get their money's worth out of them by using them as bait for the fight dogs. Shaving down their teeth ensures they can't defend themselves, which makes them easy targets. As for the ear cropping, that *is* a method of asset protection. Ears are often injured first in dogfighting, and dogs can die from infection. So ears are cut off before that can happen. Why Belle had her ears cropped was a mystery to me, since she wasn't a fight dog. Megan told me that some lowlifes think it makes the dogs look fierce, so they do it to the males and the females.

After a month with a foster family, the Andersons stepped in and adopted a broken-spirited, beat-up pooch, one who looked far more like the Beast than the Beauty, and named her Belle. Of course, the movie reference is an assumption on my part. Belle, Bella, Isabella—they're common names. That could be the whole story.

But it's not just Belle's name that has me wondering now, as I approach her cage. It's the fleece jacket the Andersons left behind for her, hanging on the outside hook. It's the same canary yellow as the character Belle's dress. And what's this underneath? It looks a bit like an infinity scarf, but it's dog-sized. A yellow fleece band, a perfect match to the jacket. For her ears! I don't know if it's because her nerve endings are exposed and the cold causes her pain, or because she needs to block gusts of wind from entering her ear canals now that she has no flaps to cover them, but either way, this accessory makes me adore the Andersons even more.

I grab a leash off the row of hooks. When Belle hears the clanging metal of the clasp, she bolts up from what I thought was a sound sleep. "Ready for a walk, Belle?"

She blinks several times, then ambles to the front of her cage. I hold out my hand, palm up, let her sniff me before I open the door. Megan's right; she's a sweetheart. She doesn't try to push her way out, like most dogs, and she's not pressed up against the back wall in fear, either. She's patiently waiting for me, sitting like a good girl, her tail thumping.

Rage flares within me toward the miserable excuse for a human being who inflicted such pain on this innocent girl. It's a miracle she trusts any humans at all. The fact that she's excited to see me, a stranger taking a turn placing her in and out of a cramped, locked cage for no reason she can discern, is astonishing.

"It's not terribly cold out today. I don't think you're going to need your jacket. Maybe just your ear band." I open her cage, block her from exiting, and grab her collar. I doubt she's an escape artist, but it's better to be safe than sorry. I drop her jacket and ear band to the ground so I can attach the leash to her collar, and as I do, she tries to stick her muzzle through the neck opening of her jacket.

"You want to wear it? I didn't realize, sweet girl. You're right, a lady must be dressed for every occasion." She bows her head and allows me to slip it on her, and then I reattach her leash to her collar. It's not until I fasten the belly strap that I notice it. Just above the Velcro strip on the side, *Belle* is embroidered in fancy script, and along with it, a flower in full bloom. The symbol of love, of inner beauty over outward appearance. Belle notices her ear band resting on the ground and nudges it toward me with her snout. I hold it up for her, and she leans her wrinkled, scarred muzzle forward, then lets me adjust it. "You *are* a beauty, Belle. Just like your name."

I take a step back to let her out of her cage. She trots toward the back door before I have the chance to zip up my jacket, her toenails clacking on the cement floor. She stops when she feels the leash pull taut, looks back expectantly, tongue out, with what can only be described as a smile. *Come on, this is going to be fun!* the look says.

I pull my hood up and open the door for her, then let her choose which way to go. She looks to the right, toward the small wooded area behind the clinic, then squats and takes an obligatory pee. She looks up at the sky as the rain settles on her fur, then shakes it off with a rattle of her collar tags and a thump of her tail.

She turns and walks to two chain-link dog runs set up alongside the building. They were installed because the only other place to walk is the parking lot surrounding the clinic, which is composed of three spaces to its front and eight to its side. It's a shame, because you can see the Town Common from the edge of the parking lot, but we're not allowed to take the dogs off the property.

We spy it at the same time: a pothole filled with rain. I try to give it a wide berth, but Belle surprises me and resists, pulling against me even as the collar digs into her neck.

"Belle, hold up! You're going to hurt yourself. We can go play. Just let me take your jacket and ear band off first."

The pothole is wide enough to ruin a car's alignment or, as it turns out, serve as a wallowing pool for a pit bull. Belle lounges inside of it and closes her eyes, water lapping at her belly while her tongue hangs out.

I crouch down next to her, and as I do, she flips over with a splash. Her belly and paws are covered with mud. I shake my head. "Oh, so it's a mud bath! The full spa experience. Go ahead, enjoy yourself—you deserve it."

The rain is starting to come down harder, and I can feel the water permeating my hood. My knees begin to ache from squatting, and as much as I want Belle to relax, I hope she decides to go to the run soon. She flips over a few more times, until the mud coats her back as well. She's managed to completely ensnare herself in her leash, so I disentangle her, then do a quick 180, because I know the full-body shake is coming soon. I'm not quite quick enough—specks of mud land all over my jacket and jeans.

"No, Belle, stop!" I brush the globs of mud off as best I can. "You know there's no bath for humans at Allerton, right? Come on, silly girl." I lead her toward the closer run, which has a cramped entryway jutting out to the right. We're in luck, I see, as we enter; someone has left a stack of fresh towels on the metal bench. I wipe down Belle and she ambles from the cement-floored entryway to the turf run.

I let her off leash and give her some time to sniff. It's a scent wonderland in here. No amount of scooping up and hosing down can erase the odor of hundreds of dogs over time. She walks by a plastic toddler pool, which holds a variety of balls and squeaky toys in the winter months. I don't know how much footage of running space there is, but even big dogs can get in five or six all-out strides before having to turn back, which is great for fetch. They can get a real workout if you bounce the ball off the insides of the cage and let it ricochet. It's a racquetball-for-dogs effect.

Belle wanders toward the far end, sniffing as she walks. I pick a ball out of the plastic pool. "Belle," I call after her, "go get it!" The ball whizzes over her head and clatters into a silver water bowl. She lets out a yelp and flattens, belly on the ground and all four legs splayed.

I immediately realize my mistake. Hurling an item at a once-abused animal? "Oh, honey, I'm sorry. I didn't mean to scare you!" I catch up and sit down on the turf beside her, even though I know it's been peed and pooped on more times than I want to consider. She's trembling, poor thing. I stroke her mud-covered side until she calms and nestles nearer to me. She looks up, offers me a cautious nudge of my hand with her snout.

"We're friends again? In that case, would you like a chin scritch?" I give her a few gentle strokes under her jawline, then reach up under the base of her ear and massage her neck. She collapses into me as she relaxes, then flips onto her back. "Goofball." I laugh. "I can't rub the back of your neck when you're upside-down." She bats my hand with her paw lightly. "What? You want belly rubs instead?" I stroke her belly, and her eyes close. Her breathing becomes rhythmic, until she breaks the serenity with a sneeze. "Bless you!" I stand up. "How about we get a little exercise?"

Belle rises and shakes, her metal tags clanging. I pick up the ball again, show it to her. "Ready now?" I roll it on the ground in front of us. She trails it in an elderly dog gait—a stiff jog instead of a bound. She favors her right, the result of the fight injury she sustained to her left leg. She lifts the ball with her mouth, then drops it, distracted by a scent she's picked up. She follows it around the perimeter of the run.

I let her sniff. When she makes it back to the run's entrance, I hand her a squeaky toy from the kiddie pool and kneel so I can stroke her back. She turns and gives me a quick lick across my mouth and nose before chomping on the toy.

"Eww, Belle, no kisses needed." I wipe her spit off, steel myself for the inevitable rush of heat, the throbbing and itchiness that signal the beginning of an allergic reaction. There will be hives around my mouth by the time we get back, maybe a swollen lip. Because it's not only dander that transmits allergens, even though Allerton's waiting room, rarely without a goldendoodle or a labradoodle, attests to the suburban pursuit of the hypoallergenic dog. Saliva does the trick just as well for me.

I press my palms to my cheeks. They don't feel flush at all. My lip feels normal-sized as well. I pick up one of the silver water bowls, examine my reflection. It's hard to tell—it's a bit like looking into a fun house mirror—but I don't see any hives. And come to think of it, no itchy eyes or sneezing from petting. Usually by now I'd be a mess. I can't explain it.

Belle is off again on another lap, sniffing hundreds of scents I will never register. Her stiff gait looks like it's beginning to loosen, and she's dropped the squeaky toy and picked up the pace a bit. Maybe she'll get a little exercise after all. I look down at the canary-yellow ear band and jacket in my hands, and rub my finger over the embroidered script. "Belle?" I call after her. "I need to find *my* Andersons. For Owen. I think . . . I think he really needs help. Nick doesn't think he does, but Mrs. Evans does think he does—I mean, I *think* that's what she thinks—and I'm so confused." Tears stream down my face, but I have no way to wipe them. My hands are contaminated with dog allergens and my jacket is covered with mud. "I think it's smarter to wait to call Owen's pediatrician until after I meet with his teacher next week. But I really need to talk to someone."

Belle stops short, and pivots. She bounds toward me with the effortless stride of a much younger dog. She's not panting when she reaches me, which is odd for an old girl like her. I crouch down, and she leans her scarred muzzle against my chest. She must have heard the break in my voice. She nestles against me for a moment, then brushes past me, and turns left into the entryway.

"You're ready to go back? Why are you cheating yourself on time?" I glance up at the clock on the wall. "We've got another five minutes."

Belle situates herself underneath the bench and closes her eyes. I look around the entryway: cement floor, metal bench, extra towels. Everything carefully selected for ease of cleaning. But for the first time, I consider the design of the two rooms. It would make much more sense to have a vertical entryway attached to a vertical run. This changing of direction isn't a big deal with Belle, but with large or aggressive dogs, it adds an unnecessary level of complexity. I guess Dr. Allerton had no choice—there's limited parking. But it really is a bizarre L-shaped design.

I smile. *Lindsay*. She's the one I need to talk to next.

I give Belle a kiss on her head. I know I'm safe with her, although I can't explain why. "Thank you for guiding me, Belle."

— 15 —

Words deserve little credit in communication.

Common Grounds has run out of lemon scones. Neither of the alternatives, maple walnut or pumpkin spice, are worthy of a four-hundred-calorie binge, so I order a salad with grilled chicken and a seltzer and head toward my booth in the back.

I should call Mom. She's expecting it, considering I didn't call on Tuesday. And Owen's well-being is certainly of greater interest to her than it is to Lindsay. But the truth is, I'm ashamed. I've already failed at college. Then I failed at marriage. And now I've failed at motherhood. I don't want to admit to Mom that Nick and Mrs. Evans noticed symptoms before me, that I confirmed this by lying to and spying on my own child this morning.

As for Belle advising me, I admit that was a moment of weakness. Who else am I going to call besides Lindsay? When you zoom through the milestones of life at warp speed, it's hard to avoid growing apart from your friends. Like leaving college to get married and have Owen. I tried to keep up my college friendships when I first moved to Boston, but it didn't take long for calls and texts to become less and less frequent, and then stop altogether. Because what did I have in common with them? Exams and dating weren't part of my world anymore, and both topics seemed insignificant in comparison to the fact that my body had figured out how to create another human being.

Before Owen was born, I worried I'd give birth to him and feel nothing. I was never maternal; I didn't want to be Mommy's little helper when Lindsay was little, and I didn't want a job as a babysitter when I got old enough. But the second the doctor handed Owen to me, something primal ignited, and I was overwhelmed by the ferocity of my love for this seven-pound, eight-ounce shrieking mass of rumpled flesh with scrunched-up eyes and a flattened nose. *So this is what it means to be a mother*, I realized, and everything I thought I'd understood about motherhood was revealed to be a two-dimensional version of the truth. There was no way to translate this to college friends who hadn't experienced that seismic shift in perspective but still seemed to think they understood. And in their defense, I didn't do a stellar job of concealing my boredom with their anxiety over legitimate stressors like graduation requirements and job searches.

I made mommy friends, once Owen was old enough to go to toddler gym and music classes, and even more once he went to preschool. But my Boston friends seem a world away now that I don't bump into them in the school parking lot. Playdates haven't happened since we moved. I don't know if that's because they're legitimately busy or making excuses, but I do know that my supposed friends have been weird about my divorce. Like Jen. Her son, Henry, and Owen were in class together for two years, and they used to have playdates twice a week. Owen and

I bumped into them at the park at the end of July, and Jen hugged me as I tried not to cry, and she said we needed to talk in private, without the boys. We texted, but couldn't find a date that worked for her, so I said she should just give me a call when she was free. But she said no, this was far too important not to be face-to-face. I haven't heard from her since.

Jen isn't the only one who reacted in an unexpected way. Stephanie tried to set me up with her cousin's best friend a month after Nick and I separated. A *month*. Kara couldn't talk to me without crying and telling me about her parents' divorce when she was *exactly the same age as Owen*, and she also told me she overheard Rebecca say that she wouldn't have settled for anything less than full custody with no visitation if she were me. So I've let those friendships fade as well. I've told myself that kindergarten would have been a transition year regardless of where Owen ended up, but now I realize how selfish that was. I should have worked harder to keep those friendships up for him, even if it was uncomfortable for me. Why should he pay the price for my insecurity?

Lindsay picks up after two rings. "Hey, Riss." I hear what sounds like a bird whistling in the background, followed by purrs. Maybe she's listening to an NPR segment about nature, or a podcast about the jungle? I imagine the Amazon rain forest: a spectacled owl, a brightly colored macaw, a spotted jaguar. But there's an echo to the sounds, a reverberation I can't pinpoint.

"Still having audio problems?"

"No, they're fixed. Can you hear me okay? It's fine on my end."

"Your voice is clear, but the jungle animals sound off. What are you listening to?"

"Humpback whales." She lowers the volume. "Really soothing. Whales are my spirit animal."

"Ohh . . . so the distortion is because of the underwater reverberation. Poor animal guesswork on my part."

There's no reason to clarify that sound travels differently under water, and my assumption of jungle animals, given the limited information I had, wasn't a bad one. I'm stalling for time while I think, because isn't the concept of a spirit animal a Native American belief? I guess Asian shamans could practice a similar tradition, but somehow that doesn't sit right. I don't ask, though, because Lindsay will assume I'm trying to trip her up.

I think of Belle. "Does 'spirit animal' always have to refer to a species as a whole? I mean, could your spirit animal be an individual animal?"

"I don't know any humpback whales personally."

"No, I mean for *me*. There's this dog where I work—"

"It's more than just picking a dog you think is cute." Lindsay's voice is pinched.

"That's not why I was thinking of her," I say, suppressing frustration. "She's not cute in the traditional sense at all. She's an old pit bull, not a puppy. She used to be used as a bait dog, before she was adopted. But you're right, I don't know the official process of picking a spirit animal. How does it work?"

"You don't choose your spirit animal. It *presents* itself to you. It's the embodiment of your subconscious."

"So it comes to you in a dream?"

"It will manifest itself whenever your mind is at rest. So, yes, people often connect with their spirit animals in dreams, or during meditation. But an animal *can* present itself in physical form, if your heart and mind are fully open—it's just rarer."

"So why humpback whales?"

"Because whales have the awe-inspiring capacity to withstand the pressures of the ocean, and the ability to break free and surface when life-sustaining air is needed."

Well, *yeah*. It's called respiration. Technically, she's right; it's amazing in the sense that it took whales' land-dwelling ancestors fifty million years to make the transition to aquatic living. But that's not what she means. It's not hard to spot the heavy-handed metaphor: "pressure of the ocean" equals "pressure of life."

"Plus, they're great communicators. The males produce the complex songs that humpbacks are famous for, but the females communicate, too, with deep pulses, barely within our range of hearing. Calves whisper to their mothers in squeaks and grunts when they swim in predatory waters. The mothers guide them and keep them safe." Lindsay clears her throat. "The male humpbacks don't stay."

I don't respond right away, because I don't know enough about Lindsay's relationship with Eric to pinpoint where their communication failed. I try to think in Lindsay-like symbolism. Was he drowning her out, while her needs were unheard? Or is she faulting herself for not joining in his plan, his "song"? She brought up calves, which makes sense, since parenthood is what broke them up. But Lindsay's depiction of it . . . well, it's pretty dark. Not all of motherhood is guiding your infant through murky waters past murderous killer whales.

I need to say *something*. "That's interesting, that the males and females communicate differently. I can see why you'd pick—I mean, why a whale would present itself to you."

Spiritual Lindsay is quiet for a moment, and then, Old Lindsay lets out a laugh. "Come on, Riss. You can do better than that. No comment about why it should be a cow?"

"Too early to fight about cows." I laugh, surprised by the memory of our FaceTime bovine spat.

When Owen was a month old, I called Lindsay and asked her advice on how to get rid of excess baby weight. What I really wanted, though, was some fluff about the mother-child bond being a sacred duty of paramount concern, so I'd feel less guilty about my flabby stomach. Instead, she said she could see even my face looked bloated, and launched into a full-scale lecture regarding my ineffective exercise routine and diet.

"Cardio's the first thing we need to talk about. You're going to have to do a *lot* more of it—ideally six days a week—and weights two to three times a week. Yin yoga on your rest day will help your muscles prepare for another week of training."

"How is it a rest day if I'm doing yoga?"

"Yin yoga isn't aerobically intense. That's what I meant by 'rest.'"

Work out every day? How on earth was I supposed to do that with a newborn? Just getting five minutes for a shower was a near-Herculean task that involved dragging Owen's bouncer into the bathroom with me, strapping him in, and singing to him while he howled, certain I was gone forever. I wanted to scream at her, *Object permanence develops between four and seven months!* I move out of this kid's sight and he thinks his meal ticket is never coming back. Everyone knows you're supposed to tell a new mom that the weight will come off through nursing. *Everyone.* The same way everyone knows you're supposed to pretend you don't notice a woman's pregnancy until she's practically in active labor, *that's* how good she looks. Why can't you just be a good sister and take the bait?

"And as for your diet, my guess is you eat way too many carbs. Stay away from junk food, and refined flours—if it's white, don't eat it. Drop sugar altogether. And up your protein. That'll give your body the nutrients it needs to build muscle, which will raise your resting metabolic rate."

"But I hate meat. You know that. Just the thought of biting into gristle makes my skin crawl."

"Then you can get your protein from beans, eggs, and dairy. Lean protein from fish or chicken is the best, but I bet Nick is a steak-and-potatoes guy, right? Don't just cook it for him and scrounge for yourself. Or—does he do all the cooking? I know it's not really your thing."

Awesome. A lecture on basic nutrition and, as an added bonus, a jab at my poor cooking skills. Lindsay didn't even ask what I ate in a day; she just assumed I was stuffing my face with doughnuts and pizza. "I can't believe you, of all people, are telling me to eat red meat! Cows are revered in Hinduism! Your expert advice is to eat a sacred animal?"

Which is when Lindsay told me that last time she checked, we were both Catholic, not Hindu, that she couldn't care less what I decided to eat, and hung up on me.

We never talked about that fight, chose instead to avoid each other for several weeks. Then Lindsay called one day, out of the blue, to see how I was doing—no apology from her for hanging up on me and no request for an apology from me for losing my temper. That's always been our pattern. She never wants to rehash our fights, but she never forgets them, either; then, at the most unexpected times, like now, she'll fashion a memory into a shared joke, offer it in peace rather than keep it on a scorecard of wrongs.

Which makes me think that Lindsay's spirit animal shouldn't be a humpback whale. It should be an elephant. There's the obvious Western saying, "an elephant never forgets," but Ganesha, the Hindu deity with an elephant for a head, comes to mind as well. He's the remover of obstacles, the patron of letters and learning. And I've got to hand it to her, Lindsay is constantly seeking Truth and Knowledge and Enlightenment, while I am constantly mocking all of the Capital Letters. I can't help it, with some of the sloppy conclusions she comes to sometimes. But it takes more commitment to search than to be snarky.

"So, Linds, spirit animals aside . . . how are you?"

"I'm good."

"No, I'm serious. How are you? This is a big deal, you and Eric, and—"

"I'm fine. Really."

I sip my seltzer, forgetting she hates when I drink while we're talking. "Oops. Sorry about the gulp. I know it's not . . . mindful."

Lindsay giggles. "That sounds weird coming from you."

"It didn't come naturally, I'll admit it." There's a silence, and I think of Jen, how we never managed to say what we needed to say to move forward. "Listen, Linds, I can tell you don't want to talk about it, and I don't know if it's because you don't want to talk to *me*, or you don't want to talk *period*, but . . . I just want you to know that I'm here for you."

"About that. I know that I . . ." Her voice is thick, and I can tell she's holding back tears. "I think the best way to encapsulate my thoughts is with the Buddhist proverb—"

Click. Click. Click. The armor is up. She's too exposed; Spiritual Lindsay must return. *Don't go*, I want to say. I don't want advice from philosophers and gurus. I want my sister.

". . . 'from the deepest and thickest mud.'"

"Wait, what did you say?" I look down at the mud stains on my jeans.

"I said, 'The lotus flower blooms most beautifully from the deepest and thickest mud.' They're amazing organisms. They have to rise above muddy water to greet the sun and bloom."

I think of the hives and swollen lip that never appeared after Belle licked me across the face, of the sneezes and watery eyes that didn't pester me. She's the only dog that's ever happened with. I think of how an animal with a long-standing injury ran with no limp all of a sudden, how Belle arrived in front of me without panting. I think of the L-shaped room she walked me to when I asked for help, of Lindsay bringing up spirit animals today. We've never talked about them before. And what about the mud?

Hmm. Answers? Belle ran without a limp because her muscles loosened up from exercise, and she wasn't out of breath because she warmed up gradually, so no oxygen debt. My immune system wasn't triggered by the proteins in Belle's saliva or dander because, as my allergist once explained, dog allergies aren't breed specific, they're *dog* specific. I don't know why my body didn't react to Belle, but not knowing something doesn't necessitate a jump to a supernatural explanation. It simply requires more hypotheses and testing. The L-shaped runs are due to parking. Lindsay quoting a Buddhist proverb is not surprising, nor is a dog jumping in mud.

Simple.

But if I'm wrong, and spirit animals do exist . . . there's no question that Belle is mine.

— 16 —

An ant cannot build a hill by itself.

It's ten past three, and Owen is decompressing with his daily half hour of after-school iPad time.

He's sitting sideways on the couch, his back against the armrest and the iPad in his lap. I can hear the sound effects of a familiar video game, but I can't remember which one.

I glance at him as I load the dishwasher with the dirtied plastic containers from his lunch and snack bags, see him making hurried streaks across the screen with one index finger, then two. Aha.

"Fruit Ninja, O?"

He nods. "I got a dragon fruit!" He frantically swipes across the screen. "They're really rare. Worth fifty points!"

It's a welcome change to see him this excited, even if the subject matter is digital produce. The old Owen. Did I imagine this morning? It feels as if I suddenly have two Owens—but one is shrouded in secret, a stranger.

There's a knock at the door.

It's Rose, I see, when I open it. Why is she here? Should I apologize for Nick's behavior, for whatever she heard last night? Or maybe she's here because she feels badly about kicking me out of her apartment with the case yesterday.

She's decked out in full winter gear, which is odd for a forty-five-degree day: a full-length wool coat with notched lapels, leather gloves, and a chenille scarf. She must be on her way out, since her coat is dry.

"Hello." I use as neutral a tone as I can muster.

"Dottie has a cold." Rose says this as if I know who Dottie is, or have reason to care that she's sick. I *do* know, in fact, because of my conversation with Lena. Dottie is Rose's less-than-polite friend, the woman I met at shiva. But *Rose* never told me Dottie's name. Lena did. Rose was too busy closing the door in my face that night to bother with formal introductions.

"I'm sorry to hear that."

I should coax it out of her, bridge the communication gap. It's the kind thing to do. I should say, Is Dottie the lady I met at your apartment? Does she need help? But I don't feel like being the better person. I have plenty of problems of my own to deal with, so—

"*Oy*, she's sneezing and coughing something terrible. Coughing, coughing, coughing."

"I'm sorry to hear that," I say again.

"So . . . ?" She looks at me expectantly, nodding, in the way one waits for a child to reach a conclusion that is patently obvious. Except she seems unaware that she hasn't given me any of the pertinent background information.

"So *what*?"

"So now Marnie has to take her to the doctor instead of taking me to—" She stops midsentence, anticipating my argument, but I have no intention of interrupting because I have no idea what she's talking about. "What, you think Marnie can leave her there, coughing like that? Dottie called me, crying—*crying*, I tell you—because they can't take me now. She has to go to the doctor. She has to be seen today."

"I don't understand—"

"Because it has to be today for me, too! I'm sorry poor Dottie is sick, but she should have called earlier, given me more time. Maybe then I could have made different arrangements. She knew this morning, but she didn't call. She didn't want me to be upset with her. Not until the last minute did she call, when Marnie showed up at her place at one. One o'clock, when she was supposed to pick me up at one thirty! On such short notice there was nothing I could do. It wasn't right of her. If she knew, she should have picked up the phone—"

"Rose! What are you talking about?"

"What? Oh—what am I thinking? That's right. You don't know Marnie. She's the spring chicken of the group. She does the driving."

"No. Bigger picture. Where were you supposed to be going?"

She stops, confused. "I didn't tell you? It's Bernie's birthday today. I have to go visit him."

Birthday? I fully admit I'm out of my depth when it comes to the complexities of mourning, but it seems odd to celebrate Bernie's birthday when he died a handful of days short of it. It makes sense that she'd like to honor him on an important day, but isn't this the sort of ritual that comes later in the healing process, when grief isn't so acute?

"I can't get there on my own. Even before he . . . Bernie was always the driver." She pleads with her eyes, then drops her gaze to the floor. She opens her mouth, but no further explanation comes. "Please," she finally says, her voice catching. "Please, would you take me?"

"Rose, I would, but . . ." I glance back at Owen; I don't want him to overhear. But he's completely engrossed in his iPad, slicing virtual pineapples and melons. Even with parental controls, that device is a portal into an alternate realm.

I turn back to Rose. At least I don't need to whisper for Owen's sake. "I can't." I point behind me. "He's never been to a cemetery before. I haven't even had an in-depth conversation with him about . . . death." I mouth the word, even though I know he's not listening. "And my ex wouldn't be thrilled about me making a decision like this without asking him first. I'm so sorry."

"Yes, yes, of course, I understand," she says, even as she vehemently shakes her head no. I wait for her to wave goodbye, to turn and leave, but she remains rooted to the ground. "But . . . it isn't only Bernie, you see, it's also . . . so it's very important that I go *today*, because . . ." A sob rises up and escapes her, followed by a larger one, which she tries to stifle in a series of choking coughs. She rummages through her handbag until she finds a hard candy, her hands shaking as she removes it from the strawberry-designed wrapper. She plops it in her mouth, sucks on it, then swallows several times. She fixes her gaze on me once she regains her composure, but now the beseeching look in her eyes is gone; her expression is flat. "I understand," she repeats, her voice now toneless, and she turns toward the stairwell.

Goddamn it. Last I checked, Rose owed me an apology for kicking me out of her apartment. Yet somehow I'm the one who ended up saying *I'm sorry*, and I still feel like a horrible person. Yes, it's true I promised Lena I'd get Rose out, and I haven't made good on that agreement, but in my defense, that was for errands and fresh air, not for trips to the cemetery with my kindergartner.

What I said to Rose about Nick is true. I *don't* think it'd be fair of me to make a life decision for Owen without Nick's input. I'd be pissed if the situation were reversed. It's a bad precedent to set.

I've never taken the time to examine what I want to pass on to Owen. I don't know if I believe in heaven. I just tossed it out as an explanation when Bernie died because I wasn't prepared with anything better, which I know doesn't secure me a spot in the Parenting Hall of Fame. As an adult, there's much greater comfort for me in the idea that Bernie's body will nourish the earth, which will, in turn, sustain plants and animals, than the image of Bernie sitting on a fluffy cloud. But there's no way to talk about the circle of life without discussing decomposition, and I don't know how much a child his age should be expected to process. I'm not willing to give Owen nightmares and compound his existing struggles because Rose is having transportation issues.

But I've never seen Rose so resigned before. Grief-stricken, shocked, proud, delighted . . . in the few days I've known her, I've seen all of these cross her face. But the Rose that just turned away—the one with the deadened eyes and the blank look—she isn't the *real* Rose, and being the one responsible for extinguishing that spark is nauseating, even though this situation isn't of my making. Have I lost all compassion? Didn't I spend my morning blubbering to a pit bull because I felt like I had no one to turn to? Rose is turning to *me*, someone she wouldn't even allow into her apartment until two days ago—so I must be her last shot.

I hear swords slicing interspersed with fruit exploding, and I pull my iPhone from my pocket to check the time. Shit. I missed the ten-minute countdown. I've got to give it to him at the ten-, five-, and one-minute mark if I want to avoid a major negotiation. "Five more minutes, O. iPad time's almost up."

The iPad! *Of course*. Maybe I can use Owen's laser-like focus on it to my advantage for once. What if I drive Rose, but stay in the car with Owen and let him fiddle around on his iPad while she visits Bernie? There must be a neutral-looking parking area I can find. It's possible I can get away with taking Owen without him having any idea where we are, with the help of that hypnotic tablet. And if that's the case, then why shouldn't I help Rose?

"Rose!" I call after her. "Where's the cemetery?"

She spins around, eyes bright and hands clasped. "You'll take me?"

"Maybe. I need to look it up on Google Earth, so I can see the layout. Then I can tell you if I can make it work for Owen."

Rose gives me a look that I see on dogs' faces at the vet clinic all the time—the one that says, *I want to make you happy, but I have absolutely no idea how.* The technology gap is too deep. There's no point in trying to explain that I can use an app on my phone to access satellite imagery of the location of her husband's cemetery.

"Where is the cemetery?" I ask again.

"Eastfield."

"Okay, but a town as big as Eastfield must have more than one."

"Are you kidding? How many do you think there are? Close to us, there is only Wayland and Eastfield."

What? Wayland is Natick's neighbor to the north, but Eastfield is a good thirty minutes south, with four towns in between. No cemeteries in any of them? What about the neighboring towns to the east and west of us? Zilch? But then I realize: Rose means Jewish cemeteries.

"What's the address?"

"The address, I don't remember off the top of my head. But how to go there, that I know by heart. You know the ice cream place, Scoops?"

I shake my head. "I'm still pretty new to Massachusetts."

Rose waves away this information. "You know the place, everyone knows the place. You've seen the sign—the two *o*'s, they are ice cream scoops. Now you remember?"

"No. Is the cemetery near Scoops?"

She nods. "Except it's not an ice cream place anymore. Now it's a Dunkin' Donuts. You take a right and it's a mile on your left."

Great. I don't know which is a worse choice for a landmark: Scoops or Dunks. Scoops no longer exists. On the other hand, in Massachusetts, there are very few places Dunks *can't* be found. Multiple Dunks on the same street isn't considered excessive here, nor is one situated across the street from another.

"What's the name of the cemetery, Rose?"

"It's just Eastfield, everyone knows it's Eastfield."

I sigh and type the keywords *Jewish cemetery Eastfield MA* into the search bar. Eastfield Memorial Park is the official name, apparently. On 472 Laurel Drive. How hard was that to remember? I type the address into Google Earth, watch the animated globe circle until it pinpoints North America, then watch it drill down to the U.S., Massachusetts, Eastfield, and finally, 472 Laurel Drive. It places a red, lightbulb-shaped icon on an aerial view of the road entering the park, which is separated from the main road by a large archway. The road is tree-lined and long, and surrounded by open land on either side. There's no street view available, and I can only find one structure, which is located to the left of the road, if you picture yourself driving on it. Surrounding the building on three sides is a medium-sized parking lot, which is enclosed by immaculately sculpted bushes. I zoom in closer until I see rows of what look like white and brown horizontal marks on the ground, beyond the trees on the right side of the street. They must be the tops of headstones. The cemetery appears to be enclosed on all four sides: on the bottom of the screen is a line of trees along the grass, the left side displays a continuation of the tree-lined street, the top of the screen shows a curvature of the road around the cemetery after it passes the parking lot on the left, and on the right is a pond. The archway is directly across from the parking lot.

It could work. The trees lining the road that enters the cemetery and the bushes surrounding the parking lot will completely mask Owen's view of the graves, and there's no reason Rose can't cross the street on her own once we're parked. We'll just wait for her. It's true I don't know where Bernie's plot is, and it's hard to judge distance, but beggars can't be choosers. She'll have to manage.

But what should I tell Owen Rose is doing? I can't tell him she'd like to go out for a walk when it's raining. I could tell him she went for a walk there the other day and lost a piece of jewelry, and now she's going to look for it. That is, if he even asks. My guess is that once I hand him the iPad, there will be minimal questions.

I look up at Rose, whose hands are still clasped. "Everything is good, with your Google?" she asks, between sporadic coughs.

I smile. *My* Google. "We can go. Just let me get a few things together." I look at her coat. No hood. "You're going to need an umbrella. I'm sorry—I don't have one to give you." I do, actually. But I have to cover my tracks from my lie to Owen this morning.

"It's raining? I need to get my cap, then. My special one. Waterproof, so my hair doesn't get ruined. I don't go to the hairdresser again until Saturday."

"Okay, fine. Go grab it, and Owen and I will pick you up at your apartment in five minutes."

— 17 —

A loud voice claims understanding; a silent one demonstrates it.

The door to Rose's apartment is ajar. I nudge it open further, knocking on it as I let Owen and myself in so that she'll know we've arrived. "Hello? Rose? Are you ready?"

"Yah, yah, almost." She motions us inside, and as she does, she shakes her head, gives us both an exasperated look. "I leave the door open for you, and still with the *klopping!*"

"Oh! I'm sorry. I just didn't want to surprise you—"

"All I need is to find my cough drops, and then we can go." She rummages through the kitchen cabinet next to the sink. She's found her cap, although it isn't a cap at all. It's an old-fashioned rain bonnet, the plastic kind that ties under the chin.

"They're in the bathroom, remember? When we cleaned up the kitchen, we took all the extra cough drops and put them with the ones that were already in your bathroom closet. It makes more sense to have them all in one spot."

"To you, maybe. I need my cough drops by the sink, in case I need a glass of water."

And there isn't a sink in the bathroom? I want to say, but there's no point. Yesterday, I left the cabinet that she's now digging through perfectly organized: mugs on the top shelf, cups and saucers on the middle one, and separate jars filled with teas, artificial sweeteners, and a sugar bowl on the bottom one. Today all the teas and sweetener packets have been shoved into one canister and moved up to the middle shelf with the cups and saucers, and the lowest shelf appears to be a depository for crumpled tissues, stacks of mail, and cough drop wrappers. The countertops, clear yesterday with the exception of a toaster oven, coffee maker, and paper towel holder, are now cluttered with an assortment of pens and notepads that I placed in a drawer in Bernie's office, along with appliances that I cleaned and stored in lower cabinets. Quite a thank-you for yesterday's efforts, this mess.

"Why don't you grab some hard candy from Bernie's office?" I know the menthol cough drops would be better, but I'm not going to spend an hour looking for them. My goal is to make this outing seem like a mundane errand for Owen, not a huge ordeal that will bear repeating to Nick, like my ill-fated driving adventures.

"*Feh*!" Rose waves away my suggestion in disgust. "Worthless for coughing. *Oy*, I hope I'm not coming down with Dottie's cold. I'm not such a young lady anymore. I don't bounce back so quick." She looks around the kitchen, her gaze finally settling on the pantry. "I haven't checked there yet. Not my usual spot, but it could be with all the rearranging that I left them there." She says this to herself more than to me, then ambles over to the pantry.

"Rose, would you mind if Owen helped himself to a piece of candy?"

Owen looks up at me with a slight frown. The butterscotch and peppermint hard candies in Bernie's glass canister don't rank high on his list of preferred treats.

Rose glances at Owen, just behind me in the hallway. "Go, go." She points to Bernie's office.

"Grab a handful and put them in your pocket," I whisper to him.

Owen looks up at me, confused. "But I don't want—"

"They're for Rose. In case she can't find her cough drops."

His eyes open wide and he gives me a serious nod, then heads to his secret mission in the office.

They'll have to do, because she's never going to find the stupid cough drops. I'll give her five minutes to putter around, and then remind her that we have to drive all the way out to Eastfield, which is a good half hour away in no traffic, exponentially longer the closer we approach rush hour, and that the longer we wait, the more sunlight we lose. That'll get her moving.

I pull out my iPhone, open Maps, and type the cemetery address into the search bar. Taking 95 will get us there ten minutes faster than either of the back road options. Waze and Google Maps agree with Apple's assessment. But I've fallen for this trap before; I've followed directions, and in the fifteen minutes it's taken me to drive to the highway's access point at the border of Wellesley and Newton, a multilane backup has developed. Maybe I should just head south on 27, ignore my GPS's commands to get on a bigger, faster road, because there's no point if—

The tinkling of piano keys interrupts my planning. What was I thinking, sending Owen into Bernie's office for candy? He's tipped a wastebasket onto its side, I see, as I enter, and is using it as a footrest.

"La-dee-dah-dee-dee-dah-dum," he sings under his breath, as he pecks out the notes. "La-dah-dah-dah-dee-dee-DAH-DAHH-DUMMM!"

It's the bridge to *Rainbow Connection*. He must have figured it out while he was at Nick's yesterday. "Have you learned the whole rest of the song, O?"

He turns and nods. "That *was* the rest of it. I mean, that's not the end. It's the part I still had left to figure out. The end was easier, so I did that first." He pauses. "It's hard to explain. That part I just played? That's the middle of the song, but the part that comes after *that* sounds just like the beginning—but then the very *very* end, it's a little different, and it slows down—so I only had to learn a little bit. Get it?"

I smile, because for all of his precocity, Owen doesn't have the basic musical vocabulary of song structure. "You just played what's called the bridge. Remember we talked about the chorus last time we were here—the part that repeats with the same music and words? In songs, there are also verses, which also have the same music, but they have *different* words. But it would be boring if you just went back and forth between chorus and verses, over and over. So there's also a bridge, which gives your ears something new to listen to, and then the chorus and verses come back. The very, very end you mentioned—when the music sounds slightly different and slows—that's the conclusion, or the end."

Owen nods obediently, although it's clear from the way his fingers are poised over the keys that he's tolerating my vocabulary lesson rather than enjoying it. "So do you want to hear it all the way through now?"

"Of course, but maybe we should ask Mrs. Klein. Remember last time? We surprised her, and she—"

But Owen doesn't wait. He's playing again. As I watch him lean into the music, something shiny and red catches my eye. A chunk of ribbon is sticking out of the piano bench.

Oh, God. It's the end of one of Joel's soccer ribbons. I must have closed the bench in such a hurry that I didn't notice. I'll just have to fix it before Rose makes her way over here.

"Hey, O, let me interrupt you for one second."

But he doesn't hear me over the music. He's playing not in fits and starts, but fluently, as if he's practiced this song for weeks. I brace myself for him to strike the wrong key, or, at the very least, mangle the tempo. Even as a layman, I can tell he's not using proper finger positioning, and I know he's not one of those wunderkinds who writes symphonies, but still, to decode the whole song, to remember it and play it back in its entirety within two days—that's impressive for a five-year-old, isn't it? I don't think it's wrong for me to push Nick to nurture this kind of raw—

"Such talent, your boychik."

I jump at the sound of Rose's voice. "Oh! You, umm—you found your cough drops? I'll tell Owen we're ready to go."

Rose puts her finger to her lips. "Let him finish."

Owen's whole body is swaying with the music, and I turn to Rose, who has tears streaming down her face. How is it that in my effort to help, I've managed to make Rose cry before we've even gotten to the cemetery? Has she noticed the soccer ribbon, suspected my deceit? I've got to get out of this room. I inch toward Owen, raise my hand to tap him on the shoulder. But Rose grabs my wrist before I can reach him.

"This is a gift your boychik is giving me."

I look at her, confused. I don't know why Joel once lived with Rose and Bernie, why the piano continued to hold such meaning for them after he moved away. How long has it been since they've seen him? Lena didn't make it seem as if it was to be a decades-in-the-making reunion between Rose and Joel on Saturday, but then again, Lena has no reason to share that type of information with me. Maybe Joel left on bad circumstances, and he never had a chance to say goodbye to Bernie. Maybe it took Bernie's death to bring him back to the family. I assumed that Joel is the son of Bernie's brother in Florida, but, now that I think about it, what sort of tragedy would have rendered both of Joel's parents—one of whom is still alive—incapable of or unwilling to care for him? Wouldn't a more likely scenario be that both of his parents died, in an accident, perhaps? Could Joel be the son of a deceased brother or sister of Bernie's?

Rose lets her tears continue to flow, doesn't attempt to wipe them away. "It's not just Bernie's birthday today. That's what I couldn't say before. It's also Joey's backward birthday."

"'Backward birthday'?"

"Yes. Bernie's is November thirtieth. Joey's, March eleventh. So the dates are eleven thirty and three eleven."

Not quite a match, with four digits to three. "I still don't—"

Rose turns to her left, quietly slides open the top left drawer of Bernie's desk so as not to disturb Owen, and pulls out a pen and Post-it note. She jots something down, then passes the note to me. On it is written:

11/30

03/11

"Now you see?" she says. She steps closer to me, so I can hear over the sound of Owen at the piano. "When Joey was little, we would celebrate with two cakes. Bernie, he didn't like chocolate so much, but my Joey had to have it. So we always had two. Even after, we always got two cakes."

After what? I want to ask. Was there a rift between them? It's true that Joel doesn't seem to be rushing back from London, but he *is* coming back, and Rose seems quite happy about it.

"That's a beautiful tradition," I say.

Rose nods.

"So we'll visit Bernie today, and then you can celebrate with two cakes on Saturday, right? It'll be late, but it's something to look forward to."

Rose looks at me strangely. "Why would I—? Today is the day, I just explained."

"I know. But I thought, if Joel is coming in on Saturday, you might want to celebrate with him then." I've managed to offend her, it seems. Maybe her relationship with Joel is fragile. "Is he . . . uhh . . . still going to be able to make it in by then?"

"What are you talking? When Joel gives you his word, it's like gold. He'll be here." She pauses, and then the bravado disappears from her voice. I lean in to hear her over the piano: "But not to celebrate his backward birthday. It's not his. It's Joey's. *Joseph's.* My son's."

Joseph.

So Rose and Bernie weren't the benefactors of an orphaned or unwanted Joel. They were the parents of Joseph, who loved Bandit, Laffy Taffy, roller coasters, and soccer; who marveled about the size of blue whales and the contours of the universe; who made model airplanes with his dad and played piano for his mom.

I glance at Rose, her eyes fixed on Owen as he plays Joey's piano, and place my hand over hers.

— 18 —

Aspire to sway with the wind, like bamboo.

Eastfield Memorial Park.

I recognize the black wrought-iron archway from the satellite images as I turn onto the narrow road, the gravel crunching beneath my tires. What wasn't visible from the aerial view were the gates below it, which are anchored to enormous white stone pillars and, thankfully, are open.

Just as Google Earth promised, the road is lined by towering trees, which is a huge relief. It didn't occur to me until twenty minutes into our drive that the images I saw might have been outdated, or that the trees might not be evergreen, leaving open the possibility of arriving with row after row of headstones plainly visible to Owen from the right rear passenger window.

Paper crinkles and I glance at Rose in the passenger seat, who's rummaging through her purse. "Aha! Here it is. The map. This one I made for Marnie. In all of the rushing, I forgot to give it to you. I know it here by heart, but if you want, you can have it."

"Rose, I'm driving . . . now's not the best time." I peek at the map she's holding up, which bears more than a passing resemblance to a pirate's buried treasure map, with circuitous routes and a big X marked in red. "Wait. You made her a map? For inside the—" I look in the rearview mirror at Owen. "For inside *here*?"

"Yah, yah. The roads, they curve around and around, and the signs are hard to see. Marnie says she needs everything written down before she drives anywhere or she'll get all *fardrayt*. We need Arad, section thirty-four."

"Section *thirty-four*? How many are there altogether?"

"Hah? That I'm not sure, maybe forty-five, fifty? You have to be on the lookout for the signs with the section names and numbers. You'll see them, they're hanging off of the stone poles. How do you call them? Same as by the entrance, but much smaller—"

"Pillars?"

"Pillars! Yes, that's the word. So, we take this road as it curves around, past the pond, and when we reach the end of the pond, we take a left and go maybe—"

"How big *is* this place? I thought it was just that area on the other side of the trees on the right. And isn't there supposed to be an archway coming up soon on the right, an entrance? And a building on the left, with a parking lot?" I'm not sure what to call it. I don't think *funeral home* is right, and even if it is, I can't say the words aloud with Owen in the back. It could lead to questions later.

"Yes, the building is coming soon on our left. But Eastfield, small? Why would you think such a thing? Everyone knows it's the biggest in Massachusetts, maybe even in New England."

"Maybe in your circle of friends."

"Uh-uh, too fast." Rose points to the fifteen-miles-per-hour speed limit sign, surrounded by manicured bushes. I've only been going twenty-five, but I brake a little, and we inch our way down a small hill. They're in view now, the archway, and across from it, the opening to the parking lot and unnamed building. I'd like to pick up the pace, but Rose is monitoring my speedometer, so we creep along the road. Finally, I pull into the tree-lined lot, park in a spot facing the building, and let the car idle. It's a one-level office, and above the double doors, in large capital letters, are the words WELCOME CENTER. So that's the correct terminology. It seems an odd fit, more suited for a tourist attraction or a college campus, but I can't think of anything better. What are the choices? Mourning Bureau? Grieving Office?

I look back at Owen. He's had the iPad for ten minutes already. I never let him use it in the car, but today I've made an exception. The goal is to digitally mesmerize him before he shows any interest in his surroundings.

"How're you doing, O?"

His eyes don't break from the screen to meet mine. "Huh?"

"Does your stomach hurt from the car ride?"

"Uh, no, I'm good."

He's hypnotized already. Normally this type of response would register as a six out of ten on the Maternal Technology Anxiety Scale and result in me taking away the iPad, because choosing electronics over actual human beings, particularly those who love you, is insulting. It's astonishing to me that I've had to spell that out for him multiple times. But today I don't remind him of appropriate behavior. For once, I'm pleased he's screen-entranced.

I turn back to Rose. It's useless to explain that my plan has been thwarted by neglecting to swipe left on Google Earth. "So. My idea was to stay in the parking lot with Owen while you walked across the street to the entrance. To give you some privacy, but also because of what we spoke about at my apartment." I gesture toward Owen with a tilt of my head.

Rose nods. "Yes, yes, I understand. If you like, you can park further up. But all that way I can't walk by myself. Not even if I was twenty years old could I walk that far."

"Got it. I was confused. I thought that archway was the only entrance. I thought the whole . . . *place* . . . only extended to the pond."

Rose's eyes grow large. "What? No, hundreds of acres!"

Hundreds? I pick up my phone out of the center console, tap to open the Google Earth, and select my last search. "What are the directions again?"

"I can't give an address. Like I said, there are section names, but that's all. That's why I made the map." She holds it up again. I examine it more closely now that we're parked, but if she wants to help Marnie avoid getting *fardrayt*—which I assume means *confused*, although I guess it could mean *lost*—then I don't see how this map could offer any guidance. There are plenty of arrows indicating direction, but very few section names listed. It seems that sections are the closest the cemetery has to street names, so leaving them out is problematic, to put it kindly, unless your illustration is perfect. Rose's is a freehand scribble.

"I know there's no exact address. Just give me directions as if I was driving now. Which way would I need to go? Bear right around the pond, and then . . . ?"

"At the end of the pond, you take a left. Then you go maybe a mile and it's the third right."

I select my last entry from the search bar and wait for the red lightbulb to show up on 472 Laurel Avenue. I follow the entry road into the cemetery with my finger until I see the lot where we're now located, and continue along it as it bends toward the right past the pond. Beyond the pond and across the street and to the left is a maze of looping roads, interspersed with open areas of land dotted with what look to be brown and white chalk marks. She's right. There's no way she can walk. And there's no way I can bring her this far and then not take her to celebrate Joey's backward birthday; it's too cruel. I glance at Owen again, who's watching cartoons on YouTube Kids. Maybe I'll be lucky enough that he won't look up during our ride. I can sit with him in the back while Rose is at the grave and further block his view. Putting the sunshade down on a rainy day makes no sense, that'll just draw attention. And maybe I'm being ridiculous. I'm not planning to wander around the cemetery with him. He isn't being subjected to watching Rose fall apart. He knows cemeteries exist—doesn't he?

The truth is, I don't know what Owen knows. I'm not sure how I've managed to get myself ensnared in a situation where my parental decision making is being shaped by Marnie, Dottie, and Rose rather than Nick, but here I am.

Rose looks at me hopefully. "So . . . everything is good with your Google?"

I force a smile. "Everything looks fine."

— 19 —

Motives, like waves, emerge from forces deep within.

There aren't any headstones. Really. Those horizontal lines I saw on Google Earth? The brown ones are bronze plaques, flush to the ground, I notice, as we creep along at fifteen miles per hour, loop after interminable loop. The white ones are benches. I'm thrilled that my data interpretation was so poor. What better way to keep Owen blind to our whereabouts than to remove all three-dimensional cemeterial evidence?

"Adar? Is that the name of the section?" I've already forgotten. All I've been able to concentrate on is how to keep Owen distracted.

"Arad," Rose corrects.

I assume that *arad* is the English phonetic translation of a Hebrew word, and that it means something funereal, like *rest* or *peace* or *blessed*. I'd like to ask Rose what it means, but I doubt now is the most appropriate time. So instead, I try to solve the etymological puzzle in my head as

I await further directions. Rose seems to know exactly where we are, and since the sections aren't consistently chronological, it's easier to let her take the lead. We edge forward until we reach section twenty-nine: Mount Sinai.

"Wait a second. All of the section names . . . are the names of *places*?"

She shrugs. "Yah, some. But all of them I don't know."

"Now it makes sense! Arad, as in Tel Arad."

Rose gives me a funny look. "Now you speak Hebrew?"

"No, no, no. *Tel* is an archaeological term. It means *mound*. When people have lived in the same spot for thousands of years, all of their belongings heap on top of each other over time, and the land eventually bumps up. Arad was an ancient Canaanite city and fortress. Tel Arad is the excavated site. I learned all about it in college."

Rose is half listening, her attention focused on the section pillars. "Stop here." She taps the window. "It's two rows back only."

I breathe a sigh of relief as I park the car. The rows of plaques are at least thirty deep; two rows from the curb means I can keep her within eyesight.

Arad is situated down a slight hill to the right of the road—my second stroke of luck. Owen's view is of two trees and the edge of the hill. To his left, outside the other window, is another section that's partially blocked by a row of benches. The only potential giveaway is the sea of bronze plaques that fan out on the manicured lawn beyond them.

I'll have to block the view with my body. Shouldn't be hard. I doubt Owen will look up much, and even if he does, he's seen plaques at libraries, parks, and museums.

I open the car door for Rose, splashing my way through puddles in my rain boots. I'd whistle, if I knew how—I feel giddy, knowing that

I'm going to get away with this escapade.

Except as soon as Rose steps from the paved street to the muddy ground, the block heels of her suede shoes sink in a couple of inches. Why she didn't swap out her shoes for boots when we stopped for her rain bonnet is beyond me, but there's no way she's making it down the hill, small as it may be, without some assistance.

I glance at Owen. It'll just be a minute. The road is completely flat, but maybe I should pull up the parking brake to be doubly safe, and lock him inside? Or is it safer to leave the doors unlocked? I weigh potential dangers, rank the likelihood of horrors that could befall my child.

Rose follows my gaze to Owen, then settles back on me. "Pull." She nods toward her foot.

"What? Are you stuck?"

"No. The shoes, they're a little tight, they don't kick off so easy. How am I supposed to walk down, with my heels sinking in with every step? Help me take them off. Then I can walk down by myself and you can stay with your boychik."

"Are you crazy? You'll get filthy!"

"What, all of a sudden mud doesn't wash off? Don't worry about your car, I'll wash my feet off in the puddles before I get back in."

"I don't care about my car. I think it's more dangerous if you take your shoes *off*. It's slick. You could slip and fall. I don't want you to hurt yourself."

"Psshh," Rose says, waving away the possibility. "What do you think we're on the top of, Mount Everest? Now go sit with him, like we agreed." She kicks the back of her heel against the curb until her right foot is freed from her shoe.

"Rose, this isn't safe! Give me a second. Wait, please!" I dash back to the front seat of the car, but she's already begun the same process with her left foot. "Be back soon, O." I use my best Calm Mom voice as I depress the brake into the locked position. "Just have to help Rose down the hill."

Owen mumbles a distracted *uh-huh*. He's buckled up in his car seat, and the back-seat child safety locks are on. If I lock the front doors, no one can get in the car and abduct him. He can't leave and get lost, either, a much more likely scenario. But what if he *needs* to get out, and can't? It's too cold to worry about heatstroke, but what if he's injured and needs help? I settle on unlocking the front passenger side only. That way Owen has a way out, if he needs one—and I'll see him leave, if he does.

Rose has tossed off both shoes and is now taking tentative steps down the hill. She's turned her left side to it, her arm outstretched toward the ground to brace herself against a fall. I race toward her, the momentum from the slope taking me faster than I'd like, until I'm standing several steps in front of her. "Why didn't you wait?" I yell. "I asked you, *nicely*, to wait! You're going to give me a heart attack!"

She stares at me for a moment, then back at the ground, as she concentrates on descending. I suddenly realize I don't know how Bernie died. Was it a heart attack? It's a common cause of sudden death, which his seems to have been. He didn't appear fragile or sickly, the few times I saw him. But then again, what baseline do I have to compare his health to?

I can't tell if Rose's expression is stony because I've said something insensitive, or because she's concentrating on getting down without hurting herself. "*Oy gevalt!*" she says in a rush as she stumbles over a rock, and then rights herself.

I turn so our bodies are aligned, both of our left sides now perpendicular to the hill. "Rose, *please*. I'm sorry I yelled. Grab on to my arm."

"No! We had a deal. No getting your boychik involved. Now, go.

Back up."

"Rose, he's definitely going to be involved if we have to call 911 because you fell down and broke a hip."

"What am I, such an *alter kaker* that I can't even walk down a small hill by myself? I make my exercises every day! How many ninety-four-year-olds do you know who can still—"

"Stop being so stubborn!" I take her bony hands and circle them around my left arm, and we shuffle our way down toward the base—which is where I miscalculate. There's a small pit in the ground covered by a puddle, and I step in it and stumble, pulling Rose along with me. We recover, but not before her purse comes loose from her left shoulder, opening in midair and spewing its contents all over the ground.

There's paper to pick up, and plenty of it. Marnie's directions, receipts, hard candy wrappers—all the rustling scraps I heard while driving now surround us, wet and muddied. But also, curiously, a rainbow-colored assortment of polished stones. They've tumbled out of a cream velvet pull-string pouch. On the front, the word ELEMENTS is printed in gold, and underneath, in silver: WELLESLEY—CHATHAM—LENOX. It must be the name of a store.

"*Oy-yoy-yoy*, my stones!"

"I've got them, don't worry." I pick up an old grocery store receipt. "Do you need this anymore? I could use it to clean the stones."

"Yes, yes, you can use. But two of them I need right now."

"Oh . . . okay," I say, although I don't know which color stones she needs or why. One for Bernie and one for Joey, I assume, but that's the closest I can get to an explanation. "Which ones do you need?"

"That I don't know. For that we must consult the chart."

"The chart?"

"Yes. In the bag."

I open the pouch. There's only one piece of paper inside. It looks like a receipt that's been folded in half, but when I open it, there's no itemized list. Instead, seven circles are printed on it, stacked on top of each other, in the colors of the rainbow. Next to each circle are two columns of text. The chart starts on the bottom left corner of the page with a red circle; in the center is printed *first chakra: root/base*. In the first column is written *hematite/garnet*, and in the second column, *stability*, *courage, survival*. The list goes up to the top of the page, each circle the successive color and number, until it ends with the seventh, violet circle.

"So," Rose says, after giving me a moment to read the chart, "there's no green stone, so we have to find the next best."

"Did we lose it? It might be hidden in the grass. If you hold all the papers I can check—"

"No. The lady at the store said the set came in with a clear stone instead of a green. And I need a green for Joey. It was his favorite color."

"Wait. You needed *one* green stone, so you bought a whole set *without* a green stone?"

"What are you talking? I needed a stone for Bernie, too, and this was the last set. It costs much, much more to buy the stones individual. This set was a *metziah*. Marked down twenty percent!"

"But who cares if it's not what you need?"

Rose taps her finger to her temple. "I'm thinking ahead. The lady said that when the new sets come in on Saturday, I can give her back the clear one and she will give me the green."

But that swap will leave the shop owner with another defective set, I want to say, but I don't bother continuing the argument, because none of this makes any sense, and Owen is waiting for me. I look up at the car. Thank God I didn't put the sunshade up. I can see his profile, partly obscured by the headrest of his car seat. His head is bent down, not at an awkward, sleeping angle, but at an iPad-viewing angle. "I don't get it. Why do we need to look at the chart if you're picking stones based on favorite colors? And what do chakras have to do with any of this? I mean, my sister, Lindsay, would love the stones, the chart—all of this. She keeps bugging me to practice Ujjayi breathing when I get stressed out, since it activates the first four chakras, although she's never really explained what chakras are. But this is a Jewish cemetery, so why—"

"The stones are instead of flowers, to leave on the plaques. I will show you." Rose takes my hand and we walk until we are in front of Bernie's grave. There's a tarp covering it, but no plaque. It startles me at first, that Bernie's grave is unmarked. Where is his plaque? But then I realize I've never once thought about the procedural aspects of a funeral. Without the benefit of clairvoyance, there's no way to have one ready in time.

Next to Bernie's tarp-covered grave is Joey's grassy one, a mixture of late November browns and greens. The edges of his plaque are rimmed with stones. I look down and read:

BELOVED SON OF BERNARD AND ROSE
JOSEPH AARON KLEIN
JUNE 6, 1964—AUGUST 17, 1986

There is a line of Hebrew, indecipherable to me, between Joey's name and the dates of his birth and death, but I don't ask what they mean. I can't. I can't get past the dates. Twenty-two years old. I've already lived six years longer than Joey did.

Rose points to the stones that line the perimeter of Joey's plaque, splotched with rain. "Flowers, they die. A stone is forever. You see?"

I think for a minute. *Forever.* "So the stones represent . . . memories?"

She nods. "Bernie and Joey will always be with me."

"That's a beautiful tradition."

"The cemetery, they give out stones for visitors, but I wanted to bring my own. Make them stand out from the ones people left for Joey after Bernie's service. I chose these because they're beautiful. Chakras, I don't know what they are."

"I think they have something to do with energy and the mind-body-spirit connection. I'm not sure if it's a Buddhist or Hindu concept. Like I said, my sister is the expert."

She motions to the chart. "So read, and we will find out."

"Here?"

"Why not?"

"Well, isn't that sacrilegious?"

She waves away my concern. "This sheet you are reading from, this is not a holy book."

It's a good point. The chart is in spiritual Lindsay-like territory. "Uh, okay." I can hear the hesitancy in my voice. But this is Rose's call to make, not mine. "How about we start with green, since that was Joey's favorite color?"

Rose nods.

"Green is the fourth chakra, the heart center. The chart lists 'love, relationships, and feelings.' It also says the fourth chakra connects the lower three chakras of the body to the upper three chakras of the mind and spirit." I pause. "That's kind of . . . perfect, isn't it?"

Rose's eyes fill with tears. "It is." She swallows twice, then says, "So. Now we need my Bernie. What do you see on the list that is good for him?"

"You want *me* to pick? Because I don't—you know, how about I just read the list top to bottom? Let's see . . . violet is the crown chakra which is connected to enlightenment and spirituality." I look up at Rose, who's smirking. "No good?"

"No. My Bernie wasn't, how you say, 'enlightened.' He was a *mensch*, my Bernie. A good man, a kind man, but a regular man."

I'm not sure how to respond. It's so ingrained, the reflex to idealize the dead in an effort to comfort the living, that to hear Rose admit to Bernie's ordinariness is shocking, a borderline act of betrayal. I suppress the impulse to come to his defense, to expound on his virtues, even though I have no right to make any character assessment of him. "Sounds like violet isn't a match. Okay, then—stop me when I get to a good fit. Indigo is the third eye chakra, which represents self-knowledge and insight. Blue is the throat chakra, which is related to self-expression and the ability to speak one's highest truth. Yellow is the solar plexus chakra, which is connected to humor, laughter, and confidence. Orange is the navel-sacral chakra and is related to passion, sexuality, and creativity, and red is the root chakra, which is the base for stability, courage, and survival."

"That's it," Rose says.

"Red?"

"Yes. And which one is for laughter, again?"

I look at the chart. "Yellow."

"I need yellow for Joey, for now, until I come back again with the green. For me, I need the blue."

But I thought we only needed two, I think, as I wipe off the stones with the receipt and pass them to her. She kisses the yellow stone, and places it on Joey's plaque. "Always, my Joey filled my heart with joy." Next she kisses Bernie's red stone, and places it on the stretch of dirt at the head of the tarp, in the spot where his plaque will be installed. "For my Bernie, who was my strength, even when I didn't deserve it." She holds up the blue. "The blue is to speak your highest truth? Am I remembering correct?"

I double-check the chart, and nod. "The throat chakra."

"How does it work, this stone? Do I have to hold it on my throat the whole time?" She centers it on the crepey folds of her neck. "No. Can't be." She takes it off. "What kind of *meshugaas* is this, talking with a stone on your throat?"

"I think you can just hold it, or put it in your pocket." I remember the black tourmaline stone Lindsay suggested Owen carry around. "But if you have something you need to, uh, say to Bernie, then why don't I give you some privacy?" I take a step back, toward the base of the hill. "I'll wait for you in the car. I'll be able to see when you need help coming up the—"

"I have been going to that shop for a long time now, maybe eight, nine years." She cups the stone in the palm of one hand and points toward the cream pouch with the other. "I have bought a lot of stones. Never have I bought a set that's come with a, how you say again . . . ?"

"Chakras."

"Yes, a chakras chart. Not once! And Dottie. Needing to see a doctor and not telling me until the very last minute. Not like her at all. She is like a clock, *always*. And on today, of all days." She pauses, gives me a probing look. "Maybe . . . maybe there's another reason why this is happening."

"Rose, I know this must be a very stressful situation for you. And I know that in times of stress, it's natural to search for answers. I know that, when dealing with loss, people—"

"'I know, I know, I know.' You say that a lot—'I know.'"

My cheeks start to burn. "I—I wasn't trying to talk down to you. I was trying to help."

"I know you were, *shayneh maidel.*" She pats my hand and waits for me to meet her gaze. "I was a pretty girl once, too. Not so like you with the curls—and I was always too skinny. But Bernie thought I was beautiful. I was already an old maid when we married—twenty-three!"

I smile. "Times have changed."

"And *how*. Today, women wait. Career first! But when I was young, women started families right away, at nineteen, twenty." She massages the stone between her hands, gives me another curious look, then concentrates on it again. "The doctors, they all said I was barren. And Bernie . . . oh, did he want a child."

She walks over toward Bernie's tarp, stands just outside the ankle-height rope that cordons off the perimeter. "Do you remember what you would say to me, Bernie?" she asks quietly. She looks at the patch of dirt at the head of the tarp and waits for a moment, as if he might reply. "'It will happen, my Roseleh. God has plans the doctors can't imagine.' Month after month, year after year, you'd dry my tears and tell me that."

I peek at Owen in the car while Rose's back is to me. He's still engrossed in his iPad. Doesn't it hurt, to stay in the same hunched-over position for so long? I want to check in on him, and, I'll admit it, I want to escape, too. Already I feel uncomfortable, like I'm eavesdropping, even though Rose seems to want me to listen. I'm stuck; I can't tell her that I'm taking off now that she's intent on speaking her highest truth. I have no idea how long this story is going to take, but she's starting before Joey's birth year of 1964, so I'm not going to put my money on brevity. Shouldn't she be sharing this history with someone she's closer to? Dottie or Marnie, instead of me? At least I can see that Owen is safe.

Rose's eyes are still focused on the ground. "Every time a friend would announce a pregnancy, I would beg you to leave me, wouldn't I? Find yourself another woman, a *real* woman, I'd say. There's still time. And what would you say back?" She pauses, then offers his words again: "'But I don't want another woman. I want *you*.'"

She pivots from the tarp, takes me by the arm, and guides me several steps away. "After a few years, I stopped crying. One day I told him, that's it! I don't want you to talk about it anymore. It hurts too much to hope. If you want me, you have to let the dream for a child go. And he stared at me for the longest time, with such a distant look—blank, almost like he was a stranger, looking from the outside in, and I thought to myself, this time I've done it! I've finally pushed him away. I didn't want to lose him—I wanted to give him a child something desperate!— but he had to *choose*, because I couldn't bear the shame anymore. And I remember, I had to turn away from him, but still I could feel him staring at me, saying nothing. Finally, I felt his hands on my shoulders, and he spun me around, and the blankness—it was gone! 'I don't have to let either of you go,' he said, 'and I won't.'"

She shakes her head and chuckles. "Stubborn like an ox, my Bernie! He never gave up hope, all those years. He didn't talk about it from that day on—he knew it would get me too upset—but I knew. If we were at a park, and we saw a little boy, he would squeeze my hand; if we were at the movies, and we saw a young family, he would put his arm around me and pull me close. And then, at thirty-seven, I got pregnant with Joey. After fourteen years of marriage! The doctors, they had no explanation. He was our miracle baby."

Rose turns again, pulls me until we are standing right in front of Joey's plaque. She grasps my arm as she lowers herself onto the muddy ground with a soft grunt. Then she repositions the stones that visitors have left for Joey—straightens up for him, but with a hint of pride, in the same way I angle the papier-mâché and clay masterpieces that line Owen's bureau. She picks up her yellow stone and shifts it to the center of the plaque, leaving the rest of the stones on the edge.

"A *vilde chaya*, Joey was, when he was little." Rose shakes her head and smiles. "So much energy! Running around, making mischief, and the *mess*! Bernie finally had the son he wanted. He taught Joey to ride a bike, to play soccer, baseball . . . they were so busy, with this team, and that team! And smart like a whip, our Joey. Always, he and Bernie were up to something together—building model airplanes, rockets, science projects." Rose glances up at me. "But of course, some of this you already knew."

A cold sweat breaks out under my arms and along the base of my neck. So Rose did see the soccer ribbon hanging out of the piano bench. Did she notice it before she asked me to drive her here? Or when Owen was playing piano right before we left? God, this is so embarrassing.

I feign ignorance. "Hmm?"

Rose gives me a pointed look. "It could only have been you."

There's no way out of this. I take a deep breath, sit down in the mud next to her. "I'm sorry. The bench opened by accident, but . . . I had no right to snoop around. There's no excuse."

She gives my arm a squeeze. "So. You saw soccer medals. What else did you see?"

"Some marked-up music. *Moonlight Sonata* and *Turkish March*."

Rose smiles. "The piano. Bernie brought it home when Joey was a little older than your boychik is now, bought it cheap from a friend who was moving. You must think Bernie was a softie, with all of the candy, but he was a demanding father. Twenty minutes a day, practice, to teach Joey discipline. It didn't come to him natural, like your boychik. But he learned to read music quick—that part he loved, figuring out the different symbols. Every Sunday night, after dinner, Joey would give Bernie and me a recital. He'd play whatever he'd learned from his instructor that week, and if he'd learned it early, he'd let me pick out a second piece. It wasn't until he was older, and his studies took up more of his time, that the recitals came less and less, and then they stopped altogether. But the piano . . . the piano was another language for Joey and me. If he noticed I was sad, he would play Mozart's *Turkish March* to lift my spirits. If I was nervous, Beethoven's *Moonlight Sonata* to soothe me. And for my birthday, every year, he would learn for me a new piece, from any composer that I wanted."

I'm not sure what to say. Joey sounds sensitive and mature beyond his years. Most children aren't attuned to their parents' moods in that kind of—

"I see . . . similarities between my Joey and your Owen."

"You do? Beyond the piano?"

"Yes. Both sensitive boys. Both loving." She clears her throat. "Both with a father unwilling to face the truth."

I stand up, stung by her words. "Rose, I don't know how much you heard, but . . . we don't *know* what the truth is."

"Neither did we. But *something* was wrong. That I knew." She looks up, and locks eyes with me. "As do you."

— 20 —

Do not wait for the snake to bear its fangs before you act.

R ose lets her words sink in, seems to be gauging whether I'll walk off in a huff. She struggles from her seated position onto her hands and knees, glances up at me, then stares back down at the ground again.

She'd like to get up by herself. That's the graceful way out of this scenario, but there's nothing she can use to pull herself up. Outside, there are no couches, chairs, or bookcases for support as she comes to standing.

I don't want to help her. I know that I have no right to complain about her listening in on my argument with Nick after I rifled through her piano bench and read Joey's journal. That's a wash. But for her to say that something's *wrong* with Owen? Even if I suspect that he does have some . . . issues . . . okay, fine, even if I know that it's more than that—who does she think she is, talking about my son like that? She's no doctor. And she barely knows him.

Her arms begin to shake with effort—she's unable to rise and unable to return to seated—but she doesn't look up at me. Insulting my child isn't the best prelude to a request for help, and she knows that.

Her torso is the next to tremble, then her legs. She only has seconds until her arms give way and she falls onto her face. I let out an irritated sigh and kneel next to her. "Rose. I'm here. Use me for balance."

She acquiesces, and we struggle together in a clumsy dance until she's upright. She gives my arm a couple pats of thanks once she's steady, then takes a few steps back from me. She wipes the splatters of mud off her hands and knees, smooths her bunched-up coat, then straightens her tilted rain bonnet. "So," she says, her eyes cast downward, "I am wondering . . . you will listen, still?"

It's the questioning tone and insecure mannerisms that break through my anger. They're so out of character, so un-Rose-like, that before I realize it, I give her a faint nod.

Rose clears her throat. "Joey's sickness began when he graduated college, while he was renting a house for the summer with friends. Joel—he was one year ahead, at the medical school—he saw what was happening, and he tried to warn Bernie and me. *Ach*, and what good did it get him?"

She turns to Bernie's tarp and stares at the patch of dirt in front of her. "You remember what you said to your nephew, who stuck his neck out for his cousin? 'Are you calling my son a nutcase, you little *pischer*? One year of medical school under your belt, and already you think you're a *real* doctor? Do you know how many so-called experts have been wrong about my family?'"

She throws her hands up in the air, looks at me as if to say, *Can you believe him?* "But then Joey's roommates called us. They said he'd been up for days, moving things around in his room every night. He wouldn't leave the house, and he'd been fired from his job as a bank teller. They were worried. So I asked the boys to leave a key in the mailbox for me. I could stop by after they left for work the next morning. It was sneaky, I know, to drop by without calling. But I wanted to see for myself what was going on. So I called the principal first thing and told him I was too sick to be around the children, even in the office."

Rose is still, and her eyes are wide with hope for a moment as she stares at Joey's plaque. She's holding her breath, and I'm not sure if it's because in her mind she's already *there*, in his house, and she's desperate to discover that Bernie's right and she's wrong, or if she's preparing herself for what she feels she must share with me—but I wish she would *breathe*.

Finally she exhales, then follows it with a huge inhale, as if she's about to dive under water. She focuses on the shimmering expanse of bronze plaques beyond Joey's, then squeezes her eyes shut, and immerses herself in memory.

The house was empty except for Joey. The door to his room was closed, but I knew he was awake. I could hear the shuffling of his feet inside.

"Joey? It's me, *hertzeleh*. Joey?"

The bitter stink of sweat grew stronger as I walked toward his room. No sound from Joey, only the scurrying of his steps from the side of the room closer to me.

"Come, Joey, I'll make you breakfast. Just open the door."

I knocked on his door. A polite *rat-a-tat-tat* first, then stronger raps, then pounding with both of my fists.

Silence for far too long, followed by jagged gasps, in and out, in and out. I turned the doorknob—it gave, there was no lock—but the door wouldn't budge! Something was blocking it.

"Joey, open up! Please!"

Still the breathing. But now a strange half whimper, half whine. Was it coming from Joey? It had to be. But never had I heard a sound like that from him before.

"Joey, you're scaring me! Let me help you, please, my angel, open up, please!"

Suddenly, a high-pitched cry through the gasps. Like a terrified, wounded animal. What was happening to my child?

I hurled myself against the door until finally, it opened, and I fell onto the back of his tipped-over dresser into his room. It was far too dark inside for the morning. And my right arm and hand—why were they wet?

Joey was wide-eyed, shaking in the front-left corner of the room. He leaned forward and craned his neck around to look in the empty entryway behind me, and then scurried over to me. I thought he was going to help me up. My cheek and ribs hurt me something terrible from the fall, and my eyes hadn't adjusted to the darkness. But no, he stood over me and patted down my sides like police officers do in TV shows, and turned and looked behind us once more into the doorway. Out of the corner of my eye, I watched as he tiptoed around the back of the dresser and glanced up at the hallway ceiling. Then he faced me again. He picked up my handbag, which had fallen on the ground next to me, and rifled through it. "Why aren't you at work?" His eyes, they were not my Joey's. Full of distrust and fear.

"Your roommates asked me to check on you. They're worried about you, and so am I."

"You could have come after school."

"I asked them to leave the key."

"You never skip school. *Never.*"

THE FORTUNE COOKIE WRITER

"There hasn't been a good enough reason to. Until now."

That's when I felt it—the drip, drip of Joey's tears on my cheek. He kneeled down and helped me to sitting, and dried my arm and hand with his shirt. Once I was upright, I could see that it was only water. A plastic cup had fallen when the bureau tipped. But I noticed, then, that towels covered his windows, and his TV and phone had been destroyed, their insides strewn across the floor.

"I'm sorry I didn't help you right away, Mom. You have to understand . . . sometimes they use the people you love against you."

I didn't want to ask. But I knew I must. "Who are *they*, Joey?"

"The FBI," he whispered. "They're monitoring me. I took care of it in here." He motioned to the ruined TV and phone. "But they're still recording me in the living room." He pointed to the door that was propped open by his tipped dresser, and put his finger to his lips. "Until I throw them off the scent altogether, I have to stay here. The problem is, they have people working on my case twenty-four seven, and I need to *sleep*. That's why I set . . ." He turned from me, and let out a frustrated gasp. "It didn't work!"

He was looking down at a thin wire, ankle height, that extended across the length of his room. On our side of it lay the fallen bureau; on the other, his bed. Attached to the base of the wall closest to us was a wooden paper clip, and atop it, a battery. The two were connected by a red-and-black wire, and there looked to be a black component as well, but it was hard to see in the dark. Above the paper clip was an electrical outlet.

"Joey, what is this?" I raised my hand to touch the paper clip.

"Mom, no!" He grabbed my hand before I could touch it. "It's my protection. So I can sleep. I can't keep guard all the time. The bureau was supposed to hit the trip wire." He slumped to the ground, grabbed my hand, and pulled me down next to him. He nestled against me like he hadn't since he was a little boy. "I can't anymore . . . I'm so tired."

He was skin and bones—when had he gotten so skinny? "We will get through this, my angel," I whispered to him. "I promise you, we will get through this."

Rose's back is angled away from me, but I can see her slight, rounded shoulders move with the exertion of her now rapid breaths. I have no idea what to do. I raise my hand to pat her on the back in comfort, then stop midair. It's such a paltry gesture. What am I planning on pairing it with, anyway, an insipid "there, there"? My mouth is ajar in shock, I suddenly realize, and Rose turns and notices before I can replace my actual expression with a more composed one.

"That's the face!" she says. "That same face was on Bernie when I told him, and he was white as a ghost. He said that Joel had been right, that we needed to get Joey to a doctor right away."

Is *that* the connection, then? Is this Rose's way of trying to convince me to take Owen to a doctor? But she overheard me arguing with Nick—shouldn't she know that *he's* the one who needs convincing? Maybe she thinks I won't stand up to him, either because of money, or because she analyzes the dynamics of marriage by her generation's standards.

But Owen's struggles can't be compared with Joey's. Unless . . . is it possible that Rose has noticed something ominous about Owen's behavior that I haven't, and decided to share her story as a cautionary tale? Should I add her to the growing list of people who see my child more clearly than I do? I wish we could just have a straightforward discussion, but what am I supposed to say? *Will you please stop sharing your deepest personal secrets; all this drawing of parallels is getting confusing?* I can't, not when she's trying so hard to tell me—*something*. So I settle on a simple, "What happened?"

"Joey was in the hospital—I don't remember how many days— and after that, he said, no more! He would go to the appointments by himself, he would face the sickness on his own. What could we do? He was no more a child. I think he took his medications, but I couldn't be one hundred percent sure. When he would come by to do his laundry, it would take him time to answer a simple question, like he was in a fog. So Bernie and I, we didn't know: Was it the medication that was making Joey feel so terrible, or was it the sickness itself, creeping back because he'd stopped taking the pills? I tried to get him to come home for the summer, tried to put some meat on his bones, but he said no. His roommates, though, they told me he was sleeping at night again. He seemed less nervous, more like the old Joey."

Hmm. Not the glowing tribute to medical intervention I was expecting. I know Rose isn't one to sugarcoat, but if she's trying to persuade me, shouldn't she concentrate on how doctors stabilized Joey, and gloss over the debilitating side effects and fear of the unknown? I rub my forehead, then my eyes. All this hypothesizing is getting tiresome. The best course of action is to thank her for helping me see the light, and then we can head back to the—

"But Bernie," she says, a flush spreading across her wan cheeks and forehead, "always he would pester me for details. Did Joey say *why* he thought the FBI was after him? What exact connection did he say the TV had? Why wouldn't he let me touch the paper clip? Did it look like a booby trap of some sort? Wouldn't that explain why he didn't want my hand, still damp from spilled water, near his device and an electrical outlet? Every night, for weeks, Bernie would pick, pick, pick until he dragged a new bit of information out of me. Then, satisfied, he'd go to sleep, while I would be up for hours, stifling my cries, awake with the memory of the bitter smell of Joey's fear, the sound of his panicked breathing and hurried footsteps. Finally, one night, I couldn't take it. Enough! I said. I can never heal if you make me relive that horrible morning every single night!"

Rose clenches the blue stone, and her skin pulls taut around her bony knuckles. "It was his way of comforting himself, the questioning. Figure out why it happened, detective-like, stop it from happening again. It was destroying me, but taking it away from him was the greatest mistake of my life. Because the next day, he brought . . . *it* . . . home."

She glances at the patch of dirt. "You remember, Bernie," she says. "Your eyes were red and puffy when you came home that night, so I knew you had been crying in the car, where I couldn't see you. You thought I didn't know, didn't you? But I knew. Of course I knew. But it wasn't in your nature to show me that you'd been suffering. A man supports his wife. A man is strong, has the answers." A flicker of disgust passes over her face. "You set it down on the kitchen counter with your wallet and keys, and I looked up at you, shocked. 'What if his medications stop working?' you said. 'What if he forgets to take them, or throws them out? It's only for an emergency. And it has no bullets—without them it's no more than a toy.'"

Rose shakes her head vehemently, as if hearing right now, for the first time, the most incomprehensible idea ever proposed. "I told you I would never touch it, not in a million years would I lay a finger on it! Joey wasn't violent. It was his mind, playing tricks on him. He was trying to protect himself, that's all! But you, you walked up so close to me that I could smell the alcohol on your breath—you stunk of it, like a common drunk!—and the *words* you spit at me! 'You listen to me, you ignorant fool of a woman! He doesn't know what's real. Do you know how dangerous that is? What happens next time, when he decides that you *are* the enemy? You think he failed with that booby trap? Hah! He was expecting men to burst into his room, not his mother. More weight and force would have pushed the bureau further and tripped the wire. If he hadn't been so exhausted and confused, he would have realized that.'"

"But Joey trusted you, Rose," I whisper. "Even in that state."

Rose startles at the sound of my voice, does a double take when I inch a few steps into her line of vision. "Yes," she says, after a moment. "This is exactly what I tried to tell Bernie. I pleaded with him, but he said if Joey got like that again, he would have no way to protect me. Joey was bigger and stronger than him. The only way to calm him was to scare him, and who was Joey more afraid of than the FBI? He stopped listening to me then, just looked at me the same way he did when we were young, like a stranger looking from the outside in, and I *knew*. I knew that I couldn't change the mind of a man who'd saved his family through blind faith once before. He'd proven the experts wrong! And then I remembered all the years that I'd let him hold on to his silly dream for a child, how I'd thought he needed hope, but I'd been wrong. It was *control* that he needed. And isn't that what he'd been trying to regain with his nightly questions? But this time I'd robbed him of it. It was *my* fault, that Bernie had brought the . . . *it* into our home. So I made him a deal. He could keep it, but he had to follow my rules. He had to show me it was empty, he had to lock it up, and he had to keep the hiding place and the combination a secret—even from me."

I can feel myself scowling at Rose's insistence that she was to blame for Bernie's decision to bring a weapon into their home. And something isn't adding up: Why would confident, stubborn-as-an-ox Bernie say yes to an arrangement with so many stipulations? "Hold on. Bernie agreed to *that* deal?"

"What are you talking? Oh, did he fight me! Why did I need to lock it up if it was empty? How was I going to get it in an emergency if I didn't know where it was, or the combination? And so I told him: We've been married long enough that I know when I can't change your mind. But you're not the only one with lines that can't be crossed. I don't want to see it in my house. Ever. If I find it, I'll throw it out. It's for you, and you only. These are my terms. Take them or leave them."

Rose pauses for a moment. When she talks again, her voice is hushed. "What I didn't consider, with all of my rules, was Joey's shame. Of his sickness, I mean. He shouldn't have been. It wasn't his fault. But for years, I was told it wasn't *my* fault I was childless, and did I listen? Nah! I cursed my body, just as Joey must have cursed his mind. Which is why I, more than anyone in the world, should have known how Joey was suffering. And now I carry the guilt of being blind to my child's shame. To this day, I don't know how Joey found out about the—about *it*. But like I said, my Joey, he was smart like a whip. It turns out that Bernie was both right and wrong. Joey *was* violent, but not toward others. He turned his pain inwards."

So that's the missing piece. Rose heard Nick admit that Owen hurt himself.

She sighs. "I never forgave Bernie. I knew he suffered terrible— even more when he found out, after, that there was no booby trap. It was only an alarm. But I didn't show him compassion. Not even a little! I was cruel, and I knew it. It felt too good, at first, to hurt him with a harsh word here, an unkind look there. I knew he would take it, that there would be no bottom to how much abuse he would accept from me. And then the months became years, and the years became decades, and I wanted it to stop. It was so *tiring*, the anger. But I couldn't. I didn't know how to anymore. It had become who we were. Who *I* was."

Rose is silent for a moment, and then she opens her palms, the blue stone now visible. She holds it up to me. "I think it worked."

"I guess so."

"So you see?" Hope blossoms on her face.

Should I comfort her? Thank her for her concern about Owen? Cut to the chase and ask if I've drawn the correct conclusion? "Uh, first let me say that I'm honored you'd share such a personal—"

"*Oy gottenyu* . . . the sun is setting!"

"So? Is there some religious significance to—"

"The cemetery closes at sunset!"

What? There's a chance I could get locked in this place? I can't even begin to imagine explaining that to Nick. "They must send staff around to see if the grounds are empty before locking the gates, don't they?"

"How should I know? I've never been here this late. All I know are the visiting hours." She clasps my hands with her bony fingers, pulls me toward the base of the hill. "Time to go. Already your boychik has waited too long."

"Wait." I disentangle my hand and take a few steps back toward Joey's plaque and Bernie's tarp. I want to say something, but "Happy birthday" and "Happy backward birthday" wouldn't do the moment justice. I think first of a childless Bernie and Rose, him squeezing her hand in the park every time they saw a little boy; next of Joey, the desperately wanted child who gave them the miracle of a childhood filled with science projects, soccer, and piano; and last, of the troubled young man he grew to be, one who couldn't see beyond his own pain to realize the destruction he would soon wield on those who treasured him. Suddenly my throat is tight, and all I can choke out is, "Your parents loved you so much, Joey."

I wipe my eyes with the back of my hand and walk back to Rose, who is waiting for me, her gaze now set on Owen.

— 21 —

Not all mountain trails lead to the summit.

Tonight's dinner, ratatouille with a white bean dip and crusty baguette, is not easily thrown together. Even though the ride back was more merciful than I anticipated, traffic-wise, there's no way I'll have dinner on the table before seven. By the time Owen and I eat, and I wrap up and deliver Rose's portion, I'll have lost another forty-five minutes, and I'm guessing she isn't a late-to-dine type of gal. But then again, what do I know? That's just me stereotyping old people. I've never even seen Rose *eat*, and from the looks of her gaunt frame, it's not something she does frequently.

Ratatouille is Owen's favorite. Not to eat; to *make*. That's because I'm tasked with the labor, and he's responsible for the artistry. I chop the onions, mince the garlic, and measure out tomato sauce, olive oil, and oregano; Owen combines the ingredients and paints the baking dish with the mixture. I slice the eggplant, zucchini, squash, and pepper into thin circles; Owen stacks them in a spiral from the outer rim of the dish to the center, drizzles the veggies with olive oil, and sprinkles them with salt, pepper, and sprigs of thyme.

Owen tends to call it a day when the ratatouille goes in the oven and focus switches to the white bean spread. There's not much room for creativity in food processing. But today he sits up on the countertop next to the sink, rinsing the cannellini beans in the colander while I assemble the machine.

"Something on your mind, Owen?" I ask brightly.

He flicks some of the viscous fluid surrounding the beans off his finger, makes a face. "No. Why?"

"Just . . . you usually don't like doing this part with me. So I was wondering."

Not that I want to open a discussion about this afternoon's adventure. I'm just as unprepared for a discussion about death now as I was before our trip to Eastfield. But if there's any confusion in that little head of his, that takes priority over this less-than-ideal educational situation, as well as the blowback I'll have to face from Nick. I'll take the pass if I can get it, but not at Owen's expense.

He shrugs. "I already used up my iPad time."

"But you could play your keyboard if you want, or color, or read."

"I know. Sometimes I just like being with you."

I feel it then, the ache of separation. There are so many types, all with different symptoms. There's the temporary separation of weekends lost to visitation with Nick; that's a blend of guilt, anger, and loneliness that reveals itself as anxiety. There's the pain of knowing that Owen will grow up far before I'm ready for it, that this pure, boundless love he has for me is finite. That's more of a dull ache in my chest combined with a burning at the back of my eyes. Newest is Owen's sudden secrecy, a wedge between us I never suspected. Is it because he fears his undiagnosed behaviors as much as I do? That unknown is an arctic chill gusting down my spine. And then there is the permanent separation Rose has endured. I can't even fathom it.

I push all the food processor parts aside and grab Owen, nuzzle my nose in the nape of his neck, and give him a kiss on his cheek. "I like being with you, too, O. More than anyone in the world. And that's saying a lot, considering how disgusting your hands are right now. You've got bean goop all over them."

He giggles and pretends his hands are claws. Goop drips onto the lip of the sink. "I'm a bean monster!" He crinkles up his hand and sends spurts of bean juice onto his shirt, pants, the floor, and my cheek.

"Owen, stop!" I say, still laughing, but he doesn't listen. It's on my shirt now, too, all up and down my arms. "Gross, it's getting everywhere!" I cover his hands with paper towel before he can get any more on me, then hoist him off the counter. "Here are two more paper towels. Wipe up your clothes then clean up the mess on the floor. You're officially fired from bean-rinsing duty."

"What can I do then? I can't cut the bread."

"Go change your clothes. Then you can either help me with the buttons on the food processor, or . . . you can make the table fancy."

"What?"

"At formal events, like weddings, there are place cards with the guests' names on them, and the napkins are folded up in a special way. I can show you how to do it."

Owen's eyes light up. "I'll go get my markers." He looks down at his bean-stained shirt. "After I change."

"No, now that markers are in the mix, don't bother. Just get construction paper—" I don't finish the list because he's already running toward his room. *Running.* I love that about this age, about *him.* The only thing that'll get me running with excitement is the thought of seeing Owen or Belle. Place cards certainly aren't going to cut it.

I think of Joey. How old was he when he made model airplanes and rockets with Bernie? My guess is only three or four years older than Owen. I try to imagine what Rose would have been like then, bustling around in the kitchen making dinner as they went about their projects. But I have no basis to imagine her young or happy. All I know from her youth is what she told me today—that she struggled to conceive for years, that she worked as a secretary—

A secretary. At an elementary school, of all places. I know very few options were available to women of Rose's generation, but Rose seems particularly ill-suited to be a school secretary. She's highly unorganized and she probably scared the hell out of the younger students.

People do have different faces at work and home, though. Sometimes the very skills people are required to demonstrate at work are underutilized at home because they're burnt out from the day: the contractor with a half-finished project on his own house, the car mechanic with the jalopy that he never has the time or energy to fix. Maybe Rose's home was always a mess, since she had to be so organized at work. Is it possible she was sunny at school because she knew it was a job requirement, but let her harsher tendencies win out in her private life?

But maybe . . . maybe Rose was once a very *good* fit for that profession. Maybe she was the smiling school secretary that knew every child's name in the building, as well as that of their siblings and parents. Maybe grief fundamentally changed who she was. I can't even begin to process what it would be like to lose Owen. And I don't mean that in the obvious, I-haven't-experienced-loss way. I mean that I actually can't imagine it.

Rose slept for part of the ride back, and I spent the time constructing morbid hypotheticals about Owen. My brain shut down mid-day-dream every time. The pictures in my head got blurry and disappeared, or I forgot the sequence of events and had to start again. And it wasn't because I was multitasking; I've ended up at home after driving on auto-pilot plenty of times before. It's because my mind wouldn't even let me consider the possibility.

Owen and I modify our fancy table setting when we discover the cloth napkins are at Nick's. Not that we would have attempted a swan fold—that's a Martha Stewart-esque skill that's not in my repertoire—but even a simple cone or pocket fold is not going to happen with my value-priced paper napkins. Owen decides the next best option is to draw a picture of a swan directly on the napkins underneath our names, overlooking the fact that covering a napkin with marker then renders it useless—but I don't want to quash his creativity, so I tell him it's a great idea. He can leave the swan napkins on top of the plates as decorative pieces, and I'll put clean napkins under the forks. I finish up the bean dip while Owen puts the final touches on the place settings. We've got half an hour to kill until the ratatouille will be ready.

We snuggle on the couch under a blanket, Owen telling me all about his day at school until the timer dings. I look at the clock. 7:12. I'd forgotten about cooldown time. That'll be another forty-five minutes, and there's zero chance I'm leaving Owen up here by himself with a warm stove, even to walk down one floor. I've more than earned my keep today. I'm sure Rose can grab something out of her well-stocked freezer if she can't make it until eight.

I knock on Rose's door: sharp thwacks that are sure to irritate her. I have no choice. My arms are full of containers of ratatouille, white bean dip, and sandwich bags filled with French bread. If they all tumble over and get the hallway carpet sticky, it won't be an easy cleanup. God, I wish the grocery stores still bagged in plastic. I know it's terrible for the environment, but I could really use a small plastic bag right now.

Rose opens the door, and I speak before she can. "Don't say it. I'm sorry about the *klopping*. I know you don't like it. Next time I'll knock more lightly, I promise, but I didn't want any of this to fall, and Owen's upstairs in bed, so I don't have a lot of time—"

"*Sha, sha.*" Rose takes the bean dip and bread from me and heads toward the kitchen. She looks back, motions for me to follow her.

I place my container next to hers on the countertop. "Ratatouille, no sprinkled parm, so don't worry. And inside your container is a white bean dip—moderately spicy. Owen likes a lot of garlic, but I didn't know if you would, so I played it safe." I glance at Rose, who is looking at me with an amused expression. "What? Did I break some other dietary rule now?"

"No, it's perfect. Thank you."

"Oh. You're welcome. But you're looking at me as if—"

"You don't even realize?"

"Realize what?"

"You said *klopping*!"

"What? No, I'm pretty sure I said 'knock.'"

"Nah, nah, nah, I heard it with my own ears. You said *klopping*." She chortles as she opens her freezer, frowns when she finds it too full, then opens her fridge and shoves all of the containers inside it. "So. This you will not believe. Dottie. She is going to be one hundred percent fine! Already she's feeling much better. She is *impossible*, that Dottie, she never listens."

"What? But this afternoon—"

"*Allergies*, not a cold. I told her! It's a dry cough that she has, that's how you can tell."

"Allergies? To what? All the pollen is gone." I think of my pathetic excuse to Megan. It's hard to believe it was only this morning that I was walking Belle.

"Mold. Dottie has dry skin, so when she starts to use the heat, she also turns on her humidifiers. She has the big ones, the kind that come up to your waist, and when she turns them on, you can smell that *farsh-tunken* moldy air all through the house. One time I said to her a couple of years ago, Dottie, how do you clean those? And she said she thought her cleaning ladies did it. And I said, if they haven't asked you to buy extra ammonia, they haven't done it."

Ammonia? Is this Rose I'm talking to, Rose of the paper-strewn kitchen and bursting cabinets? Rose knows how to clean? "Eww. Definitely sounds like a health hazard."

"Dottie told me I didn't know what I was talking about. She was sick because of the weather. It was too much for her with all of the changes in the fall—it's cold, then it's warm, then it's cold again. She got better after a couple of weeks, but then the same thing happened the next year. So again I said, Dottie, I think it's mold, and she told me that she used her humidifiers all winter long, so if she was allergic, she would have been sneezing and coughing all winter."

Rose rolls her eyes. "So you see what I'm dealing with? I said, Dottie, that's because when you start using the humidifiers in the fall, the mold that's been growing inside them all year gets sprayed all over your house, and your allergies act up. Then your cleaning ladies wipe it away, and you get better. This year, I begged her to try medication to see if I was right. And she told me that I should stop being such a *noodge*, why couldn't I just leave her alone, she's never seen any medical degree hanging on the wall in my home. But then this morning she felt so terrible that she called her doctor, and guess who the doctor agreed with? *Me.* The doctor told Dottie she has to get rid of the humidifiers altogether, not to even bother cleaning them. And already she's feeling better on the Zyrtec. That Dottie, it's a good thing I love her so much, because she drives me *meshuggah.*"

"How long have you known each other?"

"Since I was twelve years. I grew up with Dottie. She's the closest I have to a sister."

"Sounds like the two of you talk to each other the way my sister and I do. And that's not necessarily a compliment."

"*Ach*, words," she says with a dismissive wave of her hand. "They mean nothing."

"I don't know about that. My sister, Lindsay, can be pretty cruel when she wants to be. She'd probably say the same about me, but I've never *meant* to hurt her. Maybe I have, but—"

"You misunderstand me. I mean words, they are not so important as actions. Today, I was lucky, you had *rachmones* on me and took me to see my Joey and my Bernie . . . but a sister would never have left me in such a position in the first place. Dottie, I take care of her, she takes care of me, but we are not blood. Dottie's children, I think of almost as my own, so many holidays we've spent together, but neither of them came to my Bernie's funeral. They both had good reasons, they both called. But blood is thicker than water."

Is it? I think about Lindsay, about that Halloween so long ago when she gathered up those mini-Butterfingers. It was a tender childhood gesture, but maybe I've given her too much credit for it. Because in critical times, she hasn't been there for me. Like when I found out I was pregnant. Lindsay was in Thailand, discovering herself at a month-long yoga retreat. Mom was the one who heard me sobbing in the bathroom, pregnancy test stick in hand. I babbled that it hadn't been a one-night stand, that Nick and I were in love. That we had spent *three whole months together* traveling every weekend to Delphi, to Cape Sounion, to Corinth and Hydra. The more I talked, the more the vein that runs down the center of Mom's forehead popped out, the one I'd only seen when she found out my cousin Ashley, at fourteen, had been caught sneaking out of the house to meet some creep twice her age, or that her best friend Lisa's son had gotten a DUI and totaled a car within a month of getting his license. Lindsay would have known how to make that vein go away, how to make Mom understand that while I might have been stupid, I hadn't been *that* stupid. I needed Mom to stop looking at me like I was such an enormous disappointment, to be on my side, because if *she* couldn't understand, there was no hope for Dad.

I didn't expect Lindsay to drop everything and fly home, and I knew it wouldn't be easy to get in touch with her—there was the time difference, of course, and the fact that she was supposed to be spurning material possessions and focusing inward—but I didn't think it would be *impossible*. She was in Chiang Mai, a city of over a hundred thousand people, not some remote island with no cell phone or Internet access. Mom and Dad had made sure she unlocked her cell phone before she left, and she bought a SIM card when she got there. But I didn't hear from her until she got back to California, and by then, I was already in Boston with Nick. She said she'd visit me once she recovered from jet lag, but she didn't, not once, during my entire pregnancy. That stung.

Now that I think about it, where was Lindsay this summer, when my world fell down around me? Shouldn't she have offered more support than an email with a to-do list of negative-energy-cleansing techniques for my new apartment? I've been too angry at Nick, too busy trying to get my life together, too busy trying to be strong for Owen, to realize that I have a right to be mad at Lindsay. My ears start to burn and a bitterness rises in my throat. Suddenly I'm filled with rage toward my sister, what with her endless platitudes about generosity of spirit and her apparent lack of it. Hypocrite.

"You know, Rose, sisters aren't always there for each other. Trust me. Lindsay and I don't see eye to eye. On just about anything. We used to, a long time ago, but I think I need to accept that—"

"If you used to, then you will again. You must never, ever give up on a sister!"

"I don't want to, but she doesn't make it easy."

"But a sister, there is nothing like it! You can't put a price on what it is, to have a sister—"

"Look, I don't know why you believe in this ridiculous, made-for-TV, rainbow-and-butterflies version of sisterhood, but honestly, you don't know anything about it! Real life is a lot harder than you think."

Rose's mouth is ajar, but she says nothing. Then, after a moment: "I know plenty about real life." She turns her back to me, and her voice becomes flat. "Thank you again for the dinner. I'll let you get back to Owen now."

"Owen." Not "boychik." I've crossed the line. And on today of all days, after she's opened up to me. "Rose, I didn't mean it like that. I was only talking about real life in terms of dealing with a sister. I have a lot of issues with mine, and I was getting upset thinking about them, and I . . . I took it out on you. I'm sorry. Rose, turn around, please. All of my problems with Lindsay, and even with Nick . . . I know they're nothing compared to losing Bernie. And as for what you've been carrying so long with Joey . . ."

I shake my head helplessly. There are no words.

She turns when she hears his name. Her eyes are brimming with tears, but they aren't tears of sorrow, or of frustration or disappointment with me. She's smiling. I never know quite what to expect with Rose.

"It's the most wonderful thing, to hear Joey's name said by someone he never met," she says. "It keeps him alive."

The apartment is still as I tiptoe back inside toward Owen's room. I peek through the cracked door to see him, try to judge the depth of his sleep by the messiness of his blankets. He's slid halfway off the bed, completely entangled in his comforter and sheet. I creep inside and hoist him up, rearranging his covers as best I can without waking him. His hair is already damp at the temples. He mumbles something I can't make out, then flips over toward the wall.

I don't know where he gets it from, this hyperactive sleeping, if that's what you call it. Most mornings, I wake up close to the same position I fell asleep in, and Nick's a normal sleeper, too. But not Owen. Sometimes I walk in and his head is at the foot of the bed, sometimes he winds up on the floor, and other times by the door. He's the only person I've ever known who wakes up sweaty, not from one too many blankets, but from exertion. I turn out the light, wait for a moment to hear if he stirs. He flips to his other side once more, lets out a congested snort, and then quiets to a steady, rhythmic breathing.

I want nothing more than to veg out in front of the TV right now, but I'm behind on fortunes. I'm supposed to be at 290 by tonight, and I didn't even make my quota for last night. What number was I on when

Nick showed up?

I boot up my computer and take a seat on the couch. 274. So I've got to crank out twenty-six more fortunes by tomorrow night, and I need to put in a couple of hours for Smartypants tonight, too. They emailed me a list of ten toys today that need product descriptions ASAP. I'm going to be at this until midnight. I grab my charger, but the outlet between the couch and the wall is blocked.

Rose's case. I dragged it over from the kitchen and jammed it into this out-of-the-way spot last night after Nick left, then forgot about it in today's chaos.

Could it be *the* case? Or, to be more exact, *the safe*?

I type *gun safe* into the search bar, and up pops row after row of images of five-foot-tall, three-spoke-handled armored safes filled with rifles. Their product descriptions include words like *twelve-gauge steel door*, *four-inch locking bolts*, and *drill-resistant*.

But what are these others, farther down the page? They look to be smaller than Rose's, even, seem to hold one gun and little else. They lock with a combination of a digital keypad and a key. I don't see anything that looks like Rose's case. Is that because Rose's is old, and gun safe technology has improved? I don't know when digital keypads became the norm. Did Bernie buy a case that should never have been used as a safe?

I can't go by Rose's reaction to seeing it, because she never knew what it looked like in the first place; that was one of the conditions of her deal with Bernie. What, exactly, did she say when she saw it? "Why didn't he? How could he?" I replay the scene in my head, Rose holding Bernie's cords mid-air, paling when she saw the case. No—I've got it wrong. It was, "Why would he?"

"Why would he *what*?" I say aloud. "Force such a stupid, dangerous decision on their family? Buy such a low-security safe?" A gun case isn't

THE FORTUNE COOKIE WRITER

an item you should economize on. It makes no sense. When you have a lethal weapon in the house—

Bernie's words, via Rose, come back to me in a rush:

"And it has no bullets—without them it's no more than a toy . . . Why do I need to lock it up if it's empty?"

I see the situation, in a flash of clarity, from Bernie's perspective: He obeyed Rose's rules, so he believed that only he knew of the safe's location. He hadn't even bought any bullets. Why buy a drill-resistant safe with a twelve-gauge steel door and four-inch locking bolts to keep a gun with no bullets safe from himself?

Maybe, then, the explanation is simple: knowing the horror the case inflicted on them, Rose was wondering why Bernie would *keep* it.

I've got to try to open it again. But I've tested every possible combination already. I suppose I could look into ways of prying it open. How hard can it be? So I won't get to use it again as a medication safe. Fine. It'll be worth it, just to satisfy my curiosity at this point. I type *how to pry open a safe* into the search bar, and just as the screen populates with videos and links, it hits me: if this is *the* safe, Joey must have cracked the code.

There are marks on the safe, but they are ones of age, not forced entry. I pull the case out from between the couch and the wall, set it down on the ground. What would be the most common, three-digit code someone might use?

I think of my go-to username. It's DoggoFan107. I picked 107 because my birthday is October seventh. But Bernie's birthday is November thirtieth—four digits. I doubt he would have used just the first three digits; 1-1-3 would translate to either November third or January thirteenth, depending on how you group the numbers. Joey's birthday of March eleventh is three digits, though: 3-1-1. Maybe I skipped by it somehow, yesterday? I turn the numbers on the combination lock, then push the square metal tab to the right. The latch doesn't budge. I run my fingers along its sides, try to determine if the mechanism itself is broken, but I don't feel any jagged pieces. So Joey's birthday is out.

The placeholder zero! I left it out when I flipped Bernie's birth date around in my head the first time Rose mentioned it to me. But what if Bernie didn't? What if he grew used to thinking of Joey's birthday as 03-11 instead of 3-11? He would have only been able to use the first three numbers: 0-3-1. Once again, I try the combination, push the tab. Suddenly, I don't want the safe to open. Please, Bernie. Please tell me you didn't.

The latch stays firmly in place, and I breathe a sigh of relief. It was all in my head. It's late, and I should put this creativity toward fortunes, not imagining my neighbor's tragic past. I release the square, but as I do it catches and pinches the flesh of my thumb. I gasp in pain and push the square, harder this time, to release the skin.

I hear a click. The latch doesn't fly open, as I'd imagined it would, but that was definitely the sound of unlocking. I pry it apart the rest of the way, unbuckle the drawbolt lock clasps, and open the lid.

It's empty. After all that effort, the goddamn case is empty. Just the same black casing on the interior, and a swatch of gray carpeting on the bottom, fastened down by aluminum trim on all sides.

Not that I expected to find objects of much weight—after all, I've lifted and shaken the case. But maybe a letter from Joey? A picture he drew as a child, a memento of some sort?

I close the case, try to shove it back between the couch and the wall. I don't know the Lindsay-approved New Age terminology for it, but there is far too much negative energy attached to that hunk of metal.

On my second shove, I notice the crumpled-up edge of a napkin sticking out from under the couch. I pull out one of Owen's swan napkins, then two. What are they doing here? I told Owen I was keeping them, that we should use them for fancy dinners from now on.

But more importantly . . . why are our names blacked out? When I left to go to Rose's, MOMMY and OWEN, both in Owen's print, were in blue marker, above gray-outlined swans. Now they both look like inkblots.

I rub my finger across them, see if water smudged the ink. But the consistency of the paper is uniform, and the swans look the same as they did at dinner.

My stomach clenches as the answer comes to me:

Markers aren't erasable.

Owen didn't cross out our names.

He waited for me to leave, and then tried to perfect the letters.

— 22 —

*Like bubbles in a boiling pot,
the truth will surface.*

O wen is the last to get off the bus after school. He's rooted to the bottom step, and I reach my hand out for him. I've never thought about why he's always last to get off until now, why he doesn't jump off the steps and try to stick the landing, Olympic gymnast–style, like his peers. It's okay that my little guy is cautious, I've thought. But now I wonder if he chooses the back of the line because he knows he's beholden to an inner voice that doesn't always let him jump when it's his turn.

"Come on, O. The driver needs to get to the next stop."

Owen frowns. He tenses his right shoulder one-two-three times, which I think is just an adjustment of his backpack, but . . . will that shoulder tense eventually hit eight, and then have to be done on both sides? I can't help but be suspicious of his every movement now.

Owen circles his shoulder back, then gives a whole-body wiggle until the weight of his backpack is adjusted. He grabs my hand and jumps to the curb. "Can we go to the farm today, Mommy?" He looks up at me, blue eyes wide with anticipation.

It *is* a beautiful day. It's fifty-eight degrees and clear skies, abnormally warm, and the temperature is supposed to plummet to the thirties for the weekend. I should say no. I submitted my Smartypants copy last night, but fell asleep on the couch while trying to finish up my fortunes. The final three hundred are due tonight, and I'm still twenty-six short.

Owen is studying my face, awaiting my decision. There's no whining, no pleading, no bargaining to get his way. His expression is far too serious for a little boy.

Peking Foods is California-based, I remind myself. Eight o'clock deadline. I could adjust my schedule: farm, dinner, work. I squeeze Owen's hand and smile.

The Natick Community Organic Farm is a hidden gem half a mile down Route 16 from the Charles River waterfall. It's nestled back from the main road, along with one of the town's five elementary schools, and is home to several cows and goats, a flock of sheep, a herd of pigs, bunnies galore, and more turkeys and chickens than I can count. The school's tennis courts abut one end of the farm, and depending on where the cows are in the pasture, you're sometimes treated to background mooing as you serve. We park in front of where we often find Haley, the brown-and-white-spotted cow, but she's nowhere to be seen.

I asked Owen, at the time of her naming, if he selected *Haley* because cows eat hay, and he said no, it just fit her. I nodded and said I agreed, and I did; the repetition of the *h* sound and the long *a* sound in *Haley* and *hay*, combined with the semantic connection between *cow* and *hay*, did, in fact, make *Haley* the perfect cow name. There must be a psychological term for that subconscious selection process.

Owen wants to see the pigs and the chickens today, he tells me, as we walk along the dirt path.

"Not the bunnies, O? We always start with the bunnies."

Owen shakes his head. "The pigs."

This makes no sense. Owen usually tries to steer clear of the pigs altogether. He says they smell. I've explained that pigs are clean animals, that they wallow in mud to keep cool, and that it's the *pens* that smell, not the pigs. Anyone's house would smell if there was rotting food and no toilets, I tell him, but my defense of the pigs' fastidiousness has yet to win him over. The list is always the same: bunnies, goats and sheep, cows, *maybe* the chickens, and pigs only at my urging.

We veer to the left, past the maple trees that will be tapped in a couple of months for syrup, past the bunnies' huts on our right, until we reach the pigs.

"How old are the pigs, Mommy?"

"Umm, I don't know. Why?"

"This one here," he says, pointing to an enormous black-and-white sow. "She's one of the biggest. How old do you think she is?"

"Honey, I'm not sure how to judge her age just by looking at her."

"Her hair isn't gray or white."

"I don't think pig hair changes color like human hair does."

"She doesn't have any wrinkles on her face."

"Pigs don't get those, either." Owen doesn't know pigs are livestock, not zoo animals. Signs of aging don't apply. But where is he going with this? "My guess is the best way to tell her age is by her health—you know, can she run? Do her teeth look clean, do her eyes look clear?"

Owen peers through the metal fencing posts at the sow, who has now stretched out next to the water trough and is napping. "Get up, lazybones," he calls out to the pig. "I can't see your eyes or your teeth when you're sleeping." He settles his gaze next on an even larger hog, who is eating from the feed trough, and on the two pink-skinned pigs rooting in the mud nearby. "None of them are running, either. All of them are lazy, lazy, lazy today." He kicks the base of the fencing. "I'm going to the chickens."

He turns and walks toward the chicken coop. Even though he starts a couple of steps ahead of me, he quickly falls behind, since he's meandering around every brittle, curled-up maple leaf littering the ground in front of us.

"What's going on, O? You love to stomp on the leaves. Why are you being so careful?"

"Because these leaves are brown."

"I know. Those are the crunchiest ones. Come on!" I drag him by the hand toward a small leaf pile near the coop.

"No!" he screams. "Stop!" He disentangles his hand and takes a step back.

"Okay, okay." I raise my arms in *I surrender* fashion. "You want to tell me what's going on? You're acting really funny."

Owen says nothing, but his chin is quivering, and his eyes have welled up with tears.

"Oh, honey. Come here." I sit down on the ground and pull him onto my lap.

Owen's whole body starts to shake. "It doesn't make sense. I asked Mrs. Evans why, and she never answered."

"Why *what*, O? Does this have to do with the focus wall?"

He gives me a confused look. "What's a focus wall?"

Oh. That's right. The teaching term might not be written on the wall itself. "You know, the wall that has a different letter, word, and number on it each week?"

Owen shakes his head. "No. I asked Mrs. Evans about the life cycle. But she looked at me like what I said was weird."

My God. I've really screwed this one up. I piqued Owen's curiosity about death, and then I made myself an unavailable resource. So he asked his teacher, and the poor woman didn't know what to say.

I take a deep breath. "What was your question, Owen? You can ask me anything. You know that, don't you?"

"But this is a *science* question."

I hide my smile. I'm pretty sure he hasn't made it to astrophysics yet. "It's true that I'm not a teacher. But I can try."

Owen sniffs. "Well . . . okay. I asked Mrs. Evans why people are more like leaves than chickens and pigs."

It's not what I thought. But I can appreciate the strange look from Mrs. Evans. "Why do you think that, O?" I keep my voice light.

"Because of the *pictures*! From our life cycle worksheets about frogs, chickens, and pigs."

"So you learned about eggs and tadpoles for the frog, right?"

Owen nods. "And for the chicken, there was a picture of an egg, a chick, and a grown-up chicken. For the pig, there was a picture of a lot of piglets with the mommy pig. I forget her name."

"The sow."

"Yeah. The sow. For the leaves, there was a tree for each season. Get it?"

I shake my head. "No, honey. I'm trying. How does that make people more like leaves?"

Owen picks up a leaf from the ground. "There are brown leaves in the winter."

"What are you saying, Owen?"

Owen shakes his head, as if he can't believe that now *two* grown-ups can't manage to put two and two together. "The frogs and the chickens and the pigs never die in the life cycle worksheets. But the trees do. Mrs. Evans says in the winter, the trees don't have enough sun to make food for themselves, so they let their leaves die and then they hibernate through the winter. And . . . and people die. The Candy Grandpa did."

I sigh. So. The Talk is going to happen now. "People do die, Owen. Pigs and chickens and frogs do, too. It's just not on your worksheet because grown-ups get uncomfortable talking about it. But everything that's alive eventually dies. Dying is part of the life cycle."

"But in the worksheets the life cycle is a *circle*. And circles go round and round and don't end. But I don't get that, because when you die, doesn't everything stop?"

"That's a hard one to answer. The truth is that no one knows what happens. That's another reason grown-ups don't like to talk about it. We want to be able to give kids all of the answers. So what I told you when we first found out about the Candy Grandpa, about heaven? That was . . . that was me telling you what I was told when I was your age. It came out before I had the chance to think about it. But I wish I hadn't said that. How about we start again? I'll tell you what I know for sure, and then I'll tell you what I believe. Because they're two different things."

Owen nods, his face solemn.

"What I know for sure is that it's permanent."

"Permanent?"

"It means it's forever. Like, if you step on a bug by mistake, can it get better and crawl away?"

Owen shakes his head.

"It's the same with people. When people die, it's because their bodies stop working. They can't eat, drink, or breathe anymore. But they can't *feel*, either, so they're not in pain. That can be comforting—knowing the person you loved isn't hurting. But it's still very sad, because you'll never be able to see that person again, or talk to him, or hug him."

"So the Candy Grandpa *isn't* in heaven?"

I shrug. "Now you're at the tricky part. A lot of people believe in heaven—kids and grown-ups, too. And they might be right. But me, that's not what I believe. I believe that when people are buried, their bodies . . ." Ugh. The decomposition talk. The reason I initially turned down Rose's request to take her to the cemetery. I take a deep breath and start again. "I believe that when people are buried, their bodies feed the earth. The soil, I mean. And that soil will then feed a tree, which will grow leaves. And maybe a caterpillar will eat some of the leaves, or birds will use them, together with twigs, to build a nest for their eggs. Get it?"

Owen gazes up at the maple trees that surround us, then kicks at the dirt and nods an unconvincing yes.

I point to a huge oak tree. "Look. What if the soil feeds a tree, like that one there? What will you see under it in the fall?"

"Acorns," Owen says, spying the empty caps scattered beneath the tree.

"That's right! And who loves acorns?"

Owen's face lights up. "Squirrels! So maybe . . . maybe the acorn will feed a squirrel?"

"Exactly! That's the meaning of 'life cycle.' It goes round and round in a circle, because even when there's an ending for one living thing, it's the beginning for another."

I search his face for clues as to how I've handled the discussion this second time around. Clear and concise—that was my plan if it came up again. Owen doesn't push for further clarification of my vague and flowery "bodies feed the earth." Which means, I think, that part of him knows he isn't ready to hear more.

He stays nestled in my lap, grabs a stick, and picks the bark off it. Is there more he wants to talk about, but doesn't know how to? "O? You don't have to worry about Dad or me dying, you know. That's not going to happen for a very long time. Not until you're a grown-up, with kids of your own. And . . . you don't have to *do* anything to keep bad things from happening."

Owen gives me a wary look. "What do you mean?"

"Have you heard of superstitions? Like knocking on wood for good luck, or stepping over cracks in the sidewalk? Sometimes people think the things they do will keep the people they love safe. Do you ever do anything like that?"

He's silent.

"It's okay, honey," I say softly. "I *know*. I know you're not satisfied unless your letters are perfect. I found the swan napkins last night, and I've seen your schoolwork. I know how upset you got at Dad's last weekend when he messed up the nighttime routine. I know about the tapping on the floor and the wall, the running up and down the stairs. You don't need to feel like you have to protect us, Dad and I are—"

"That's not why I do it!" Owen bursts into tears.

No? With all this talk about the life cycle? "Then why, O?"

"I don't know! I just *have* to. Until it feels right. And then I can stop. I can't explain it any better."

I wipe his tears, kiss the top of his head, and pull him even closer. "I bet you feel like you're the only person this has ever happened to."

"I'm not?"

"No!"

"It's happened to you?"

"Uh, no . . ."

"Daddy?"

"No, but that's not . . . the point is, I'm going to take you to see Dr. McClaskey. And I bet, when we see him, he'll say, 'I know another doctor you should see.' And *that* doctor will be able to help us a lot."

"You think?" There is hope in Owen's eyes.

"I do. But promise me one thing?"

He nods.

"No more secrets, okay?"

He smiles at me for the first time today, gives me a bear hug, and then clambers out of my lap. He pulls my hands with all his might, and I jump up as if his strength has lifted me off my feet.

"I don't want to see the chickens anymore, Mommy. Can we go see the bunnies?"

Friday night is usually Mexican night, but our go-to recipes aren't easily modified for Rose's dairy-free diet. So tonight's dinner—our final one— won't be black bean and cheese quesadillas, but chicken marsala with asparagus. I omit the butter and use olive oil only. Although it's Rose-friendly, Owen is less than thrilled with the result.

"I'm sorry, O. Rose says butter doesn't make her stomach feel good. I put extra olive oil in. Do you hate it?"

"No." He takes a delicate bite. "It's just . . . different."

"Well, sometimes different is good."

He picks up a piece of asparagus from his plate, holds it up like a moustache, and giggles.

I give him a stern look. "Playing with your food at the table?"

Owen freezes. I can tell he's trying to figure out if I'm serious.

"Always use your fork." I stab two pieces of asparagus with mine. Just as Owen's smile begins to fade, I grab them off my fork and hold them up, one on either side of my front teeth. "What am I?"

"A walrus!"

"Or?"

"What do you mean 'or'?"

"Isn't there an animal from *Ice Age* that I could be, too?"

"Oh! A saber-toothed tiger!"

"You got it! Winner gets to eat all of the asparagus."

"*That's* what I get?"

"Kidding. But you like asparagus. Weirdo."

"But asparagus is healthy. You said so!"

"No, you're right," I say, smiling. "I'm lucky to have a kid who eats his veggies without complaining. Now finish up. When you're done, we'll take Rose's meal downstairs to her. This is the last time, you know."

"The last time we're going to see her?" Owen's words are garbled by his chewing.

"No . . . I'm sorry, that was confusing. The last time we're cooking her dinner. We were helping her out until her family could come into town, and her nephew is coming tomorrow. But we'll see her around like we did before."

"So . . . not really."

"Yeah," I admit. "I guess not really. How do you feel about that?"

"I feel kind of bad that she's all alone. I think she liked it when I played piano for her."

"So why don't you come down with me and tell her that you'd like to play again for her sometime? I think you're right, I think that would make her happy."

"Can you do it? 'Cause I don't know how to say it right."

"Okay. You can just come along, and I'll do all the talking."

Owen shakes his head. "It makes me feel . . . I don't know. Embarrassed. Can I just stay here? Please? And if she wants me to come back to play another time, I will. I promise."

I knock on Rose's door, lightly.

There is no "yah, yah, I'm coming," no "enough with the *klopping*, already." Instead, I hear footsteps and the flip of the dead bolt, and then the door opens a couple of inches. Rose peeks out, but she says nothing.

"Rose, hi! I'm just bringing by dinner," I say, as if she hasn't figured out why I'm carrying plastic containers. "Owen is upstairs, so I'm going to drop off quickly, if you don't mind. The chicken—"

"No. No need." She closes the door, and the dead bolt clicks.

What?

Honest to God, this is the third time this week I've had the door shut in my face by this woman. I gave her a pass the first time because of my faux pas, and the second time because of the case. But this time . . . and after what she shared yesterday . . . seriously, what the hell?

"Rose!" I bang on the door, *klopping* be damned. "Rose, what is going on?"

The lock turns once more, and the door opens, this time enough for me to see her whole face. Her eyes won't meet mine. "Excuse me for my bad manners. But there's no need. I *know*."

I'm so irritated I don't think about the fact I have no idea what she's implying. I go on the offensive right away. "Well, you know what *I* know? I know that you have a habit of kicking me out of your apartment, and it's getting old. Now I've made chicken marsala and asparagus for you, no dairy, which Owen wasn't too excited about, so if you don't eat it, then I've ruined his dinner for no reason."

I wait for her to motion me in, but she doesn't open the door farther. Nor does she offer to take either container from me. "Wait a minute . . . you *know*? You know *what*?"

Her eyes narrow. "All of it!" she spits at me. "Joel is coming tomorrow. A couple of hours ago he called to tell me when he'd be in. And he told me he spoke with . . . *her* . . . and that the two of you had come up with this *farkakte* plan. That there never was an email from the management to all the tenants. That she has been *paying* you." Her voice is dripping with disgust.

"But why . . . why would he tell you *now*?"

"I caught him in a lie! He asked me how your meals had been, and I asked him how he knew who you were. And he's always been a terrible liar, ever since he's been a little boy, he stammers and he laughs, and I said, Joel Klein, something funny is going on, you'd better tell me the truth. So he told me that . . . that woman . . . called him after she spoke with you."

Of course Lena called Joel. It makes sense she would let him know of the ruse, would want him to know that Rose was taken care of this week. My cheeks begin to burn. Thank God I let Owen stay upstairs. "Rose, I know making dinner is something I should have done out of kindness, but what did I do that was so terrible? I kept my end of the bargain. I cooked you meals every night, and I even brought you to visit Bernie and Joey."

"Don't! Don't you *dare* say their names."

"But Rose, before you said it made you happy to hear Joey's name said aloud by people who'd never met him. That it kept him alive."

"*Sha!* That was before."

"Before what? I'm still the same person! And I shared plenty with you about *my* life. Lena didn't pay me to do that. I don't know your sordid history with her, all I know is you won't even utter her name, but for some reason she seems to care about you. She drove in for the funeral, and then she devised this plan when I bumped into her in the hallway—"

"What are you talking? She didn't go to the funeral!"

"She said she did. I don't know why she'd make that up."

"She—she came to temple? Or the graveside service?"

"I don't know about temple. But she said she stayed in the back at the graveside ceremony."

"No! Can't be. I would have seen her. Everyone took turns."

"Took turns what?"

"Shoveling the dirt, of course."

I try not to show my surprise. The mourners fill the grave?

Rose catches my expression and softens. "To show respect for the dead. And to help the living."

Help? "How? It sounds . . . traumatic."

"Yes. There's no forgetting the sound of dirt and stones hitting the casket that holds your husband. Or your son. You must face reality. And only then can you begin to heal. You see?"

I nod, but I can't help thinking that Rose never healed after Joey's death, nor did her marriage. She may have been able to take that first step—to face reality—but she could never forgive Bernie for taking away the person she loved most.

I don't know what to say next, even though I know she's waiting. "Look," I say, finally, "I've only met Lena once—this past Sunday, in the hallway near the mail room. I don't know where she was or wasn't during the funeral. All I know is that she seemed genuine in wanting to help you, but too scared to knock on your door. So why is it that you hate someone so much who is going to so much effort to help you? Who *is* this mystery woman?"

Rose's face pales. "It's ancient history. Not worth repeating."

"But—"

"Now that I know the truth from you, too, I must say no to dinner. Goodbye, Marissa." Once again, she closes the door.

— 23 —

One cannot journey forward until he has learned from previous travels.

"Goodbye"? What does Rose mean by that? Goodbye for now, or goodbye forever? I stomp up the stairs. That makes three times in five days that she's shut the door in my face.

Enough. I've *more* than kept up my end of the bargain. Most people would have called it after one round of sparring with Rose, but not me. No, apparently I'm a glutton for punishment. I heave the plastic containers onto the kitchen counter, but luckily, they don't spill.

"Mom?" Owen peeks his head out from his room.

"Yeah, honey?" I offer what I hope is a convincing smile. I don't want to explain the whole story; taking money to feed a grieving widow wasn't my noblest moment. But I don't want to lie to him, and I don't want to evade the truth if he asks. Not after I made him promise not to keep secrets from me.

Please don't notice that I've brought the food back, O. Please don't ask why Rose didn't take it.

Owen looks down at the carpet, drags a circle in the matted plush with his foot. "So I was thinking . . . can I have a little extra iPad time tonight? I know I have to take a break now, but—"

I exhale with relief. This is about the iPad? "Sure, sweetie. You know what, why don't you use it now?"

Owen blinks several times. "Now? Really?"

I smile, a real one this time. "Don't give me a chance to change my mind."

He grins and disappears back into his room.

I walk into the living room and drag the case out of its wedged position between the couch and the wall. I'm not going to attempt to bag it. If no one's at the trash room, I'll drop it off, and if someone's there, then Rose is going to get a delivery. She can figure out what to do with it. Her problems are mine no longer.

I kick the case ahead of me as I head toward the door—far too hard, but who cares now that I'm dumping it? With each kick, the lid opens a sliver and then slams shut. I must not have refastened the draw-bolt clasps completely after the triumph of finally cracking the code last night.

As much fun as it is to beat up this piece of junk, I'm not going to get away with an anonymous donation to the trash room if I make this much noise in the hallway. So when I reach the door of my apartment, I walk in front of it to fix the clasps.

Goddamn it. I've managed to jam the left clasp. It's resting over the nose of the lock, but it's angled to the right instead of lying centered. I can't snap the bottom portion of the lock into place, and I can't loosen the clasp to realign it over the nose, either. I turn the case against the kitchen wall, place my foot against it for leverage, then pull the clasp forward while pushing back the lid at the same time. I give it a couple more solid kicks for good measure, because, my God, how hard should it be to get rid of this useless hunk of metal? Plus, it just feels good at this point. I kick it because it's unfair that Rose was rude to me after all I've done for her this week; I push it because of the sinister forces swirling inside of Owen, torturing him from within. I kick it because of my crushing guilt for not noticing his pain earlier; I push it because my inattention forced him to choose to confide in Nick over me. I kick it because of Courtney, whose face I have never seen, but whose presence is so intrusive that I now imagine it on librarians; I push it because of Lindsay's spiritual musings, worthless when spoken by a careless sister.

The metal clasp releases! It falls down before I have the chance to stop pushing the lid backward, and the case swings open, the lid hitting the wall.

That's when I notice it. The writing.

The battle has dislodged the gray carpeting that lines the case from the metal trim in the front left corner. Underneath it is what appears to be the back of a photo, and visible, in a scrawl, are the letters *l-i-a*.

What is it with this case and writing? First it dredged up Owen's illegible swan napkins, and now it's revealing another handwritten riddle?

I run to the kitchen, grab a pair of scissors from the odds-and-ends drawer, and cut through the thin carpet. There are three photos, all facedown—I assume they were placed that way so as not to have the images damaged by the scratchy underside of the carpet. Only one has an inscription, and now I can see it in full: *At Delia's, 12-20-85*.

I flip it over. The photo is of a young man and an auburn-haired woman of the same age. The man is kissing the woman on the cheek, and she's laughing, as if he's caught her by surprise. It's hard to tell where they are. They're at a set table, but behind them the taupe wall is free of art or photos, offering no clues as to their whereabouts.

The next photo is of the same woman, now with a different man, seated on her other side. He's older than her by several decades, and everything about him seems . . . well, *inflated*. His hair is bushy, straining against the gel he's used to slick it down; his lips are fleshy and exaggerated; his neck is thick and veiny; and the buttons of his shirt strain over his chest and stomach. He looks like the kind of guy who was once very muscular, but now age has added a layer of fat into the mix. Regardless of his body mass index, he cuts an imposing figure. He's smiling, posing for the camera with his arm around the young woman, who's leaning in to him.

I pull out the last photo. It's of the young man in the first picture, and the woman seated on his other side. She's several decades older than him, rail thin with short black hair teased and blown back from her face.

Rose and Joey.

It's a candid shot, both of them smiling at each other. Rose's gaze is fixed on Joey, her face filled with pride. There is a slight blur around Joey, as if he was looking elsewhere, sensed her gaze, and turned to meet it. Did Bernie take this shot, or was the photo given to him by someone else at the table? The man with his arm around the woman, maybe? Someone else not photographed?

12-20-85. Joey died in the late summer. August 1986 was engraved on his stone. So this picture was taken eight months before he died. Was he already struggling at this point? Are these the last photos before tragedy struck?

The young woman. Is she Lena? The woman in the photo has auburn hair, and Lena is blond. I look closer at the first photo for signs of freckles, of skin coloring that might be a giveaway for the woman's natural hair color, but it's too faded for that level of detail. Not that freckles would be conclusive evidence. They can be covered up by makeup, which Lena is clearly adept with, and hair color can be changed. The way to tell is by examining her facial features—the angle of her jaw, the slope of her nose, the shape of her eyes. But I've only met Lena once, and this picture—if it *is* of her—is of a thirty-five-year younger version of the woman I met on Sunday.

"At Delia's." Lena said her full name was Darlene. Maybe the man with her is her father, and *Delia* is her family nickname? But, on second thought, if the photos were taken at Lena's family home, wouldn't Bernie caption the photo with her parents' names instead? "At Sue and Bob's," or whatever their names might be, would make more sense.

I suppose Delia could be Lena's mother's name, but there's no woman in any of these photos who might give credence to my theory. It's possible Lena's mystery mother was there—that she was cooking or serving, if she was the hostess. Or maybe no one took a picture of her, or the pictures didn't turn out well and were thrown out. 1985 was before digital photography.

But then again, maybe my theory is flat-out wrong. A kiss on the cheek doesn't necessarily signify a romantic relationship between Joey and the young woman, and the young woman may not be Lena. Lena might not be Delia, and her mother might not be, either. The problem is that I have a suspect pool of one.

I pick up the picture of Rose and Joey, and hold it gingerly around the edges. I'm almost afraid to touch it, now that I know I have an item of such immeasurable value in my possession. I walk to the door, because regardless of what Rose thinks of me, I have to get this photo to her . . . and then I stop short.

Bernie *hid* all of these photos from Rose. Why?

It's time to call Lena. The ruse is over. She can tell me if she's the woman in the photos—or she can choose not to tell me, I guess. But I have to try, because if it *is* her, then she has a right to at least one of these photos.

My phone rings, and the display lights up with "Mom." Part of me wants to answer. I need to talk to someone about Owen, and I always seem to get sidetracked with Lindsay. Why wouldn't I confide in Mom? It's ridiculous that I'm this humiliated to talk to my own mother. Look what I've caught Owen doing this week! His behaviors are mysterious and frightening, but not once have I been embarrassed by him. He's my child, and he's struggling; I want to help. That's it. Why do I assume my mom feels any differently about me? I slide the bar to accept the call, but it's too late. It's gone to voicemail.

The phone vibrates again. At first I'm impressed with my mom for her diligence, but then the display lights up, and I see that it's Nick. We haven't spoken since he walked out Wednesday night, but considering Owen's confession at the farm, I pick up.

"Hey, Nick."

"Hey. So, you know Greg Broderson?"

"Uhh . . ."

"From work? You met him once. Remember, at Jim's retirement party? Brown hair, balding . . . a little shorter than me?"

"You've just described about half of the male population over thirty-five."

"Okay, fine. Doesn't matter. The point is, he has tickets to a concert on Sunday. Boston Youth Symphony Orchestra. And he can't go. So he gave them to me."

"That's great," I say warily, because I'm not sure where he's going with this.

"They're doing *Peter and the Wolf*. And Greg says the kids can go in early and touch the instruments. I thought Owen might like it."

"What time on Sunday?"

"Noon. Do you have other plans already?"

"No, but . . ." I'm torn. Owen would love it, he really would. And the fact that Nick wants to foster Owen's love of music—*that's* certainly new. I should encourage Nick, let him see Owen's eyes go wide with delight as the hall fills with music. That would do more to help my piano crusade than any amount of nagging could possibly do.

But this is *my* weekend. We have a visitation plan for a reason. It gives predictable structure to Owen's life, which will "decrease his anxiety during a turbulent time." That's what all the literature says. "Planning leads to stability, and stability affords a child with a sense of inner calm."

Except . . . I'm really good at planning. Cleaning and planning are my areas of expertise. And Owen doesn't seem anywhere near calm.

I look down at the photo of Rose and Joey. It hurts to look at, to see the radiant joy in Rose's face, knowing she will soon be robbed of it.

Joy.

That's what I want for Owen.

I've never been to the symphony. But I imagine now the violins, flutes, French horns, clarinets, bassoons, and drums working together to tell the classic tale, the music swelling and filling the hall. I imagine Owen's mouth agape in wonder and amazement, and before I can stop myself, I'm crying. Not a delicate, feminine whimper; I'm sobbing, gasping for breath in between torrents of snot, tears, and hiccups.

"He'll—he'll love it," I choke out, after several attempts. "You should take him."

"What? No. I wasn't trying to steal any of your time. It's your Sunday. I was planning on giving the tickets to you. I just wanted to see if you'd already made plans."

Kindness. The bastard. My throat aches as I fail to stifle my sobs. If he would just go back to being a jerk for a minute, like he was on Wednesday, I could get it under control.

"Riss, are you okay?"

"You were right! And I was right, too! And I wanted both of us to be wrong—more than anything that's what I wanted, but then when Owen didn't want to see the bunnies first, I *knew* something was wrong, but—"

"Hold up. 'You were right, I was right'? 'Bunnies'? What are you talking about?"

I lower my voice, even though I know Owen's in his room. "I spied on him before school yesterday. You're right, he taps when he thinks no one is looking. More than that—he has these elaborate routines, and . . . it's what I thought it was, Nick, what I was scared about. You *can* get it this young—I looked it up. And Owen admitted it to me today. He's been miserable, and I've been so wrapped up with my own issues that he didn't feel like he could turn to me. That's why he turned to you when he was getting bullied—"

"Picked on."

"Fine, *picked on*. That's not the point." I think of Joey playing *Moonlight Sonata* or *Turkish March* for Rose. Yesterday I was surprised that a child could be so attuned to his mother's feelings; today I discovered that my own has been so sensitized to mine that he chose to keep his struggles a secret rather than heap any additional pressure onto his overloaded mom.

"Look," Nick says, "maybe Owen sees that you're stressed out sometimes. But that's not why he confided in me."

"But Wednesday you said he was trying to impress me because I'm—"

"Wednesday we were mad! We both said things we shouldn't have." He lets out a deep sigh. "Choosing me doesn't mean he trusts me more. Don't you get it, Riss? He chose me because he's already lost me."

"What? That makes no sense."

"Sure it does. That's why he can show his flaws to me. He can't afford to lose you."

I hear a sharp intake of breath, followed by several gasps, then a high-pitched squeal. I think he might be crying—or maybe swallowing his cries. I've never heard Nick cry before. "I've failed him, and for what?"

For Courtney, I want to say. *Remember her?* But I can't bring myself to hurt him when he's this vulnerable. I can hear him breathing, and I realize suddenly how much I miss the sound of it. How much I miss the steady, reassuring presence of him next to me in bed every night.

That's how I always felt with Nick: reassured, protected. I'm sure he was petrified when he asked me to move to Boston, and soon after, when he asked me to marry him, but if he was, he never let on. He always seemed to have a game plan. If we were going to have a baby, he said, we needed to think about practical things, like health insurance. Had I checked into Yale's policy while on leave? Or if my parents' policy would cover me if I was living across the country? At the time, I'd given him credit for being levelheaded while I was falling apart, but now I realize he was following his father's script, just as he did when he parroted stories about his cousin Alex in Greece. I was the next female after Aunt Nora who needed rescuing, and Nick's dad dispatched him.

But we're different people now. Nick doesn't want to be the kid who takes orders from his dad anymore, and I get that it pisses him off that his dad forced our marriage on him. A spouse is the only family member you can choose. There are few bigger decisions than the selection of who to share your life with.

As for me, I don't need to be rescued anymore. I don't even like the sound of it. I'm not some damsel in distress, and I'm not someone's mess to clean up. I'm a lot stronger than I realized, and it's not a question of *Can I be strong?* when it comes to Owen. I have been strong for him and I will continue to be strong for him. There is no choice.

Nick clears his throat. "So . . ."

His voice pulls me out of my thoughts. "So?"

"So Sunday?"

I think of Rose, how her marriage survived in name only because she was never able to forgive. My marriage is over, but maybe my relationship with Nick is still salvageable. I have the power to forgive, if I'm ready.

"*You* should take him. Really. And Nick? You didn't fail Owen. You're a good dad."

— 24 —

Once the clouds pass, the stars cannot be ignored.

"Do you want blueberries in your pancakes, O?" I call over my shoulder as I pull out the orange juice.

"No, they mess up the shapes when they're inside the pancakes."

"Good point." I turn to face him. He's wearing his favorite fleece pajamas, the ones with giraffe spots on the pants and a giraffe appliqué on the top. He's holding Geri, who looks every bit as morning-disheveled as he does; her neck has a dent in it the exact size of Owen's head, and it's flopping over, the stuffing now misaligned and unable to support its weight. Owen has a red impression across his face from the seam in Geri's neck.

He pulls a measuring cup from the drawer, then raises his hands in the air. I pick him up and place him on the countertop next to the stove, on the opposite side of the burner I'm using for the pancakes, to be safe.

"Be careful, O. The pan's still hot, even though—"

"—my side isn't on. I know."

I place the bowl of batter next to him, and he scoops the half cup into it, then pours the contents into the pan. Our rule: no circle pancakes. Too boring. The only exception is if the middle is scooped out to make an *O* for Owen. The person with the most imaginative description of the pancake gets to eat it. It's a Rorschach test of sorts, but deviating from a mundane response gets you breakfast instead of a diagnosis.

"It's a cloud," says Owen, as the pancake puffs up in the pan.

I give him a look. "You've used cloud before. You sure you don't want another chance before I go?"

"No, no, no, wait!" He waves his hands to ward off my turn.

It's bubbling in the center, so I flip it. The top is golden brown. "Looks like it's going to be tasty. And I'm sooo hungry. Tick, tock. My turn in ten, nine, eight, seven—"

"Stop! It's a . . . a camel! See? The hump, and the swoopy neck?"

"I *do* see it! I was going to say snail, but you're right, the batter drippings near the bottom look like legs. You win." I lift the pancake with a spatula and slide it onto a plate.

Owen shimmies off the countertop, belly down, then grabs his plate and a napkin on his way over to the table.

"Oh, I meant to tell you," I say as I spritz the pan with cooking spray, "Dad called last night. He has tickets for *Peter and the Wolf* tomorrow. It's a symphony—all classical music. It's a story about a little boy and a bunch of animals. All the characters are different instruments. I said I thought you'd want to go."

"But . . . tomorrow I'm with you."

"I know. But I thought it might be nice for Dad to see how import-ant music is to you. It's just for a couple of hours. Go grab your iPad, and we'll look it up, and you can decide if you want to go or not."

He does want to go, he decides, after watching a couple of minutes of the Vancouver Symphony Orchestra's production of it, which was posted on YouTube. But the story's synopsis concerns him—specifically, the demise of the duck who lived in Peter's yard.

"He's okay, O. It says you can hear him whistling at the end."

"But he has to live in the wolf's belly. Forever."

"Well, the duck isn't *really* a duck—it's an oboe, remember?"

"I know. But I still feel bad for him."

"How about we go feed some real ducks this morning, then? Will that assuage your oboe-duck guilt?"

"What does 'assuage' mean?"

"I'm asking you if you'll feel better if we go feed the ducks."

"Oh! Uh, do you mean the Wellesley ducks or the Natick ducks?"

"Your choice. But remember: we only saw the Angry Goose once." I check the pancakes, then flip them over before they burn.

The Wellesley ducks live by a stream outside of Town Hall, which looks more like a castle than a public administrative building, with its stone façade and cone-capped rounded towers on either side. This was Owen's preferred duck-feeding spot, until the Angry Goose stalked him on our last visit, honking. Petrified, Owen chucked his entire piece of bread at the goose and ran crying in the other direction. The Natick ducks, by contrast, are more elusive. They live on the Charles River by the South Natick Dam, which is surrounded by guardrails. You can't get as close to them, but on the upside, you won't get into an altercation. Owen likes watching them line up, their tail feathers hanging over the edge of the waterfall.

I put two pancakes onto a serving plate, point to the one closest to me. "This one looks like Africa."

"You win. But the other one? It's an elephant superhero. See the trunk? And there's the top of the cape."

I hold the serving plate out to him. "Elephant superhero? I can't beat that."

Owen smiles and stabs the pancake with his fork. He takes a bite, then stops midchew. "Maybe we should save some. For the ducks."

"The ducks are on a no-pancake diet, O. No more bread from now on. It's not good for them. I didn't know until we saw the sign. Let me see what we can feed them before we go." I scan for my phone and spot it on the coffee table. I type in "Wellesley ducks," and click a link on the first search result, a page on the town's website devoted to them. It states that the wild ducks—the mallards and Canada geese—are not to be fed, or they'll lose the ability to fend for themselves. The domestic duck and goose population, cared for by the Town, is comprised of "around nine domestic ducks and geese: four white Embden geese, four mixed-breed geese, and one Pekin/mallard mix."

One Pekin duck.

Shit! Those twenty-six fortunes I was supposed to finish after my visit to the farm with Owen? I completely forgot about them. Between dealing with Owen's confession, getting kicked out of Rose's apartment again, and discovering hidden photos in her safe, fortunes haven't been in the forefront of my mind. Is it better to send an apology email with the 274 I have right now, or should I finish them all first? It's Saturday, so no one's going to notice until—

The phone rings, and "Lena Scolani" lights up on the screen.

Now? I *do* want to speak with her, but at some point, I need to prioritize my own family. I can't keep getting pulled into an ungrateful woman's past. My finger hovers over the red Decline circle.

But the photos.

Lena's my only shot to learn more about them. I have to pick up.

"Hi, Lena."

"Oh, hi! I'm so glad I've caught you! I was worried it might be too early, with it being the weekend—"

"Not at all. I have a kindergartner."

"I remember those days. How long have you been up?"

"Couple of hours. He slept in until seven. Super late for him."

Lena laughs. "I'm sure you have a busy weekend ahead of you. I won't keep you. I just wanted to thank you for helping Rose this week. I know it wasn't easy."

"Joel will be in tonight?"

"Yes, as planned. He called yesterday to let me know he spilled the beans by mistake, but by the time I picked up the message, it was too late to call you. Did things go okay yesterday?"

I let out a snort. "No. They did *not*. She kicked me out, for the third and, thankfully, final time."

"Three times? I thought only once before?" She sighs. "I'm so very sorry. I didn't realize she'd be quite this difficult. I wouldn't have dragged you into this had I suspected she'd act this inappropriately. At the time it seemed like a reasonable solution, but then again—"

"Lena?"

"Mm-hmm?"

"Umm, I'm not sure how to say this, but . . . I found three old photos of Bernie's. Rose doesn't even know they exist. Here's the thing: I think you may be one of the people in two of them. If I take a picture of the photos and text them to you, could you tell me if it's you?"

Lena hesitates. Then, brightly, "Of course! But why don't you . . . why don't you explain them to me first? Just for curiosity's sake."

"Okay. The first is of Joey, I think, and a young woman with auburn hair. He's giving her a kiss on the cheek. I can't tell where it is—the wall behind the two of them is pretty nondescript."

Lena lets out a gasp. "You know about *Joe*? Rose told you? She won't let you in her apartment, but she opens up about—that makes no sense, no sense at all! What *happened* this week?"

"It's a long story. But we . . . we went to visit Joey's grave on his backward birthday, and she opened up."

"'Backward birthday'? What are you talking about? Joe's birthday is March eleventh."

"Right, but if you take the digits of his birthday and flip them, you get November thirtieth."

"You get November third."

"Well, it depends on if you count March as a three or an o-three. And Rose and Bernie always counted it as an o-three, because Bernie's birthday—"

"*Bernie's* birthday?"

"Look, it doesn't matter. The point is, on the back of the photo, someone wrote the date. I don't have it in front of me right now, but it was in December, 1985. I can't remember the exact day. And it says 'At Delia's.' So I thought maybe that was a family nickname of yours. You said your full name is Darlene, right?" I stop short of mentioning my theory that perhaps Delia was her mother's name, because who am I to question her like a private investigator? Even posing this one theory must make me seem borderline creepy.

"It must be a stray mark," she says, after a moment.

"What?"

"I bet it's an *l*, not a *t*. 'Al Delia's,' not 'At Delia's.' It's an Italian restaurant. *Was* a restaurant, at least. Been out of business for a long time."

"Does 'al delia' mean something? Is it a cooking term, like 'al dente'?"

"I don't think so . . . although I could be wrong. I'm not the best chef. I always assumed it was the owner's name. It was a popular restaurant back in the eighties in the North End. Fancy, for special occasions."

"So . . . it's you, then? And Joey? I can tell it's Rose in the other photo, but there's one man, he doesn't look like Bernie. He's a . . . bigger guy, with thick, wavy hair. He's hugging you in one of the pictures. Your dad?"

"That's him. No more hair, though."

"So you and Joey were . . . ?"

"Engaged. We were out celebrating with our parents that night. It was winter break of our senior year."

"Did you know he was sick?"

Lena pauses. "You did have an eventful week." Then, in a quiet voice, "Yes—and no. Joe and I were together from the time Joel set us up our freshman year. Joel dated a sorority sister of mine, Susan, and they introduced us. My guess is Joe's symptoms started long before I noticed them, but I can't be sure. We never lived in the same dorm, so I didn't see him every day. Once I remember showing up at his room and glancing through the half-open door. He was sitting on his bed, his back to me, books and notes strewn around him. He was muttering and gesturing, staring at the far corner of the room, but he was alone. I knocked as I entered, and offered to help if he was prepping for an oral presentation. He flinched, and when he turned, his face was creased with worry and confusion. He looked like he hadn't slept in days. I told him to forget what I'd just said. He didn't need help studying, he needed a break. Looking back, I wish I'd let him speak first. Because now I think he may have been talking to someone only he could see. And I wonder what he would have said, had I not provided him with an excuse for his behavior and a graceful exit from the situation.

"We rarely argued, but I do remember that when we did, it was usually over him not looking at me. I'd get frustrated, tell him he should stop being so self-absorbed. That I had problems, too. It wasn't until years after Joe died that Joel told me he'd probably been looking away from a hallucination in my direction, not me. Trying not to engage with it. It eats at me, knowing that when he needed help the most, I lashed out at him.

"But the final straw came about four or five months after that photo was taken. My brother, Darren, was a junior in high school, and he was considering applying, so he came for an on-campus visit with my parents. They took Darren, Joe, and me out to dinner that night. Joe hadn't been acting like himself that day—he was so withdrawn—and my dad asked if there was anything either of us would like to share with Darren. You know, did we have any words of wisdom, as seniors. And Joe suddenly perked up, and he launched into this whole tirade about how only specific sections of the campus were free from cameras, how you had to be careful that government agents weren't tracking you through your student I.D. card, and how the staff at the main dining hall had tried to poison his food once. And I was shocked! I mean, Joe *had* gotten more particular over which sections of the library or student center he'd sit in, but he'd never told me *why*. And I watched my dad's face redden, and my mother's eyes widen, and there was no recognition on Joe's face that what he was saying was completely untethered from reality, and I *knew*, I knew then that something was really wrong."

"So . . . what happened?"

"That was it. My dad called off the engagement. I loved Joe, but . . . I was scared. I didn't know what to do. I hated my dad for taking charge and forcing me to cut ties with Joe, but I was also relieved. It was so much bigger than me, his illness, and I was so young. As a parent, now, I can see how clear-cut the choice was for my dad: he'd only met Joe a handful of times, and here he was confronted with a young man struggling with paranoid delusions. I don't know if he even knew what schizophrenia was—I certainly didn't—but it's such an easy decision, to step in while you still have some authority and remove an obstacle from your child's life. That's all Joe was to my dad. An obstacle, a risk to my future happiness. I went back home after we graduated, and sometimes I'd sneak out and see Joe. At first he seemed to be getting better, but then he got so, so skinny, and I wondered if it was because of what he said at dinner that night, about people trying to poison him. I reached out to Joel, told him he needed to talk to Rose and Bernie. They wouldn't even take my parents' calls, so I knew they wouldn't talk to me. They blamed me for breaking Joe's heart—they assumed that's what caused his decline."

I can't think of what to say. I know how terribly that conversation worked out for Joel. Joel, who had just finished his first year of medical school, and then went on to become a psychiatrist. I want to thank Lena for sharing such private memories with me, but I'm not sure how. "You stayed in touch with Joel all these years?" I ask, after a moment.

"Mm-hmm. That sorority sister of mine, Susan? Joel ended up marrying her. Without Susan, I'm sure I would've lost touch with Joel. The only reason Susan wasn't called in to help Rose this past week is that she and Joel have recently gone through a bitter divorce, and Joel's kids live far away. We decided that Rose's hatred for Susan is fresher than her hatred for me. And I wanted to help. For Joe." She sniffs a couple of times. "I hadn't visited his grave in a very long time. I stayed behind after everyone left Bernie's service and spent some time with him."

"Would you like the pictures? The one of you and your dad, of course. But the one of you and Joey, too?"

"*Me?* I would love them, yes—but you said they were Bernie's, didn't you? Shouldn't they go to Rose?"

"I'm not sure. Bernie hid them from Rose. She has no right to the picture of you and your dad, even if Bernie took it. That leaves the picture of her with Joey—which absolutely needs to go to her—and the one of you and Joey. I don't know Bernie's reason for hiding them, but my hunch is that he feared she'd rip up the one of the two of you. So I think it's safer in your hands than hers. Fairer that way, too. Both you and Rose will get one picture with Joey. I'll text you a picture of the photos. If they're what we think they are, let me know, and I'll mail you the originals."

— 25 —

Assumptions make one as blind as the mole shrew.

orn, lettuce, peas, oats, seeds.

Search Engine Master Owen Karalis typed in "good duck food" while I was on the phone with Lena and solved the problem. He also mulled over his duck outing options, and as much as he wanted to be fair and take turns, he wasn't sure the Angry Goose was in the mood for company. He hoped the rest of the Wellesley ducks wouldn't be too upset, but we were going to have to see the Natick ducks two times in a row.

The upside of Owen's selection was the South Natick Dam's location: next to a charming brick and stone library. After seven duck sightings and a liberal spraying of the Charles River with vegetables and seeds, I coaxed him inside. A half hour later, we had eight new books. The perfect solution to keep him busy while I churned out my final fortunes.

But Owen needed help reading two of them. Three others, once started, were pronounced boring and tossed aside. And I couldn't think of one original fortune. All of my gems were trite or laughable. After two wasted hours, I emailed an apology to Peking Foods, attached the 274 I'd had since Wednesday, and noted I would get the final twenty-six to them before Monday.

When we woke up this morning, Owen announced he needed to dress up in his fancy clothes for *Peter and the Wolf*, which I assumed meant a button-down shirt and khakis. But no, he needed to go full-on dress pants and zipper tie for the event, because "that's what conductors wear." *It's not necessarily what five-year-old audience members need to wear*, I felt like saying as I thought of the dry-cleaning bill, but I held my tongue. No need to spoil the magic. And he did look adorable, I had to admit.

I look at my phone. 11:34. Nick and Owen are probably at Symphony Hall already. I drum my nails on the kitchen counter and consider my options.

It's only a five-minute errand.

But I'll need to make a quick stop in Wellesley first, for twenty minutes, and round-trip travel time is an hour. I'll have to hustle to make it to our meetup spot in Newton in time.

I check the Weather Channel app one last time before I go: chance of precipitation is 0 percent. Winds one to two miles per hour, which according to the Beaufort Wind Scale counts as "light air" to "light breeze." Weatherspark.com clocks average wind speed at seven miles per hour, so today is an unusually still day in Eastfield. Lindsay would say the universe is speaking to me.

My phone rings, and Lindsay's name pops up on the screen. "Linds! I was just thinking about you."

"But we just talked on Thursday."

"Most people answer with, 'Really, about what?'"

"Mom thinks you're mad at her."

"Because I called you twice this week instead of splitting up the calls?" I leave out the voicemail I've yet to return. "A week ago she was staying at my apartment, so it's not like it's been forever since I talked to—"

"It's because of the brochures."

"What?"

"Did you get any this week?"

I think back to Wednesday's cleaning battle with the showerhead and my heated argument with the Boston College brochure. "One."

Lindsay lets out a snort. "Get ready, then. Mom was so excited you talked to her about going back to school that she called every university in Massachusetts and asked them to send you a brochure. I told her you could get all that information online, that she's just killing trees for no reason, but she didn't listen. Your mailbox is going to be stuffed."

What is with Mom's obsession with my mail? First the negative energy sachet for my bills, and now—

I smile, realizing my mistake. It was never meant to get rid of bills. She placed the herbs in my mailbox to pave the way for good news from colleges. I want to laugh with Lindsay over the oregano debacle, but I can't, considering Mom's postal antics were inspired by Lindsay's email, which I mocked.

"So she thinks I got a bunch of brochures. Why would I be angry?"

"For interfering. She had to give out your name and address."

"Who cares? It's public information. Universities send out mass mailings all the time. It's weird she didn't bother to check which schools offer my major, though."

"Mom doesn't research like we do. She covers all bases and calls it a day."

"Like we do"? When I think of Lindsay, *research* isn't the first verb that comes to mind. I associate research with objective data, empirical evidence, the scientific method. But if you take the word at face value, *to research* is a shortened form of *to repetitively search*—and who is better at that than Lindsay?

"So since I knew Mom would blow off the research . . . I've done a little for you."

"What?"

"Have you thought about Northeastern?"

"Yeah," I admit, surprised. I haven't told anyone where I'm planning to apply.

"Perfect! Their mascot is a Siberian husky. Second only to the pit bull as the most misunderstood and maligned breed. Where else?"

"BU, Brandeis, and Tufts."

"BU's mascot is the Boston terrier, so I'd keep that on your list. Brandeis's is an owl, and Tufts's is an elephant. So those are a bit more concerning. But interpret as you see fit."

An owl. Not sure what I think about that. When Lindsay and I first spoke about spirit animals, and she was listening to whales, I mistakenly thought I heard an owl. Is there some meaning there? And an elephant. I wonder—

Wait. What am I thinking, letting myself get pulled into Lindsay's warped logic? Mascot and spirit animal compatibility is *not* a legitimate criterion when evaluating universities. I have to be disciplined when it comes to something as serious as college, because that is the only way to keep Owen safe—

Safe.

I haven't thought about college once since Wednesday afternoon, when Mrs. Evans called and I first suspected Owen *wasn't* safe. The exact time my hypothetical fears were replaced with an authentic one.

Let's break down the first hypothetical fear: that Nick will try to weasel his way out of child support with a new baby, leaving me in financial ruin. There are a host of enforcement mechanisms in place to force him to comply. And I do have my settlement money. It won't be fair if I have to spend it to make up for his delinquency, but Owen and I won't end up on the street. I'll have time to come up with a plan. And it turns out I'm pretty good at that. I searched for a new apartment and lined up three jobs in the span of a couple of months, and I haven't given myself a lick of credit.

And what about fear number two, that I'll have an allergy attack, lose my job, and Nick will take me to court on the grounds that I can't care for Owen? Surely *Doctor* Allerton would understand that allergies are not my fault, give me a reference, and I'd get a new job. Maybe not a stellar job, maybe not one with a fantastic career trajectory, but a job nonetheless. Worst-case scenario, what will a judge say, if Nick takes me to court? Probably that I've been quite resourceful thus far. A judge has already determined once that Owen needs me—me, *without* a bachelor's degree—so why have I been making myself crazy?

College has never been about Owen. It's been about me. Yes, he'll benefit, but I want it for me. I don't have to conflate every goal with motherhood now that I have a child. I don't know how or if I'll be able to make it happen, but it isn't selfish to try. Nick's ambitions didn't disappear when he became a parent, so why should mine?

"Listen, Linds, thanks for all the research. I have a lot to think about." I want to share more, but there's too large of a gap. Lindsay's never been married or divorced, doesn't have kids and doesn't want them. It's too hard to explain.

"I didn't get it." Her voice is quiet.

"Get what?"

"When you left school. I mean, I knew it was a big deal, but I'd left school, too, and for me it was a relief. I'm talking about the pregnancy."

I'm not sure what to say. Lindsay's never been pregnant, so where's this newfound source of wisdom?

"I want kids, you know. Eric and I both did. We tried, for a long time. We couldn't."

"But you told me that you didn't know if you even wanted to get *married*, that Eric wasn't willing to accept any alternate journey."

"Right. I said I had doubts about marriage. I didn't say anything about kids."

I stop to think. She's right. I was the one who assumed that statement meant marriage before kids, that she'd been trying *not* to get pregnant. I shake my head in disbelief, let out a sigh that ends in a chuckle. "Wow. I guess I jumped to the wrong conclusion. But . . . if it was a long time . . . why didn't you tell me?"

"I don't know. Maybe because Eric and I never really knew what was going on. When I couldn't get pregnant after a year or so, we started seeing specialists. And we did all sorts of tests, but everything was always normal. It's called unexplained infertility. I tried meds and insemination, which didn't work, so then I tried shots and insemination, and that didn't work, either. When it was time to move on to in vitro—I didn't want to, and Eric did. It felt like he wanted kids more than he cared about the stress it was putting on me. So we broke up."

All that talk about humpback whales guiding their calves through killer-whale-infested waters—I'd assumed the predatory waters in her metaphor represented the dangers that might befall a child, when they symbolized the adversities she faced in *becoming* a mother.

"Oh, Linds. I wish you'd told me."

"No way. You were barely holding it together."

So both Owen *and* Lindsay decided I was too distracted and self-involved to reach out to me over the last several months. God, that is humiliating.

"But I'm hopeful. There have been signs that children will be part of my future."

Signs? I let the comment slide, but I don't want to hear any New Age fluff on this topic. It's too important. Owen is the most amazing gift I've ever gotten, and I want that for Lindsay, too. I don't want her to tell me that words like *growth* or *creation* kept popping into her head one day, or that she mistakenly walked into an OB-GYN office instead of her primary care's, and that's why she knows. I want to pepper her with questions: What percentage of women with unexplained fertility go on to have successful pregnancies? Would she consider going through in vitro with a different partner? By herself? What about adoption? Surrogacy? Shouldn't she choose science over signs on something as critical as this?

Which is when it occurs to me: Lindsay already *has* chosen. When she had a medical problem, she didn't rely on herbal remedies and meditation. She went to see a doctor—many times. And it didn't work. I feel a sudden surge of compassion for my sister, who never gives up researching. My Sister the Seeker.

"Linds? Wherever your next journey leads you—"

"Stop talking like that."

"What? I was just trying to—"

"Talk like yourself."

"Fine. Don't shut me out anymore, okay? You're—you're my sister."

"I love you, too, Riss."

Elements doesn't have shelves stocked with herbal candles and geodes, racks of incense sticks and beaded bracelets. It's in Wellesley Square, a shopping district populated with boutiques, galleries, and salons, not healing arts shops. The stones, it turns out, are mere novelty items at Elements—an impulse buy, after your purchase of a glass vase, a silk scarf, a piece of handmade pottery. It takes a bit longer for the saleswoman to dig through her new deliveries in the back room than I'd hoped, but after five torturous minutes she comes back holding one bag of red stones and one bag of green ones. The stones are crystals, not gems, which is why they're so inexpensive.

She places the bags on the counter. "Are you sure you only want the two colors? Because they also come in a rainbow assortment."

"So I've heard."

She leans over the countertop and says in a lowered voice, "This one little old lady—you won't *believe* this—I had a rainbow set, but the heart center stone was defective. Clear instead of green. I offered her a discount, but no, that wasn't enough for her. She told me that unless she could come back and swap out the clear one for the green one, she wouldn't take it. Some people, right?" She shakes her head, her copper leaf-shaped earrings swaying in emphasis. "For anyone else, I would've said no, saved myself the hassle by damaging the set out and sending it back to the manufacturer, but she's a repeat customer. She buys a lot of crystals. Nothing else, ever. But a lot of crystals. She'll show up at some point."

I nod because it's easier to agree, even though it doesn't sit right to side with this woman over Rose. "Two red and two green are all I need."

The saleswoman opens up a cream pouch, slides in two small slips of paper along with the stones as she runs my card. She gives me a rote "Thank-you-have-a-good-day" and passes me the pouch and the receipt.

I nod and wave goodbye as I pull the first slip of paper out of the pouch and push the door open with my back. There's a picture of the green stone, and underneath it I read:

Heart chakra color:
green

Associated gemstones/crystals:
emerald, malachite, jade, amazonite, petalite

The fourth chakra is also known as the heart chakra. The Sanskrit word for heart chakra is *anahata*, which means *unhurt* and *unstruck*. A person who holds on to past hurt has a heart chakra that is closed. Showing compassion to others is the best method of opening your heart center, allowing you to live in a state of *anahata* rather than bitterness.

I stop, one foot in the store and one on the sidewalk, and look at the saleswoman while holding up the paper. "Have you read this? About opening your heart center? Maybe, when that little old lady comes back . . . you might ask her *why* she buys so many crystals. Just a thought." I offer her a bright smile to take the edge off my words, then turn and walk down the street to my car.

I slide into the front seat and set the pouch down on the passenger seat, on top of a manila folder wrapped inside a plastic bag. I pull out the second slip of paper and read:

Root chakra color:
red

Associated gemstones/crystals:
garnet, red jasper, hematite, bloodstone

The first chakra is also known as *muladhara*, which means root support or root base in Sanskrit. In your body, your root support is your tissue and bone. Ganesha, the remover of obstacles, is the god of the *muladhara* chakra. To honor him, you must connect to your body, your spirit, and the earth.

Ganesha! The Hindu deity with an elephant head. The one that made me question Lindsay's choice of spirit animals. And root support . . . *that's* why Lindsay and I keep struggling to understand each other despite being so different. We're connected; part of each other's root bases, part of each other's tissue and bone.

Suddenly, I think of Rose and Dottie. "We grew up together," Rose said. But she also said they met when they were twelve. I'd just assumed Rose and Dottie and Bernie had all emigrated as young adults. But now I realize my poor assumptions about Lindsay might not have been my only ones this week.

I do the math. Rose is ninety-four, she said at the cemetery, which means she was born in 1927 and met Dottie in 1939. She married Bernie at twenty-three. I don't know when she met him, if she knew him in . . . well, what country? I'm assuming Germany, because of the last name Klein, but that's her married name. I don't know her maiden name. Maybe Rose is originally from Austria or Poland.

First names, then. Bernie is short for Bernard. It's a German name. But Dottie is an American nickname for Dorothy, isn't it? I've assumed

Dottie speaks with the same slight syntactic clumsiness as Rose and Bernie, but that's because I've heard her speak so little. All of Dottie's words in the humidifier story were paraphrased by Rose, so they were laced with Rose's accent. And the one time I did meet Dottie, she spoke in Yiddish, pronouncing my lasagna to be *treif.* But . . . now that I think of it . . . what did she say, when she opened the door last Monday night? "You're looking for Rose? Rose! You have a visitor." A brittle voice, the voice of an elderly woman. But no trace of an accent.

That would mean Dottie was born in the U.S., not whichever country I can't decide upon for Rose. But focusing on Germany versus Austria or Poland is missing the forest for the trees.

Rose is Jewish.

Did Rose's whole family make it out, and resettle in Massachusetts near Dottie's family? That seems like a near impossibility for 1939. Did she lose a sister in the war? Is that why she has such an idealized view of sisterhood?

Or is it something more devastating? Did Rose lose all of her family, perhaps get rescued by a humanitarian organization and fostered by Dottie's family? Did Dottie have a sister? Was Rose jealous of their relationship?

Question after question pops into my head. There's so much I'd like to ask Rose, so much I'm ready to learn, and now it's too late. I sigh and check the clock on the dashboard. I've got to make up some time on the road.

Arad. I only have to turn around twice to find it, so maybe half-*fardrayt,*

if there's such a thing. I wish I could ask Rose if there's a word for "only a little bit confused." I toss Marnie's map on the passenger-side floor and pick up the stone-filled pouch and the manila envelope, covered with a plastic bag.

I park in the same spot I did three days ago, walk down the hill that is no longer muddied. Bernie's tarp looks a bit higher off the ground than I remember it, and the red stone that Rose left for him is nowhere to be seen. Joey's yellow stone still rests on his plaque.

So Joel and Rose haven't been here yet. They couldn't have come yesterday; the cemetery is closed on Saturdays. I doubt they've already come this morning. Rose would have swapped out Joey's yellow stone.

There isn't a cloud in the sky. Still, I'm glad I have the plastic. I set the bag on the ground, between Joey's and Bernie's graves. I place the green stones on the two corners on Joey's side and the red stones on the corners on Bernie's side. At least it's not muddy, like last time. That would've spoiled my plan.

I think of Rose sitting in the mud in the very spot I'm standing now, telling me her highest truth; of Belle, splashing in the mud puddle in the parking lot at Allerton; of me, covered with Belle's mud as I ask her who can help Owen. Belle the Beauty, with the flower on her canary-yellow jacket.

The flower.

It wasn't a daisy, or a carnation, or a tulip.

It was a rose.

I shake my head. L-shaped kennels. What was I thinking? Belle was nudging me toward Rose, not Lindsay. It's so obvious. And I never made the connection until now.

What was it Lindsay said, though, when I called her after I walked Belle? "The lotus flower blooms most beautifully from the deepest and thickest mud." It took Rose far too long to fight her way toward the sun, but she did, for a brief moment, when she decided to tell me her highest truth. I wish she'd unburdened herself decades ago, wonder if that would have helped her relationship with Bernie begin to heal. I kneel and touch the green stones, the heart stones for Joey, but I can't help but think that Rose is the one who needs them. She's the one with a closed heart center, living in bitterness rather than *anahata*.

Not a tree branch or blade of grass is rustling in the wind. The envelope *does* have four stones weighing it down, but I'm too nervous to leave it.

I look at Bernie's bumped-up grave. A groundskeeper must have been by to fill it in—that's how the first red stone disappeared. I scan the thirty rows of plaques ahead of me until I see, on the very edge of Arad, the telltale signs of cemeterial maintenance: a shovel and a wheelbarrow.

It doesn't seem respectful to run along the grass, even the outer edges that are meant to be pathways, so I make my way out to the road and then sprint over to the wheelbarrow. Yes! It's filled with rocks! Ugly, heavy gray rocks. Exactly what I need. I don't see any groundskeepers in view. I pick up two medium-weight rocks and return at a slower pace.

"Hi Bernie, hi Joey." I place the rocks on the edges of the plastic bag. "It's Marissa again. Will you hold on to this for me, keep it safe? It's just for a couple of hours. You should be the ones to give it to her."

— 26 —

If your neighbor's plate is empty, even the sweetest plum will taste like rotten fish.

Peter and the Wolf turned out to be an enormous success.

"Did you know that there are four groups of instruments in every orchestra?" Owen unbuckles his seat belt and climbs out of the booster seat in Nick's car. "And did you know that the strings are always in the front? And that the woodwinds are in the middle, and the brass and percussion in the back? And did you know that all the musicians tune their instruments to the oboe's *A*?"

Nick rolls his eyes and smiles. "Prepare yourself. The didjaknows have just begun. I got quizzed the whole way back. And I *do* know—I was there!"

"So you had a good time?" I ask Owen, as I try to avoid looking at the booster seat. It's a point of contention between Nick and me, his recent switch away from a car seat with a five-point harness. Owen's not the minimum weight of forty pounds yet, I pointed out when I first saw it, and his shoulders aren't above the top strap slots on his car seat. Nick said there was no law against switching him earlier, and I told him when Owen's safety was concerned, his go-to for advice shouldn't be the law. It should be the pediatrician, who'd said that Owen was still too little. Nick got defensive after that, and—

". . . so can we do that when we get home, Mommy?"

"I'm sorry, honey, what?"

"I want to watch it again. On YouTube. So I can show you some things. Who were we watching yesterday?"

"Oh! I think it was the Vancouver Symphony Orchestra."

An irritated look crosses Nick's face. "You watched the whole thing online yesterday?"

"No, no, no." I shoo away the accusation with my hands. "Just a couple of minutes, to give Owen an idea of what it would be like."

Nick gives me a slow nod, then squats down so he's the same height as Owen. "I'm glad you had fun, O. Give me a hug, okay?" Owen throws his arms wide. Nick lifts him up in the air, and he squeals with delight. Nick gives him a couple of pats on the back, then sets him on the ground. "Now go get yourself belted up in Mommy's car." Nick nods toward the parking spot next to his. "I want to talk to her alone for a minute."

Owen scoots behind Nick's car and opens the rear door of mine.

"I'll see you Wednesday, buddy."

"But no more Courtney?" Owen glances back at Nick.

Nick blushes and takes a few hurried steps over to Owen. "That's right, just you and me, kiddo." He closes the door, leaving Owen to buckle himself.

No more Courtney? I look down at the ground so as not to embarrass Nick, but he's silent. Finally, I say, "No more baking?"

"No more anything."

"But on Sunday—"

"I know. Look, Owen had a rough evening on Wednesday. He had a tantrum because of the baklava."

I wait, because Nick knows he owes me more of an explanation than that.

He sighs. "Courtney thought a Greek dessert would be fun, because—"

"I get it. What happened?"

"You have to butter every phyllo sheet. Quickly, before the others dry out. And Owen, he had to cover *every single spot*. And when she tried to hurry him, he—he went ballistic. When we spoke the next day, she said she wasn't ready . . . anyway, we broke up."

So Owen fell asleep in the car on Wednesday because he was tired from his tantrum. That's why Nick was already in a bad mood when he arrived at my apartment, and why he was so quick to label my need for cleanliness and order as the genesis of Owen's troubles. And then I told him Owen's anxiety was because he'd replaced me with Courtney and the next day Courtney dumped him. Now Nick's words about Owen—"I failed him, and for what?"—make sense. I almost feel bad for him. Almost.

"I think Owen will be fine with it," Nick says. "It's not like they were close."

I nod.

"Also . . . I owe you an apology."

"For what?" I ask, in my best offhand voice.

"For not taking the music seriously. I thought you were blowing things out of proportion. But it's important to him."

"Yes. Very."

"He told me he wants to take piano lessons."

I don't say anything, because Nick knows this isn't news. What he's saying is: *I asked him without you around, to see if you were telling the truth.* And I can't blame him for it. I do the same thing, all the time. I look away, so that my silence doesn't seem accusatory.

"I know you've done some research already. Why don't you look into it some more—and then we'll talk. Owen says he hates soccer and he doesn't want to play in the spring, and he doesn't want to try baseball, either. I don't know if I'm willing to give up on baseball before he's even tried it, but if he doesn't like soccer, we can take the money and reallocate it. So that's a start. What do you think?"

What do I think?

I look up at him, notice for the first time he's wearing the azure button-down I bought for his birthday two years ago. I remember thinking at the time that the color would be great on him, that it would bring out his eyes, but it wasn't the real gift, we both knew that. Nick couldn't care less about clothes. "What did you get for yourself?" he asked with a slow smile, and I held up a Victoria's Secret bag and said, "Oh, do you mean this?" When Nick puts on this shirt in the morning, does he remember that night? Or is it no different to him than any of the other button-downs in his closet?

I think of all the Nicks I know: the one who dutifully went to Greece to care for Aunt Nora when his father was too selfish to do what was right; the one who took turns in the hospital with me for three days when Owen was admitted with pneumonia at age two; the one who decided our marriage wasn't worth salvaging, and conspired with a lawyer to turn my life upside down; the one who has caused me more pain than anyone I have ever known, but who also has given me the most joy, in the form of Owen.

But of course, that's not what he means.

"Yes," I say, finally. "It's a start."

Ten minutes, fifteen tops. That's the amount of time I thought Owen would invest in our YouTube viewing of *Peter and the Wolf*. But no, he was all in for a complete viewing—the full twenty-nine minutes and thirty seconds, replete with his running commentary. I pull him onto my lap and snuggle with him as he jabbers away.

My heart aches for Rose. She had this once.

It's hard to believe I've only known her a week. Not even a full one. Just six days. It's Lena I met a week ago. I picture Lena in her black sheath dress and Christian Louboutins, three crisp one-hundred-dollar bills and a check in her hand, an offer I couldn't refuse. The fortune bursts into my consciousness, fully formed: A MAN WITH A BOWL OF HALF-COOKED RICE RARELY DECLINES AN OFFER OF ROAST DUCK.

The events of the past week flash through my mind.

Rose, nose turned up at my lasagna. It's obvious that NOT EVERY RABBIT IS DELIGHTED BY A CARROT. Owen, noticing before I did, that Rose's piano was tuned despite its age. It's clear that THE OWL MAY BE SMALL, BUT HIS EYES ARE LARGE. I think of the struggles beneath Owen's smile, and realize that UNDER THE LAKE'S PLACID SURFACE LIES A TURBULENT WORLD. I see Belle, guiding me to Rose through my confusion, and it's evident that WITH AN OX, THE FARMER VENTURES INTO FIELDS HE CANNOT MANAGE ALONE. I replay my pained phone conversations with Lindsay, two vastly different personalities bound by a root base, and it makes perfect sense: EVEN FROM ONE BRANCH, TWO PEARS MAY NOT TASTE THE SAME. I picture Rose at my doorstep, with no choice but to ask me to take her to visit Bernie and Joey, because AN ANT CANNOT BUILD A HILL BY HIMSELF. I think of myself, of my incessant planning for the future, and it's plain as day that A SPIDER MUST SPIN AN INTRICATE WEB FOR HIS DINNER. I see Rose at the cemetery, warning me through Joey's story: DO NOT WAIT FOR THE SNAKE TO BEAR ITS FANGS BEFORE YOU ACT! Last, I picture Owen at the farm, revealing his secret to me, because LIKE BUBBLES IN A BOILING POT, THE TRUTH WILL SURFACE.

The fortunes flow out of me, and I type them into my phone discreetly, right hand only, so that Owen doesn't know I'm only giving him partial attention. When I'm finished, I count how many I've written: twenty-five! Just one short. I'm sure I can think of a last—

"Mommy?"

"Uh, what, honey?"

"It's over. Weren't you watching with me?"

"Yes! I just had to write down one—"

Owen flings the iPad on the coffee table, and it lands with a clatter. Thank God we bought the childproof case.

"Owen! You can't throw the iPad. It's delicate. And *super* expensive." I sigh. "Look, I'm sorry I got distracted, especially when you were sharing something that's really important to you. That wasn't fair. How about we head outside for a bit? Maybe go to a park?"

Owen gives me a guarded look. He's interested, but he doesn't want to admit it yet.

I sweeten the deal. "How about Far Away Park?"

The actual name is Warren Park. It was renamed by Owen, since he can't keep any of the real names straight. It's only fifteen minutes away by car, but the name has stuck. It's his favorite, since it has so many sections to explore: a large play structure with multiple slides, a yellow winding ladder that Owen has dubbed "the caterpillar," a quieter area for swinging, and an open field to run in.

He shrugs. "Well, if *you* really want to go, I guess we could."

I smile. "Why don't you get yourself a snack first? Grab a piece of fruit from the fridge. Then get changed. I have to drop off this . . . thing . . . in the trash room." I point to the case, which is still pushed up against the kitchen wall.

Owen hops off the couch and scrambles into the kitchen. Not even a glance toward the mysterious case that arrived in our apartment several days ago and will be disposed of today. For him, it's no different than an Amazon delivery.

I've never seen Freckly Maintenance Guy around on a Sunday, so I don't even bother trying to stuff the case into a garbage bag. I live on the edge and drag the unpackaged case down the stairs and into the trash room. I'd like to crush it, destroy it before some unsuspecting soul walks in and decides to take it for himself, like Bernie did with the *farshlugginer* humidifier. I should've thought ahead, put a sign that says BROKEN on it. I look around, trying to figure out how best to damage the case so no one will want it.

I should hide it! I pull bag after bag of trash away from the wall until I clear a spot. Then I pile all the trash bags on top of the case again. There. No one will find it now.

Except Freckly Maintenance Guy. I can't risk it.

I kneel and rip open the bottom of the bags resting on top of the case. Coffee grounds and filters, used tissues, chewed-up gum, and a host of disgusting items fall out. Excellent! I rip the bag further. The remains of dinners and napkins, empty toothpaste bottles and a half-empty can of soda add to the litter. I rub the coffee grounds into the case with the soda can, then spill out the remaining liquid. There. No one in their right mind would see any value in this case anymore. I feel guilty for creating a mess for Freckly Maintenance Guy, but I can't risk this case and its horrific history becoming part of anyone else's present. I pull some more trash bags from along the other side of the wall, cover up the ripped bags, and appraise my work. It'll do.

It's when I'm walking up the back stairs that I hear a voice from below: "What, you want an old lady should have to run to catch up with you? Already I'm *schlepping* two bags."

I turn to see Rose at the base of the stairs. She has a reusable grocery tote slung over her slight shoulder and is dragging a kitchen trash bag behind her. She drops both to the ground and pulls my manila envelope out of one of the totes.

"Joel took you?"

She nods. "He wanted to pay his respects. The photo is . . ." She stops, starts again in a quieter voice. "There are no words. It was in the case?"

"Yes. Along with two others. One was of Lena and her father, and one was of Lena and Joey. I was planning on giving those to Lena. Unless—"

"There is another with my—with Joey? And she wants it?"

"Very much so. She really loved him, Rose. It was her father who called off the engagement. Even when she knew you weren't accepting her parents' calls, she still tried to help. She's the one who got Joel to talk to you and Bernie."

Rose's eyes are wide. "But . . . but Joey got so terrible *after* Lena broke up with him! It was the heartsickness that did it! That's what Bernie said, that's what Dottie said! And I . . . I *listened* to them, because the doctor I couldn't talk to. Joey wouldn't let me."

Because Joey wanted to face it on his own. He thought he was an adult, at twenty-two, just like I thought I was at twenty-one. I think of my mom in the bathroom with me and the pregnancy test, the vein in her forehead popping out as I explained how I was in love. For the first time, I see that it wasn't disapproval on my mother's face. It was fear. Because now I know that fear, the sickening dread that swirls inside of you when you're powerless to help your child.

"Of course you listened to them, Rose. You trusted Bernie and Dottie, not Lena. But she saw Joey the most. The first time she noticed symptoms was in the middle of their junior year together. That's a year before the photo was taken, a year and a half before doctors became involved. And who knows when the symptoms actually began? That's just when Lena noticed. It sounds like Joey was very good at hiding them until . . . until things spiraled out of control."

Rose ignores my timeline insight. Instead, she gingerly pulls the photo out of the manila folder, then turns it toward me. "I was fifty-eight in this picture. Joey would be fifty-seven now. A father, maybe a grandfather. I can't even imagine." She wipes a tear before it can land on the photo. "I knew Lena would fall in love again, that she would marry and have children. And I hated her for that. I hated her for *living*—for experiencing all the things Joey never would. I tried to cut her out of photos that we had of her and Joey together, and ended up ruining them. Bernie was so angry with me! But I needed the hate to survive."

"Rose, if it brings you pain to have the picture, I'm sorry. I thought—"

"What are you talking? There is no better gift." She pulls a green stone from her pocket. "I went to the store, and returned the clear stone. But Joey, he has your stones now. So I am saving mine for another time."

My eyes fill. The heart center stone, in Rose's hands.

She pauses. "I think you are right. If what you say is true . . . if I have been unfair to Lena all these years . . . then she deserves the other photo." She nods once, then multiple times, as if trying to convince herself. "But can I—can I look at it first? Before you send it?"

"Of course. You can come up now, if you have time. Why don't you hand me your bags?" I look at the grocery tote and plastic bag by her feet. The tote is stuffed, and now that Rose is no longer blocking the plastic bag, I see a box that's about two feet too long sticking out of it. Why are all her belongings oblong and difficult to move?

She passes the tote to me, which, despite its width, isn't heavy. I give the loops of the trash bag a tug to test its weight, and it slides across the floor. It's light, too. I should have assumed that, given that Rose was managing them both until now.

"It's all for your boychik, anyway." Rose huffs as we climb the stairs.

"What? I don't understand. There's no need—"

"He is home now? Or he is with Nick?"

"He's home. But if this is because—"

"What, I need a reason to bring a gift?"

"Well, it's not his birthday yet. Not until next month."

She waves away my words. "*Ach.* Enough with the excuses."

We reach the second floor, and I unlock the door to my apartment. "O? We have a guest. Mrs. Klein is here. And she has . . . some gifts for you. So we'll go to Far Away in a little bit, okay?"

Owen appears from his bedroom, iPad in hand, a curious look on his face. "Gifts?"

He's eating an apple—in his bedroom, not the kitchen, like he's supposed to—and he's still wearing his suit pants and button-down from this morning's grand event. It's unbelievable how slowly kids move sometimes. How can he not have finished an apple and changed his clothes by now?

"So handsome, so grown-up!" Rose says. "Why are you dressed up? Did you go to church?"

"No, my Dad took me to see *Peter and the Wolf.* The symphony."

"Owen, Mrs. Klein might not know *Peter and the Wolf*. There's no piano in it."

Rose rolls her eyes. "*Pssh.* Your mama thinks I don't know Prokofiev! Maybe no piano when the symphony performs it, but there is sheet music you can find. So! This brings me to gift number one." Rose pulls out the rectangular box that's testing the limits of the tote bag.

Owen looks up at me, waiting. "Go for it," I say, and he rips the box open, instead of lifting the top.

"Owen! I meant open it *nicely*. What if—"

"I know what these are!" Owen says excitedly, pulling a clear, zippered plastic package from inside the box. In it are stacks of large interlocking foam puzzle pieces. "We have them at gym. If you have a lot of them, you can make a big mat. But there are only . . ." He stops to count. "Only six." He looks up at Rose, confused.

I jump in, try to think of something that could be done with such a small number of pieces. "Well, I can think of lots of things they'd be perfect for. You could practice forward rolls or cartwheels. You could use them as baseball diamonds. You could put your sleeping bag on them, and we could—"

"*Sha, sha.*" Rose waves away my furious explanations. "Your boychik is correct. There are not enough for sports. But I will give you a clue: all of these gifts are connected. So. It is time for gift number two. Number two is for you, Marissa." She pulls a business card from her jacket pocket. MACKENZIE BROS. MOVING, it says, and on the next line: BIG MOVES OR SMALL, BOOK ONLINE OR CALL! The name *Jeff Mackenzie* is written in shaky cursive next to the contact information.

"I don't understand." I'm out of creative ways to be thankful, because this makes no sense.

"Gift number three!" Rose nods at Owen, who is already peeling the long, rectangular carton out of the kitchen trash bag. "Yes, that's the one. For the little *nudnik* who can't keep his hands to himself."

He struggles to remove the top half of the box. "I'll help you, O," I offer, but before I can, he rips it in half.

"Owen! What are you doing? What if we need to return what's inside?"

But Rose is laughing. "Of that I'm not so worried." She looks at Owen. "*Nu?* What do you see?"

Owen peers inside. "It looks like a really long pillow."

"Mm-hmm. But not for your head."

"What?" Owen looks confused. "What kind of crazy pillow isn't for your head?"

"The last one!" Rose pulls out a blue plastic bag from the bottom of the trash bag. On it, I see a familiar logo, one of a musical scale, and atop it, the name of a store: *The Music Market*. That's where I've seen foam puzzle pieces and pillows together outside of a gym! I see the tops of pages, and I know what must be inside, how all the gifts fit together.

"Music books for the piano, Mommy!" Owen squeals.

"What is the pillow for, then?" Rose arches an eyebrow.

"For the bench!"

"For your *tush*," I say, and Rose looks at me with surprise.

I laugh. "Lots of people know that word. The gym mats—you stack them to use as a footrest, right? So kids can have proper positioning while playing?"

"That is what the lady tells me. Much better than the wood one Joey had. When he grows, you take away a puzzle piece. Easy-peasy."

"But *my* gift, Rose. Do you mean—?"

"Your boychik needs the piano. I have arranged with Jeff, all you need to do is call and he will move it for you."

Owen is looking back and forth between us, as if watching a ping-pong match. I can tell by his face he's not quite sure what's happening, but he knows the future of the piano hangs in the balance.

When I started scouring books of Chinese proverbs for inspiration, the first quote to capture my interest was IF HEAVEN DROPS A DATE, OPEN YOUR MOUTH. I tried to modernize it for Peking Foods—spent far too much time trying to rewrite it—but in the end, I moved on, because there was no room for improvement. The original was the best.

I don't know why, but Nick has decided to help me find a way to pay for lessons and Rose has offered to give us a piano. All I need to do is open my mouth.

And yet it feels wrong.

I don't want to take music out of Rose's life. I know her piano hasn't been played for decades. Bernie kept it tuned for a ghost. I don't know if he found solace in the ritual itself, as some do in tending to loved one's graves, or if he was maintaining it as an offering of atonement to his wife. But it was his way of coping, of keeping the past alive, and it seems unfair to take it from him now that he can't say no. I'm already giving away a photo of Joey that was once his.

"Rose, I can't. *We* can't—"

"*Ach*, you with the manners! Why can't you take it? Your boychik has talent. He needs to practice."

"Maybe we could practice at your place, then? A couple of times a week? We could arrange a time."

I know it's the right answer even as I say it. We can fill Rose's home with music again. Rose's choice of composer even, once Owen gets good enough. She will see a boy grow and laugh, and we—

But Rose is shaking her head. "No. That is not how practice works. You must practice every day—"

"We could come every day, if it's not inconvenient."

"—and it is not how *inspiration* works. The piano needs to always be available. That is how my Joey used it. He would have ten, fifteen minutes free between homework and soccer practice, or before he would go to bed at night, and he would tinker on the piano. Or sometimes he would—"

"Who's Joey?" Owen asks.

Rose and I stop interrupting each other. We look down at Owen, then our eyes lock. I give Rose a slight nod. *Yes,* it says. *You can tell him.*

"My son." Rose's voice is tinged with loss and pride. "He loved to play the piano, just like you. I think it would make him very happy to give it to you."

"He doesn't play it anymore?"

"No, not for a long time. So I think the piano is lonely. And it would like to live here, if it is okay with your mama."

Owen turns to me, his eyes pleading. "Can we, Mommy? Please? I'll be very, very careful with it. And I'll, I'll—I'll make my bed every day, and your bed, too, if you want, and I can, umm, I can clear the table after dinner, and—"

"Owen! You don't have to pay me back with chores. That's not the problem." There's no way to explain it to him. He's hugging the music books against his chest. He turns back toward Rose, and as he does, he drops one.

Rose picks it up. "Ah, *Dalton's Piano Classics*. This one is for when you get a little further along. The first time my Joey had a concert for Bernie and me, it was from songs he learned in this book."

The concerts! *That's* the answer. "Rose, I think I have a solution. Remember when you told me that Joey would treat you to a concert at the end of every week? I would be willing—I mean, I would be *honored* to accept the piano if you would agree to come to dinner and a concert once a week."

I think of Lena's words outside of Rose's apartment last Sunday, the words that drew me into Rose's world: "Do we have a deal?"

All this week, I've delivered food for Lena, but food wasn't what Rose needed. Her refrigerator could barely contain all of it. The only way to fill Rose's plate is to deliver what Lena couldn't, not when Joey was struggling with illness, and not when Bernie died.

Her words.

I repeat Lena's question, now destined for Rose's ears, and as I await her answer, the last fortune for Peking Foods—the twenty-sixth of this final batch and the nine hundredth overall—writes itself in my mind.

ACKNOWLEDGMENTS

Much gratitude is owed to:

Susannah Noel, editor extraordinaire. She has an eagle eye for detail, is a whiz at streamlining prose, and kept me smiling during the editing process with her upbeat comments.

Asya Blue, for her innovative cover design and interior layout. She indulged my missed deadlines, stringent punctuation specifications, and color change requests with patience. In the end, I chose a fitting color for the cover: blue.

Caroline Leavitt, for her early reading of the manuscript. Her insights inspired me to write in unexpected directions, and the book is richer because of her.

My grandparents, Anna and Alan. While the characters of Rose and Bernie are not based on them or their relationship, the Yiddish phrases sprinkled throughout the novel are well known to me because their voices were a joyous part of my childhood.

My mother, for her love and support, and for referring to me, several times, as Owen. She is the savior of the title *The Fortune Cookie Writer*. When told I'd been advised to discard it, she held her tongue, but her pained expression upon hearing its replacement spoke volumes. She was right. A year later, I listened.

My older son, tester of floors and tapper of doorframes, and my younger son, for all they have shared with me and taught me.

My husband, for being my most trusted friend, an exceptional father, and the person who makes me laugh the hardest. He supported this book long before I let him read a word of it, and buoyed me up during the arduous process of bringing it into the world.

Those with schizophrenia who have bravely shared their stories through documentary, interview, or lecture.

Alan Posner, for his explanation of Massachusetts divorce law. If errors exist, they are due to my misinterpretation, not his counsel.

Trish Wesley Umbrell, of the Natick Community Organic Farm, for granting permission to set a pivotal scene in a place dear to so many. May the new barn bring good fortune to the farm.